Advance Praise for *Destined to Fail*:

"I related to this novel on such a deep emotional level. I have been through a lot of the same situations that I most of the characters have been through and to see it from another perspective is very surreal. Almost out of body experience surreal. I was angered by obvious poor decisions and inspired when characters stood up for themselves and elated when there was hope. I was so deeply moved by this novel that I cried through most of it and wanted to call my boyfriend to tell him how amazing he is." —*Jenn @ Booksessed*

"There are a couple of very heavy topics that are brought to life in this novel, all of which Samantha delivers with a delicate hand but not making them too weak so they have a powerful revelation behind them. It wraps up a little too "happy ending", but after taking the journey with Jasmine through her year, it is exactly what is called for. A very strong start in the writing career of Samantha March and I'm sure the following novels are going to be just as entertaining as this one was."
—*Michelle @ Just Jump*

"Samantha March has brought forward a strong tale of survival, friendship and courage, one that all women should read and recommend to their girlfriends."
—*Shannon Hart, author of Until the End of Forever*

Destined to Fail

A Novel

This is a work of fiction. Names, characters, places and incidents are either the product of the author's imagination or are used fictitiously, and any resemblance to actual persons, living or dead, events, or locales is entirely coincidental.

Cover Design by Ashley Redbird
Copy Proof by Kira Matthias

ISBN: 978-0-615-54692-6

Destined to Fail

A Novel

Samantha March

Marching Ink LLC

To my mother, my friend

Prologue

THE BLOOD WAS TOO MUCH FOR ME TO HANDLE. I couldn't stomach the rusty smell. I couldn't figure out what was happening to me. Why was this happening to me?

I tried to force my eyes open, to keep my thoughts coherent. Why wasn't Nate here? He needed to be here; something was wrong.

My thoughts were becoming hazy, mixing together with reality and nightmare. I heard Becky order me to lie down, and I did just that. She had spread a dark blue towel on the bathroom floor and I sank down, propping my head on the bathtub. I hoped Cari wouldn't get too upset that I was destroying her bath towel. Becky was asking me questions about my doctor, and I tried to work past the fog in my thoughts to respond to her.

I heard Becky yelling for Kiley, and I saw the pale face and trembling body of my friend make her way into the bathroom. Her eyes widened when she saw me laying there, blood in between my legs, sweat shining on my forehead. I couldn't look her in the eyes. I had kept a terrible secret from her, from everyone.

Becky was giving instructions to Kiley, who stood frozen in the door frame. Becky shouted once, making her daughter run into the bedroom. I heard Kiley on the phone, saying my name and our address on campus. Were they sending an ambulance? Everyone would know my secret if they sent an ambulance. I wanted to shout at Kiley, tell her not to tell, but my body couldn't respond. I was too weak. Weak and pathetic.

I know I should have felt something at being half naked, covered in blood in front of my friend's mother, but I couldn't feel self-conscious at the moment. Worry was overtaking me, pulling me under. I needed Nate. I needed my doctor. I needed help.

Chapter One

I WOKE UP ON A HUMID SATURDAY MORNING IN August struggling to breathe. I opened my eyes to darkness, feeling sweat trickle down my forehead. It felt as though an elephant had taken up residence on my chest. I tried to scream for help, but my shrieks sounded muffled in my ears. I tore at whatever predator was trying to kill me, thrashing my legs and flinging my arms. I was only nineteen; I was getting ready to go off to college in less than a month. How could this be happening? An intruder must have broken into the apartment I lived in with my mom. I needed to escape.

Right before I really started to panic, my vision suddenly cleared. I blinked in the harsh sunlight streaming through my open bedroom window, breathing in sweet freedom mixed with the scent of lilacs. But where was the intruder? Had he gotten my mom?

"Mom!" I gasped when I saw her sitting on my desk chair beside my bed. "What the hell?"

She watched me with an amused expression, arms folded casually across her chest. "You need to pack."

I sat up in bed, still feeling dazed. "I have to what?" I looked around me then, and realized that half my wardrobe was piled on my bed. I was being suffocated by my clothes. "Mom!" I yelled, pushing the dresses and shirts away from my body. "What were you trying to do—give me a heart attack before I turn twenty?"

"No, I'm trying to get you to get serious about packing. Three weeks is not a lot of time, and you haven't even brought up your suitcases from storage yet."

"But I can't pack up all my clothes yet! What am I going to wear for the next three weeks?" I argued, still trying to calm my racing heart. My mother could act more like a teenager than a grown woman sometimes—well, most of the time.

Mom just shrugged. "I only want you to go get your suitcases down from storage and start rounding up some cardboard boxes. You don't have to do all your packing today. But it will be a start."

"So you decided to take out half my closet and dump my clothes on me? That helps so much. Thanks," I said sarcastically, swinging my legs out of bed. What a mess. I was going to have to spend the morning putting my clothes back on their hangers.

"Oh, come on, JJ, lighten up," Mom said, using the nickname many of my friends called me. My name is Jasmine, Jasmine Jones, and I get called everything from JJ to Jas to Jazzy. "You're going to be gone before you know it and then who am I going to get to pull pranks on?"

"Yeah, yeah," I grumbled, walking out of the bedroom. "You better make me some breakfast to make up for this!" I called over my shoulder as I walked into the bathroom.

Thirty minutes later, I was stuffed with gooey apple cinnamon French toast and a side of chocolate chip pancakes.

At least my mom was good at cooking. That slightly made up for almost causing me to go into cardiac arrest that morning.

I drug my pink suitcases up the stairs to our second floor apartment. Mom and I spent most of the morning going through my belongings, deciding what could stay, what could go and what needed to be tossed. Beside my scare of waking up, the day was a good one. Mom and I had been having more bonding days than usual due to my impending move to college. We would no longer be living together, and I would no longer be living in Julien.

I didn't want to think about moving day. My mom was my best friend. I couldn't stand the thought of not seeing her every day—that I couldn't come home and gripe about my classes or friends while she made supper and I read celebrity gossip magazines aloud to her. But I knew college was the right choice for me and I wasn't too sad about leaving Julien, my home of the last nine years. It seemed overnight it had changed from a quaint Iowa river town along the Mississippi to a place where you couldn't take a walk past nine at night. The violence, especially among teens, was at an all-time high.

"What time are you going to Nate's?" Mom asked me, right before we took a break for lunch. She took her glasses off and wiped the lenses with her shirt, inspecting them before slipping them back on. Her blonde hair was dyed almost the same shade of champagne as mine, and was gathered into a low ponytail. When she wore her hair that way, she could almost pass for my older sister instead of mother.

"I'll probably leave here in an hour or so," I said, sitting back on my heels. I surveyed the mess in my bedroom. It was like a clothes bomb had exploded. The neat piles we had started out with were now pushing into one another and there was little organization that met the eye. I sighed. "Oh, how I hate packing."

"Oh, woe is you. Don't worry. We'll get you all squared away before you have to leave," Mom said, patting my leg. "Why don't we be done for the day so you can get ready while I make you a quick lunch?"

"Thanks," I said gratefully. "But now I have to figure out what I can wear in this mess."

Mom helped me find an outfit—a black skirt just an inch too long to be called a mini and a white silk top with pink lace overlay. Both were in my to-go pile but made the perfect outfit for a night out with my boyfriend.

After a quick grilled cheese sandwich, I climbed into my Plymouth Breeze and headed my car for Nate's house, out in the country of Julien. As the summer days ticked down, I was getting more and more anxious about my move to college. I was leaving behind my mom, my little brother, my boyfriend. At least I had my best friend coming to college with me. That thought helped put me at ease but I was still nervous about starting over in a new city. My family had moved to Julien when I was nine, and I had an easy enough time finding new friends. But now as a teenager—an adult—that task could prove a lot tougher.

I tried to focus on happy thoughts during my ride. The summer day was a beautiful one, yet probably scorching to most people. I loved the high temps, bring on the humidity. I would much rather be sweating than in the middle of a snowstorm. I was getting ready to move away from this faltering town, away from the violence in schools and on the streets. And I was going to be the first in my family to go to college, a fact I was very proud of. I may not have been sure what exactly I wanted to achieve with my life, but I knew college was the place I needed to be to figure that out.

I hated the inevitable question, "So what do you want to do with your life?" Heck, I didn't know. I had just turned nineteen, fresh out of high school. I couldn't tell you what I was going to do tomorrow, let alone with my whole life. I knew I loved writing, and flirted with the thought of going to journalism school but decided that wasn't practical. Everyone wanted to be a writer or a journalist. That would be like me moving to Hollywood in hopes of becoming a movie star. Probably would never happen. So I chose the sensible route, accepting an offer from Irving, a business college in Des Moines.

I hoped while I was there I would make great friends and find a fabulous career. One that hopefully paid a lot of money and could help put my family's life back on track. Put my life back on track.

ഓരുഓരു

I waited outside, small white sunglasses shading my eyes, focused on the hill Nate would be climbing up. His father insisted that even though the temperature crept towards one hundred and five degrees, the farming chores still needed to be done. And with Nate's older brother already gone away to college, Nate was all they had left.

I scraped the hair off my sweaty neck and pulled it into a high bun. The five minutes I had been waiting seemed more like fifty. The sweltering summer sun beamed down, leaving all who dared brave the outdoors a sticky hot mess. Heat rose off the blacktop driveway, warming my ankles and lower calves. Without a cloud in the sky and no breeze to relish in, the summer day begged for air conditioning.

Another five minutes dragged on. I bit my lower lip, hoping Nate hadn't passed out in the heat. His family field stretched on for miles behind the house, a deep slope dipping into the confines of the woods. I knew the black kitten heels I was wearing wouldn't stand a chance against the grassy hill, so I couldn't go look for him. Especially since I could see muddy patches poking through the green, remnants from the two severe thunderstorms we suffered last week.

I glanced at my watch, tapping my finger against the glass face. Mom let me borrow her favorite timepiece for that night, after I haggled with her for twenty minutes and laid the guilt on thick about her morning prank. I thought the watch was sophisticated, and paired with my gold necklace I knew I nailed my date night outfit. Now if I could only find my date.

"Jasmine!" His voice was faint, but enough for me to hear. I ran along the walkway until the cement stopped and the grass loomed, not wanting to ruin my heels. About halfway down the hill stood Nate—shirtless—treading his way up the steep slope. Since we had only been dating for three months I hadn't had many opportunities to see Nate with no shirt. But even from my stance at the top of the hill I could make out his chiseled chest and toned muscle definition. I wanted him shirtless more often.

I waved so hard my elbow cracked twice. "Hi!" I yelled down, watching him get closer. When he finally reached the top I lunged for him, but caught myself and withdrew at the last minute.

Nate laughed. "Yeah, you might want to have me shower first before touching me. Let's get inside. You shouldn't even be out in this heat."

"I'm fine," I protested, but grateful at the thought of the indoors. "I wanted to wait for you."

Nate—always a gentleman—held open the door for me and I took another appreciative glance at his body. His tanned skin looked even darker than when I last saw him four days ago, and glistened with sweat from working in the heat. His bicep muscles flexed when he held the heavy door open for me, and I had to restrain myself from touching them.

"If you want to watch some TV or something I'll just shower quick and then we can head. You look beautiful as always, by the way," Nate said, bending down to kiss my cheek.

I beamed at his compliment, stepping into the airy open kitchen. "Thank you. And, yes, that's fine. Take your time. Are your parent's home?"

"Nope. At my uncle's house. Be right down." Already halfway up the stairs, Nate disappeared onto the second level. The groan of the water pipes filled the aging farmhouse, angry they were put to work. Stepping across the sleek hardwood floor, I settled onto the couch, flicking the television set to life. Not even two minutes later the water shut off and floorboards creaked overhead. How do guys do that? I couldn't have conditioner in my hair in that amount of time.

Nate dressed faster than he showered, and less than thirty minutes later we arrived at Marta's Grill, the number one steakhouse for a Saturday night date. Pale yellow walls danced in the flickering lights of the multiple fireplaces and dim lighting gave the ambiance a cozy romantic vibe. Each table showcased a unique centerpiece of brightly colored flowers, and ours held deep red tulips surrounded by yellow marigolds.

The host presented our table with a flourish. "Luca will be your waiter this evening," he announced in a grandeur voice, placing our menus on the table. "Enjoy." After a slight bow he left, off to take his hosting duties seriously elsewhere in the restaurant.

Nate glanced at me over his menu, sticking his nose in the air. I laughed when I realized he was making fun of the host and his uppity demeanor. I eased one pinky away from the menu, and Nate joined in my laughter.

We calmed down only once Luca arrived, clad in the standard all black uniform complete with a skinny black tie. He wrote down our orders of steak dinners, then scampered off to retrieve our sodas.

"Two more weeks, babe. Getting nervous?" Nate opened the conversation with talk of my impending move. Four hours away, down to Iowa's capital city of Des Moines. The real world loomed on the horizon.

"Oh, I don't know. Not really nervous. Just going to miss everyone. A certain boy, especially," I said, giving Nate a wink.

"Which boy?" Nate asked, sliding his elbows back on the table as Luca set our drinks in front of us.

"One with curly hair. Usually shows off a farmers tan. Goes by the name Tate. Or Nate, not sure which one."

"Sounds like he might not be that special to you," Nate teased.

"Ah, that's where you're wrong, sir." I reached across the table, placing my palm over Nate's wrist. "He's very special indeed. The specialist, some may say."

"All right, now you make me sound like a doctor," Nate said.

I laughed, knowing Nate's ability to make me smile was what sparked my interest in him. When I first met him three months ago I wouldn't have taken a second glance if it wasn't for his humor. Nate was a farmer boy, complete with the scruffy boots, dirt under his fingernails, perma tan from working long hours outdoors. I lived in the city of Julien with my mom, was head cheerleader of the varsity squad, kept up my blonde highlights and waxed my eyebrows monthly. Me, date a farmer? Unthinkable.

But when his infectious humor kept a smile on my face and the butterflies flapped each time he called me 'miss,' I figured I should take this farm boy seriously. And to think I almost didn't go to the dreaded house party that led me to Nate, all because I was still licking my wounds from a messy breakup with Kameron, my first boyfriend and first love. Sometimes, I still couldn't believe Nate was interested in me. Or that he seemed like such a decent guy. It was almost like I was waiting for his bad boy persona to let loose, to finally show some characteristics that didn't belong in the pro column. I shook myself from thinking these thoughts and tried to concentrate on what Nate was saying.

"So I have to get the combine out tomorrow. We'll have ourselves a busy day with all the crops in our field and grandpa's field. I can only hope the heat won't be as bad as today," Nate said, losing me at the word 'combine.'

"Ah, yes, the combine," I nodded my head, trying to sound farm knowledgeable. "For all those crops."

"You have no idea what I'm talking about, do you?"

"You're talking about crops and fields! And…combines. Okay, yes, I have no idea what a combine is." I admitted defeat.

Nate laughed. "No reason to feel bad. I didn't know what an eyelash curler was until last week. That's a scary widget." I smiled, remembering how horrified he seemed when I tried to curl his lashes. The scene in my bathroom was hysterical. "But a combine is just a machine we use—think of a really big tractor—that harvests the crops like wheat and corn."

I nodded. "Okay, I get that. Kind of. I've seen all sorts of machines down in your field. They look huge. And expensive."

"Like you wouldn't believe. Hundreds of thousands of dollars for just one of them."

I nearly spit out my Sprite. "Are you serious? I can't imagine spending that much money on a machine!" An all-inclusive vacation to the Bahamas, maybe. And then another vacation to Italy.

"Well, you have to realize these machines keep our farms running, which keeps income rolling in. Without those expensive machines, work would be done by hand, meaning longer hours and more manual labor than I want to think about. So the cost really isn't so bad."

Our dinner continued smoothly. The food was excellent as usual, and our conversation didn't stop. Nate and I didn't have much in common. I was more into celebrities, fashion and traveling while he preferred the rugged outdoors, but that didn't stop our talking. We were open to each other's worlds. I finally got Nate to buy a few brown polo's for the fall—the season's "it" color—and he got me to paddle a canoe over the summer. Fair trade.

I loved that Nate helped me push limits, go beyond my comfort zones. We enjoyed a fantastic summer, one that would be unforgettable. But now I was about to leave, moving away from Nate and our still-budding relationship. Nate was only going into his senior year of high school. It would be another year before he could find a college near me. Could we survive the long distance?

"You're looking sad again, JJ. What's on your mind?" I had been quiet on the ride home, my thoughts filled with questions on my relationship. But I didn't want Nate to know my worry, that I had doubts we could make it.

"Nothing, babe. Just so full of steak. I can't believe you let me eat that whole thing." I leaned over and pecked him on the cheek, inhaling his scent of body wash mixed in with hay and the outdoors. So manly. No one I met at college would compare to Nate. They just couldn't. He was everything I wanted in a boyfriend: caring and affectionate and treated me like a princess. But he was also rugged and pure alpha and knew what he wanted to do with his life and could one day provide for me. Not that I was thinking marriage already. It was much, much too soon for those grown-up thoughts.

We reached my apartment at last and I invited Nate inside. A note on the table informed me Mom was out with Aunt Janet, so the place was ours. "Do you want anything to drink?" I called to Nate, who veered left into the living room while I stood in the kitchen, minding my hostess duties.

"No, thanks."

I walked the fourteen steps from the kitchen to the living room and joined him. Mom's apartment wasn't huge, but the two bedrooms and one bathroom were enough for me and her. I thought the apartment was cozy and in a good location for the price we were getting. After Mom's money troubles we were lucky to be on the west end of town at all and not banished to the east side in low-income housing.

I found Nate staring at an eight-by-ten photograph, my favorite picture in the living room. It was a family portrait with Mom, my older sister Grace and little brother Jeremy. The three kids were standing behind Mom, all huddled close together with bright smiles shining. Jeremy and I looked somewhat similar, the same shade of light blonde coloring our hair and sharp noses paired with high cheekbones. Grace, with her strawberry-blonde hair and more relaxed facial features, didn't blend as much with us, but all three children looked similar to Mom. I loved that I got her eyes, deep green jewels shaped like almonds. I've had complete strangers compliment me on them.

Nate cleared his throat in that awkward manner that meant he was uncomfortable. "JJ, are you ever going to tell me about your dad?" he asked, looking at me with questioning eyes.

My back stiffened, reacting like the allergy doctor gave me my seasonal shot. The story of my dad. Nate didn't need to know that. "I've told you before, I don't have a dad."

"Everyone has a dad. Or a father, a biological father," Nate countered with. "I can understand if he did something that upset you but he would still be your father. And you can tell me, talk to me."

As if. Nate's parents were happily married after twenty-one years. They ate family dinners and went on camping trips together. He wouldn't understand. My family past was far from perfect but I was doing the best to make up for what had happened. No need to relive the past.

"It's nothing, Nate, really. I don't have a dad. Lots of families don't have two parents. It's the twenty-first century. Big deal," I shrugged my shoulders, turning away from him. I heard him take a breath—probably to argue with me—but cut him off before he could say anything else. "No. Not right now, anyways. Maybe some other time we can get into it." *Like never.* "But your curfew is in two hours and I don't want to spend that time talking family. Now come here."

The finality in my voice kept Nate's mouth shut and he begrudgingly wrapped his arms around me. "You're lucky you're wearing that skirt or you wouldn't get off the hook that easily."

Lowering his mouth onto mine, I settled into his strong arms and let his kisses fill my mind, erasing all the dad talk from my thoughts. Nate would never turn on me like Stuart Romney, the man's name on my birth certificate. The father I never had the chance to meet.

ଘଠଊଠଘଠଊଠ

During the next two weeks, I went along my business getting ready to move: cleaning out my bedroom, packing boxes, sending thank-you cards for my graduation gifts. I tried to squeeze in as much time with Nate that I could, but between his busy farming schedule and my going-away tizzy, that time was limited.

My mother puttered around our apartment during the last two weeks, offering her input and trying to be helpful, but generally just getting in my way. I could sense her sadness about my move. Well, sense it, and I saw her making sad eyes while staring at my senior picture last week. When I asked what was wrong, she shoved the framed picture under her pillow and turned her back to me. I inherited my unwillingness to talk about my feelings from her.

"Now, don't pack your winter clothes. Just keep those here. Why are you packing your DVD player? I thought Abby had one?"

"Well, just in case. What if hers breaks?"

"Then you come home and get yours. It's just going to be another object in your box and something that will collect dust at your apartment. Leave it here."

I obliged, setting the silver DVD player back on the shelf. It was best not to argue with her when she thought she was being helpful.

"Is Abby getting excited?"

"Eh, she hasn't said much the past few days. I think her and Jason have broken up for good."

"About time. He's scum. But who am I to judge who you love?"

I chuckled. "You sounded pretty judgmental right there, mother dearest."

"Just trying to be helpful. Which reminds me, make sure you find a good dentist down there. You *are* going to keep looking into Invisalign, aren't you?"

"Mom!" My smile wasn't that bad. I had one crooked bottom tooth. One. Not a big deal. "Just—I'm trying to pack, okay? Either help or go read a book or something."

She narrowed her eyes at me but stayed quiet for the next few moments, watching me deposit a pile of summer shirts into a waiting cardboard box. I filled the box to the brim with tank tops, tube tops and halter tops, and tried squeezing in a few swimsuits as well until the box was ready to bust. I didn't want to leave any of my favorite shirts behind. Mom wordlessly handed me the packing tape, and I stretched the handle around until satisfied my clothes were not going anywhere.

"Is Nate coming tomorrow to see you off?"

"Yeah, he plans to be here around eight or so."

"Sad?"

I looked up at my mom, curious. The last time I tried to talk to her about leaving Nate I got teary-eyed and Mom changed the subject. Even though now she was only saying one word, it still caught me by surprise. It took me an extra moment to find a response.

"Well, yeah. Yeah, of course. It'll be weird not having him just across town. But I'm going to come back home a lot, and he'll be able to visit me some weekends. So it'll be fine. Just fine."

Mom must have noticed me trying to reassure myself with that speech, as she seemed to choose her next words with consideration.

"You know, Jas, long-distance relationships can be tough. Once you get down to Des Moines and settled in you'll be busy with classes and college parties and making new friends. You might not want to come home every weekend or every other weekend."

I just shrugged, letting her words go in one ear and right out the other. Why wouldn't I want to come home and see my boyfriend and my mom and my little brother and all my high school friends? Well, the ones who hadn't already moved away for college themselves. Mom was just trying to protect me, trying not to let me build up my expectations.

"Mom, please don't worry. No need. Now, can you help me pack up the bathroom stuff? I want to make sure I don't steal anything of yours."

I walked into the bathroom, glancing over my shoulder. Mom stared back at me, her eyes filled with worry and doubt, and something tugged at my heart. Things would work out—they had to. Besides, what could be the worst that could happen?

Chapter Two

THE CITY OF DES MOINES STRETCHED BEFORE US, filled with the promise of new adventures. I always thought Julien was a large city but my former town had nothing on Des Moines. I could see the downtown area from the interstate, sprawling across miles of land with a river stretching down the middle. Skyscrapers like the ones I had only seen in New York tried to touch the sky, the windowed exteriors on most looking sophisticated and polished. The gold dome from the capitol building glinted under the light of the sun, proudly looking over its city. I imagined the people inside, dressed in their suits and ties and the women in heels, frowning into their cell phones while scurrying from meeting to important meeting.

I took Exit 4A off the interstate, riding the exit ramp until I stopped for a red light. Abby Freeman, my best friend of six years, sat in the passenger seat beside me, her head buried in a Cosmopolitan magazine. The four-hour drive had been excruciating, with Abby barely uttering a word to me. I thought she was missing her family after the morning goodbyes, but she had to cheer up sometime. We were starting a new life together, just what we had always wanted.

"Almost there!" I tried to inject as much pep into my voice that I could muster, grinning in Abby's direction.

"I'm hungry," she replied, flipping a glossy page. She didn't even bother to glance out the windows as downtown passed us by. Her mousy brown hair hung limply past her shoulders, as Abby didn't feel bothered to use a flat iron or hot rollers. Her blue eyes were makeup-less, another necessity for me that Abby didn't mess with.

And while I took great care in choosing my outfit for that important morning—our move-in day at college—Abby looked like she just rolled out of bed. My long white shorts that stopped just above my knee had been freshly ironed by Mom last night, crisping them to perfection in hopes they wouldn't wrinkle too bad in the car. I wore a deep purple tank top, low cut enough to be sexy without skanky, with three long silver necklaces attached to the material. I teased my blonde hair that morning until the crown made a perfect pouf and slipped a sparkly silver headband over top. With silver sling-backs and no other jewelry besides the five piercings in each ear, I was picture perfect to extend my hand and start making new friends and acquaintances.

Abby looked the complete opposite, like she didn't give a damn who she was meeting and the impressions her appearance would leave on people. Her gray sweatpants looked horrendously baggy and she wore a t-shirt—a t-shirt!—that boasted our school, Washington High, across the chest. With no jewelry, no makeup and a sour expression on her face, nobody would want to shake her hand.

"Aren't you even just a little bit excited today? On our own! Freedom! A new town!"

Nothing. No smile, no laugh, no enthusiasm.

The next three minutes crawled by, and I couldn't help squealing when the electronic sign on Irving's campus came into view. WELCOME STUDENTS!! kept flashing on the screen, the neon letters giving me goosebumps of excitement. College!

I took a right onto Tower Street then a quick left to enter the parking lot. Cars, trucks, and moving vans dominated the area, all vying for a spot in the cramped lot. I whipped my small Plymouth Breeze into a no parking zone, hoping no one would yell at me in the chaos.

Placing one heeled foot on the pavement then the next, I slowly climbed out of the vehicle and took a quick stretch. The parking lot resembled a zoo, where all the animals had escaped and were running for their lives. Parents and students scrambled back and forth, trying to quickly unload all their belongings so they could get up to the apartments and start unpacking. Entire houses seemed to be with some of these students. I saw full-size beds being taken down from trucks, a couch being pushed across the parking lot and one girl had a clear tote filled with only stuffed animals.

The vibe in the air screamed hectic, but an excited hectic. Students glanced at other students, sizing each other up, wondering who would be their first friend on campus. Wondering where their new roommate was and if they would get along. I didn't have to worry about either of those questions. I had my best friend and roommate right beside me. Abby's presence helped calm my fluttering nerves. I knew I could make new friends, that had never been a problem for me, but just being thrown in the gaggle of new faces and experiences and the unknown was proving daunting at that moment.

I took a deep yoga breath in and out, reminding myself to be calm. Everyone was new, everyone in the same awkward boat.

"Well, let's go get our keys!" I smiled brightly at Abby, patting my hair to make sure everything was in place. Abby followed behind me, dragging her feet like a sulking toddler. She stayed quiet during our short welcome speech from a Kathleen at the front desk, who helped us sign in and attach our keys to our new Irving lanyards. She didn't speak when our fifth floor room was pointed out to us on a campus map and we began to climb the stairs. I hoped once Abby actually saw our apartment she would cheer up.

"We're here!" I exclaimed, throwing open the door to room 521. Finally!

"I'm starving." Abby dumped her purse and small duffel bag on the minuscule kitchen table Irving supplied. "Let's eat."

"Let's explore first! Check out our view! We can see the capitol building from here!" I stood on our fifth floor balcony, taking in the unfamiliar surroundings, giddy with excitement. "The buildings here are huge!"

Abby still stood by the front door, not stepping foot into the living room yet. "How 'bout we get the rest of our bags and then go search for a Happy Joe's? I could use some pizza ASAP."

My smile faltered. There was no way I could handle Abby if that was her permanent mood. She didn't seem the least bit excited that we were on our own, living as roommates just like we had planned for so many years.

"Anything wrong, Abs?"

Silence.

"Oh, Abby. You want to talk about anything?"

More silence, followed with a small shoulder shrug.

"I'm not going to take you to dinner unless you start talking to me," I tried to threaten her. "And we have no groceries yet so you very well may starve."

I got her to crack just a hint of a smile. Slow success. Sometimes with Abby it's like chipping away at a chunk of ice. Almost impossible to break through her frosty exterior.

"You're not going to like what I'm going to say," she warned, finally stepping into the apartment. Our living quarters were small and basic. The kitchen had about a foot of tile and came with a refrigerator, stove, microwave and plenty of dark wood cabinets. The living room was off the kitchen to the left, with two small green couches breaking up the space and a tall desk in one corner. The standard college apartment. We would share a bedroom and bathroom, both small but better than sharing with a whole group of girls. And much better than the tiny dorm rooms other students were forced to live in at the state colleges.

I frowned at Abby's words, wondering if she was about to piss me off. I threw myself down on the far right couch, digging my feet into the comfort of the cushions. "Okay. Sup? I could tell something's been bugging you all day."

She rolled her eyes, taking a seat on the opposite couch. "Yeah, yeah. I figured you would. I just know you don't want to hear about it. About him."

Ah. "Jason?" I knew I didn't even need to ask. The only 'him' in Abby's life the past four years consisted of Jason.

"Yep." She blew a puff of air out, suddenly looking too tired for the clock only reading twelve noon. "We, uh, we've been talking."

My eyebrows reached towards my hair. Abby told me she stopped talking to Jason. They broke up—my assumption for good—almost three weeks ago. Since the break-up, Abby had barely uttered his name in a sentence. I supported the cold turkey method. That was how I got over Kameron.

Seeing my facial expression, Abby let out a groan. "I know, I know. I should have told you. But I knew that you wouldn't want to hear it, you wouldn't approve or think I was crazy, but..."

"But? Whatever. Let's not even get into that. Just, whatever. What did he say that's got you so upset?

"He wants me to stay in Julien."

"Why would he want you to stay in Julien? And, hello, you're no longer in J-town. You're in Des Moines. Just getting unpacked. Starting school, starting *college*, in two days."

"I know! But how can I ever make this relationship work if I move four hours away from him?"

"Abby!" I sprang up from my position on the surprisingly comfortable couch, enraged at my best friend. "What is wrong with you? Why should you have to stay in Julien? He's the one that said he would move to Des Moines with you, then bailed just before signing the paperwork. You can't seriously want to move home already. We've been here five fucking minutes!"

"This is exactly why I didn't want to talk about this with you. I knew you would freak out."

"Freak out? Sorry for trying to protect my friend. Sorry for trying to knock some sense into you. When are you going to figure it out, Abs? He's not good for you. Hasn't been for a long time. I've tried to be understanding, because I got it. I stuck with Kameron through hell. I get it. But you've got to move on, girlfriend."

"But, I love him. And he loves me, I know he does. It's just a phase. Relationships go through phases."

It's just a phase. My motto for Kameron. Therapy taught me that cheating and abuse is definitely not a phase. It was the way of life for some guys.

"It's not a phase. It's not. You know, deep down somewhere in there you know it's not right. You deserve better. Someone who will treat you right and answer your damn phone calls and not frequent the strip clubs like you know he does."

"There is no one else. Who else is going to want to date me?" The tears started flowing, the part I hated. Whenever Abby cries, I cry. Instantly. I brushed away the first tear and moved to the couch Abby sat on. "I don't have your looks or your body. I'm not funny and can make jokes without thinking.

And all my family baggage is too complicated. Who would want that? Jason's the only guy who stuck around."

"Girl, you're talking crazy. Just because I know my way around a mascara wand and inherited my mother's cup size doesn't mean shit. Look at my family baggage. At least you know your dad. He even comes around every once in a great while. You can find someone who will be accepting of that. I did."

"Nate's different. He's the only decent guy in that town. And you got him. So that leaves Jason or any of the other losers for me. I'd rather stick with Jason. I already know him."

Our conversations before their breakup sounded the same. Cry, cry, cry. Abby would beat herself down. I would end up sounding like a broken record. Always repeating the same advice, same comforting words. I refused to have a pity party just moments after getting to campus. Wasting an hour crying in the living room about boys? No, thank you! Our new classmates, potential friends, were still milling around the parking lots and hallways, ready for us to meet them. Time to get out of the room, away from Abby trying to be a Debbie Downer.

"Look. We have a lot we need to do today. My car is still packed with boxes and we need to make this apartment start looking like a home. And you need some pizza in your system. And my cell phone needs charged. So let's just pull ourselves together, get going, and we'll talk more tonight if needed. Sound okay?"

Her head bobbed. "I am hungry."

"Great! Let's get the last of these boxes up and go get food. Maybe we can rope some hot guys into helping us." Winking at my friend, I headed out the door. Time to make a change, for Abby's sake and my own.

&ℛℰℛℰℛℰ

By the time the second week of school started, I developed a comfortable pattern and a growing list of new friends. Irving, a small private college nestled near the downtown area of Des Moines, didn't compare to the larger universities such as Iowa State. Only three buildings held classrooms, all connected by cement walkways breaking up beautiful green gardens. The main building where I lived, Williams, housed students, classrooms, administration offices, a computer lab, laundry facilities and the Activities Center. The AC became a favorite hangout of mine, holding a full gym, weight room and cardio room, jammed with treadmills, ellipticals and stationary bikes. Activities also coordinated student events such as the Welcome Week festivities, dances and intramural sports.

The major I chose, Tourism and Travel Management, came in as the smallest major on campus. The other majors included accounting, business administration, entrepreneurship and medical transcription. The limited number of majors meant limited number of students, a fact I saw as an advantage. It was impossible to know everyone at Washington High. There were over four hundred students in my graduating class alone and I didn't know all them, never mind the faculty and staff. At Irving, the feeling rivaled a small town community, and I even met the president of the school on my first day. I never met my principal during my four years at Wash.

Another perk about Irving—no Friday classes. Irving was a "working college." Therefore, classes began at 7:30 but released no later than 2:00 so students could still work half days at their place of employment, and full Fridays. I planned on securing a job in Des Moines, just not right away. I wanted to have time to settle in, get comfortable with my classes and homework load and of course—make new friends!

"Hey, I'm eating at the diner this afternoon with Cari and Kiley. Want to come?" I asked Abby. We were in the bathroom getting ready for our 7:30 US Geography class. With a steady hand, I drew a perfect black line above my eyelids with my newest eyeliner pencil. Abby wrestled with her matted hair, trying to force the flyaways back into a barrette. Two minutes until we would be considered late.

"Nah, I don't think so."

"Do you have other plans?"

"No."

"So.....why don't you want to come? The diner makes decent food. I promise you'll like it."

"No. I just don't feel like it. I'm tired. I'll probably nap during break hour."

I bit my lower lip, concerned about my friend. While my calendar filled up with different parties and lunches with new friends, Abby seemed to be getting more and more desolate. I made sure to invite her to each and every activity I attended, but she never accepted. Instead, she would sit at home, saying either she didn't feel well or was too tired to go out.

I didn't say anything else as we rushed out of our apartment and down the stairs. All the travel classes took place in Williams on the bottom floor, a major benefit to the travel students living in that building. As we slipped into our seats side-by-side, a flicker of annoyance pulsated through me. I wished Abby would participate more, attempt to make friends on campus or just be social. I felt guilty about going out, but she couldn't expect me to sit at home all day and night with her.

ഇരുൽഇരുൽ

"So, why isn't she coming?" Cari asked later that day.

I munched down on a crispy chicken strip, still hot from cooking. Two of my new friends, Cari Ryan and Kiley Miars, sat across from me, each with a cheeseburger basket placed in front of them.

"Don't know. It's like she just wants to sit at home and sulk over this stupid breakup. Nothing I say will bring her out of that apartment."

"Have you tried talking to her about her feelings?" Kiley asked. I loved this girl. Reaching six feet tall, with legs for miles and a stacked rack, my first impression of the bombshell brunette had been first-class snob. My judgment couldn't have been further from the truth. Kiley was the mother bear, always caring and concerned without a hint of snob or conceit in her bones. She was majoring in medical transcription, learning how to transcribe doctor notes and orders and other medical jargon. I knew Kiley would excel at whatever she put her mind to; she had that go-getter attitude about her.

"Yeah, all the time. I know it's about her ex-boyfriend, but I hate him. I hate them together. Have for the past few years. And I keep no secret about that." Shrugging my shoulders, I continued, "And that's not going to change. I can't stand to see my friend get hurt. I'll try to keep protecting her until I can't anymore."

"Anymore?" Cari questioned, her white eyebrows furrowed. Cari lived across the hall from me and came to Irving to study a buyer career, in particular, a shoe buyer. Cari's fashion sense rivaled fashion majors, always carrying the latest handbag and showcasing the highest heels. She never dressed down—even her sleepwear looked like she could walk a runway at any moment. If she wasn't just shy of 5'1". Cari's body was the exact opposite of Kiley's: petite, rail thin and flat as a pancake. Her white blond hair and pasty pale skin looked even whiter sitting elbow to elbow with Kiley's perfectly tanned body. I loved Cari because of her attitude and ability to dish it to me straight. Beating around the bush was not one of her strong points.

"I'm afraid she actually wants to move back home. To Julien." That was the first time I spoke those words out loud. They sounded strange on my lips.

"But we just started school!"

"Is she crazy?"

Kiley and Cari's voices overlapped one another, putting a smile on my face for a brief second. It faded when I responded. "I know, I know. I keep trying to convince myself she won't really do it but I'm starting to feel a little helpless. I don't want my friend to rot away in our apartment unhappy, but I don't want her to go back home to an unfair relationship and be unhappy."

My new friends could only gaze at me in sympathy. Both had met Abby and I had a feeling she didn't leave a strong impression with them. Mopey, moody and generally unfriendly could describe how Abby responded to meeting Cari and Kiley. What else could I do? Abby would run her life the way she wanted no matter what I said or how much advice I spit out. I could only hope she would make the right decisions.

₧₧₧₧

Abby was on the balcony when I got back to the apartment. She had propped open the door with a chair from the kitchen table, and the fresh air and sunlight made our small apartment more inviting. I could see her leaning against the railing, her cell phone pressed to her ear. I could bet she wasn't appreciating our view of the downtown skyline, or the smell of summer, or the orange and gold butterfly that landed on the railing next to her.

I set my purse down on the table and flicked on the TV. Abby must have heard the noise from the television, because her head whipped around and I could feel her eyes on me. I didn't bother looking at her, instead settled into the couch, wrapping my arms around a small throw pillow.

"I got to go now," I heard her mutter. "Yeah, yeah, I know. Okay, love you too. Bye."

I rolled my eyes, still facing the TV. I assumed she was speaking to Jason.

"Hey," she said to me, walking in from the balcony.

"Hey," I replied.

"So… how was the diner?"

"It was fun. They have great chicken strips. And orange soda," I tried to brag. Abby loved orange soda.

"Cool." She didn't sound impressed.

"Who were you talking to?" I had to ask, even though I knew the answer.

Abby plopped down on the loveseat next to me. "Just Jason."

I nodded mutely.

"He wanted to know if we were coming back this weekend. He wants to take me out. On a date." It was like she was trying to make him sound like he was proposing or buying her a new car. *Ooh, a date,* I thought bitterly to myself.

"I hadn't planned on going back. Cari and Kiley invited me to go to a party with them on Saturday night."

"So? You don't even go to parties. Please, let's go home. I really want to see Jason."

My anger level was rising. "I go to some parties, Abby. I can still be social and not drink. And I want to meet new people on campus. There's nothing wrong with that. We already said we were staying in town this weekend." Abby didn't own a car or her driver's license, so the only way she could get back to Julien was through me. And I was not going to budge. I wasn't missing the weekend just so she could go back and see Jason.

"Come on, Jasmine. You can see Nate, I can see Jason, everyone's happy. Why are you being this way?"

"If Jason wants to see you so bad, why doesn't he come here then? Huh? He has his own car. He wouldn't have to inconvenience anyone else," I shot back. I wasn't going to let Abby make me feel guilty. And I knew Jason couldn't be bothered to give up a weekend in Julien to come to Des Moines, especially to pay for gas money on top of that. I hated thinking of the sleaze ball in my apartment, anyways.

"Whatever. You can be so selfish sometimes." Abby got up and stormed into the bedroom, slamming the door behind her. Tears smarted in my eyes, and I was mad at myself for getting upset. I was trying to be a good friend. Abby needed to stay away from Jason. I shouldn't have to give up my plans just to satisfy her.

A flicker of worry passed through me. Could Abby and I lose our friendship over a guy? Abby had been my best friend for six years, ever since the first day of the seventh grade when we showed up to homeroom wearing the same shirt. Instead of getting mad over the matching outfits, we had bonded instantly. We had so many good times under our belt and I assumed we would be best friends forever. But I was starting to feel the crack between us and I didn't know what to do about it. I just wanted Abby to act like her old self again. I wanted my friend back, the girl who enjoyed going to the mall with me and ordering an extra large cheese pizza, light on the sauce, and trying all thirty-one flavors with tiny pink spoons at Baskin Robbins. Not the girl who was moody and sulky and had no interest leaving the perimeters of our apartment.

I sat on the couch for a few extra minutes, trying to calm myself down. When that plan didn't work, I grabbed my cell phone and called Nate. Hopefully, he wouldn't be on the farm and could listen to me.

"I'm sorry, babe. But you held firm. You can't let her push you around. I'm sure Abby just needs to settle in more. She'll get used to the new situation soon enough and everything will go back to normal again between you two," Nate said after I told him about our fight and my thoughts.

"Yeah, I know. It's just so stupid." I was walking outside, the only place where I could get some privacy. Abby wouldn't leave the bedroom and I didn't want to risk her overhearing me on the phone elsewhere in the apartment, so I decided a walk would be nice. The sun was just beginning to fall, coloring the sky with deep pinks and purples. I wished Nate were there to enjoy the sunset with me, to hold my hand while we walked, the setting sun providing the perfect romantic background. I just wanted him to be with me and not two hundred miles away. My guard seemed to finally be retracting. Maybe Nate was the real deal. Maybe he wasn't going to turn into another Kameron or Jason.

"I miss you," I blurted out suddenly. I couldn't help myself; I was overwhelmed with feelings of wanting to see Nate. He could always make me laugh, always cheer me up. Maybe I should be rethinking going home on the weekend.

"I miss you too," he said, and I swooned when I heard the tiniest accent in his words. I loved the cowboy in him. I loved the way he was such a man and could build things with his bare hands and drive a huge tractor, and…everything else about him. Every part of him. My heart skipped a beat. Was that love? Did I love Nate?

"Sorry, what did you say?" I asked, wiping my sweaty palms on my capris. My thoughts were skittering back and forth, unsure about what I might just have realized.

"Just said I miss you. Next weekend can't come soon enough," he repeated.

"Yeah, next weekend," I said absently. "I'm back to my apartment now so I'm going to let you go. I'll call you tonight before bed." I hung up and slipped the phone in my pocket. I wasn't back to my apartment yet. I was still outside, but I had to get my thoughts straightened out. Why had I thought I loved Nate? We had been dating for four months. That wasn't long enough to fall in love. Or was it?

My mind wandered back to our first meeting. I had known from the instant I met Nate Ketcham that he enchanted me. I didn't want him to, but there was just something charismatic about him that drew me in.

I had attended a house party at the end of the school year with my friend Jessica, another cheerleader on my squad. I didn't usually go for the party scene. I didn't drink alcohol, so I avoided the house parties and weekend keggers, but Jess persisted that I get out and have some fun after my messy breakup with Kameron. I agreed—cautiously—and warned her just because I was going out did not mean I needed to drink to have fun.

Everyone at that party was wasted. The boys tried their hardest to impress the ladies, challenging each other to arm wrestling contests and beer chugging races. The girls giggled while watching and cheering, taking long gulps from their red plastic party cups.

Bored in minutes with the drunken mess, I took up a spot on an empty picnic table placed inside the biggest living room I'd ever seen. High-beamed ceilings pointed up to a skylight and the south wall was made only of windows, the thick glass showcasing an immaculate garden outdoors. Beautiful photographs that looked more like art hung on the walls, and crystal figurines took shelter inside their glass case.

As I sat, chin in one hand, a group of girls I didn't recognize came along and sat on the benches. They were squealing, high-pitched and freaking out over something just "so totally unbelievable" and "like, I know, right." I kept scooting my body along the length of the bench trying to get my eardrums away from the assault.

"Keep moving like that and you'll take a tumble, miss," a gruff cowboy voice had said. I looked up to find a cute guy standing there, watching me closely, a small smile playing on his full lips. He wore a blue flannel shirt that clung to his broad chest, faded blue jeans, and a tan that not even my thrice weekly sessions with the hotbed could achieve. If the voice didn't give him away as a farmer then the flannel shirt and dirty black boots did.

His soft brown eyes took in the scene, me not drinking, visibly annoyed by the girls interrupting my table space, and said, "How about we go get you a drink and away from these crazy women? You wouldn't want them to brainwash you to their, like, so totally freakin' crazy ways."

I laughed, a genuine laugh brought on by the cowboy. "I'd like that, but I don't drink."

His eyebrows rose slightly. "A lovely lady like you avoids the sauce? That makes you a rarity around these parts. What's your name?"

"Jasmine. Jasmine Jones." I stuck my right hand out to shake his, always remembering my manners.

"As in Princess Jasmine? A real princess before my very eyes. Well, Jasmine, let's find something that will please you. After you, my princess." He bent at the waist in a deep bow, cracking another smile on my face. A funny cowboy. Cute, too.

"And what's your name, sir?" I asked, surprised at how my body reacted to his. My skin tingled when he lightly held my arm, guiding me through the living room, down one hallway, then another, then finally into the kitchen. I liked being near him, having my hip brush into his when we stepped through the doorway.

"Ah, you, Jasmine, you can call me Aladdin."

Maybe it was cheesy, maybe a pick-up line, but I didn't care. The cowboy had made me laugh and didn't bat an eye when I told him I didn't drink. Most guys found that to be a huge turnoff. But Nate was different. From that party we talked constantly, soon becoming boyfriend and girlfriend.

I remembered the tingles that shot through my arm when he first touched me. Kameron had never caused me to have a reaction like that.

I trudged up the steps to Williams Hall, pausing to let a group of students out the swinging doors before I entered. As I placed my key in the lock of the apartment, I had a suspicious feeling that I was falling head over heels in love with my own Aladdin. And I had no idea what to do next.

Chapter Three

I HAD BEEN A COLLEGE STUDENT FOR ONE MONTH. Thirty full days of living on my own (well, with Abby) creating new friendships, attending classes and making important decisions—such as which house party on Friday night would be the best to show up at and should I really add lowlights to my hair? Important college decisions.

I loved waking up each morning and prepping for a day of classes. Most days I liked to dress up, put some effort into my appearance. Skirts, dresses, high heels and jewelry were the norm. But on occasion I wore jeans (never sweatpants like some students) or casual shorts. Those days usually happened after I pulled an all-nighter either studying or socializing with my new friends.

My classes were flowing along, challenging me but not to the point where I felt frustrated or too confused. I especially loved Geography, and enjoyed learning about different states, airports, hotels, area attractions. Whatever the lesson plan had mapped out, my brain agreed with.

Abby, on the other hand, was not so agreeable to all things college.

"Abby! Abby, wake up. Aren't you going to class?" It was 7:15 on Thursday morning. Geography started in fifteen minutes and Abby hadn't budged since the alarm went off.

"No, I'm sick today. Just tell Reba I'm ill. My homework is on the table. Will you turn it in for me?"

And with that Abby flipped over, pulling the dark pink comforter over her head. I stewed for a moment before leaving, wondering if I should start jumping on the bed and pulling her down to class with me. She missed Tuesday classes as well and we only had four-day weeks!

As I slid into my seat and pulled a pen from my purse, I wondered if Abby could be faking her sickness. She locked herself in the bathroom most times, but I had heard her throwing up maybe once or twice. She didn't seem to be eating anything besides soup and bread, unusual for her. I wondered if she had an eating disorder. I asked her about going to the doctor once, but she didn't have any health insurance and didn't want to spend the money. But she couldn't keep missing classes at the rate she was going.

"All right, everyone. Let's settle down." Reba Marthaus, the travel instructor, tried calling the class to order. Her eyes scanned the room, taking visual attendance, and she glanced at me once, noticing Abby's desk stood empty again. I just shrugged my shoulders, unsure what to say. I liked Reba, she was younger and laidback for a teacher and her classes were by far the best on my schedule. It was easy to see she enjoyed teaching and interacting with the students, and her love of travel was greater than my own. But I wasn't sure I felt comfortable yet talking to her about Abby and what could possibly be going on.

"Today we have a quiz over the Eastern region." Groans met that statement. "But," she continued, smiling at our moans, "you are allowed to leave once you are finished. Anyone interested in joining THP, please meet back here during the break hour."

THP stood for Travel and Hospitality Professionals, the travel majors "club" on campus. I had been hearing whispers about the students taking some international trip, but I wasn't sure if the rumors were true. I definitely planned on signing up and I hoped Abby would, too.

I flew through the quiz and headed back upstairs to check on my friend. At least she was out of bed, a good sign, but the bathroom door was closed. I quietly leaned my head against it, trying to hear anything from inside. When a terrible retching noise reached my ears I jumped away, disgusted. She was throwing up again.

I decided not to wait around for her to come out, instead heading to my second class of the day. Abby was also in the class, Introduction to Microsoft Office, but I made the assumption she would not be in attendance. I would try to get her to come with me to the THP meeting, but something told me I wouldn't get far.

And I was right. I walked back into the travel classroom alone, looking for a friendly face to sit with. I spotted Raine

Strabla, a non-traditional student, with an empty spot next to her, so I flung myself down in that chair.

"Hi, Jasmine!" She greeted me with enthusiasm, blue eyes sparkling underneath four pounds of eye makeup. Raine was one of the prettiest women I'd met, but I could never tell if it was her natural beauty or all the makeup she wore each day. It must take her an hour just to put the stuff on. She always dressed impeccable, no sweats or jeans for her. She even wore fitted business suits some days, making me wish I could pull off the pencil skirt trend. Raine was in her late twenties, which was why Irving classified her as non-traditional, and told the class she returned to college for her degree after studying to be an artist. Between that unique fact, her style, and that she could quote every episode of *Sex in the City* made her fascinating to me.

"Hey, Raine! Any word on this trip yet?"

"Not so far. The second-years have done a good job keeping it pretty hush-hush."

Just then Reba walked in, followed by the second year students. The class immediately got silent, waiting in eager anticipation.

"Okay, so this is everyone interested in joining THP. Great." Reba started off, scanning the bodies filling the classroom. "First things first, I'll have the officers introduce themselves and then let them explain what we are all about."

Twenty minutes later I left the classroom in a daze, cheeks flushed with excitement, fingers fumbling for my cell phone buried in my purse. An international trip! I was going overseas!

"Mom! Mom, guess what?" I shouted into my phone, racing up the stairs to get to my apartment.

"Um, you flunked out of college?" Mom always had a witty comeback to the 'guess what' question.

"No! I'm going to Amsterdam!"

"Amsterd—like Holland? The country?"

"Yes, the country! Can you believe it?"

"JJ, you're going to have to back up. Are you there now? Are you arrested in the Red Light District and this is your one phone call? Do you have pants on?"

I burst through the front door, startling Abby who was eating a bowl of soup at the table.

"Mom, you are so weird. No, I'm still in Des Moines, in the United States. And no, I actually have a dress on, thank you very much." A powdered blue dress with a fitted bodice, wide belt, and full skirt. If only I had pearls and a hat, I could pass for a Stepford wife. "Do you remember that trip I was telling you about? With the travel class? Well, they announced today that it's six days, five nights in Amsterdam! Can you believe it?"

"Wow, that's incredible. A school trip to the land of sex and XXX. Or are those the same things?"

"Mom!"

"I'm kidding, I'm kidding. I'm thrilled for you. Really. Just seems like an odd place for students, but hey, spring break, baby. When do you go?"

"They said sometime in March. We get to plan the whole thing—flights, hotels, attractions, transportation. So it's a learning experience on top of a vacation. Ahhh, I'm just so pumped!"

"Can visitors come? Your lonely old mom could go for a vacation or two."

My heart panged at her words, even though her voice still sounded cheerful. My mom was lonely? Sure, we had done almost everything together back in Julien—shopping, dining, movies, plays, even worked together when I was an assistant at the medical center she worked at. And though there were times I suffered from homesickness, I hadn't considered Mom and how she felt. Wasn't my brother Jeremy visiting enough? Were her sisters too busy with their own lives to have dinner with her?

"Aw, Mom, what's going on up there? Not enough visitors?" I asked, the worry clear in my voice.

"Oh, no, I'm fine. I just call the landlord when I get too lonesome." I could see Mom's wicked smile through the phone line.

"Mother!" She loved to talk about the hot landlord (hot to her, not me) who was probably around Mom's age and never wore a wedding ring with his tight jeans. Gross.

"Ah, take a joke. I only called him once when the shower was acting up. He didn't even stay for dessert—if you know what I mean."

"Alright, now I'm getting off the phone, you perv. I need to tell Abby about this trip."

We exchanged goodbyes and I made a mental note to call Jeremy and hound him about visiting Mom. She might try to play it off like she was fine but I worried about her all alone in that apartment.

"Going on a trip?" Abby asked, slurping on broth. She had heard my entire conversation with Mom, but didn't look enthused like I thought she would.

"Yes! Aren't you excited? We're going to be international travelers! It's going to be the best!"

Another slurp. "How much money?"

I paused, twisting my lips. "Enough. But Irving gives us some money and we can volunteer to work events like hockey games and concerts at the Taylor and Taylor Arena to raise more. The rest does come out of pocket, though."

"And you think you can really afford that?" Abby sneered at me.

I recoiled at her harsh tone. "Yes, I will figure out a way. I'll get a job earlier than I anticipated. I'll figure it out. Why are you being so, so..." I wanted to say "so bitchy," but I wasn't sure I really wanted to pick a fight right then. I wanted to hold on to the euphoric feeling about Amsterdam.

Abby shrugged, turning back to her soup. I realized then she hadn't smiled once during the exchange about Amsterdam. Did that mean she didn't want to go? "Just trying to be realistic. You know your mom isn't going to loan you any money for it," she said.

I clenched my teeth together. She really needed to go there, right when I was so obviously excited and happy? "Yes, I'm well aware of that fact, Abby, but thanks for shoving that in my face right now," I snapped at her, turning on my heel to walk into the bedroom. "Let's try this conversation again when you aren't acting so immature!"

With that I slammed the bedroom door, and just for good measure, opened it and slammed it once again. Immature? Yes. But did I care? Not at all. Abby picked the wrong time to push a sensitive topic.

₭ℙ₭ℙ

The next day, Friday, Abby and I were still on shaky terms. She hadn't apologized to me about the money comment and I didn't feel I should be the one to break the ice. I left in the afternoon to go shopping with Cari, leaving Abby by herself in the apartment.

"Why are you two fighting?" Cari wanted to know on the drive to Hollow Creek Mall. I was behind the wheel because tough-as-nails Cari was terrified to drive on the interstate. Her hometown consisted of four main roads and one stoplight, so I could see how interstate and highway driving could be daunting to her.

"You've seen her attitude. I don't know what her problem is but I'm tired of the constant 'woe is me' thing she's got going on. It's been a month now, get the eff over it."

I turned in Hollow Creek's parking lot, inching my car along the pavement. Pedestrians filled the sidewalks, tugging their light jackets and sweatshirts on now that fall was approaching. The wind was wild, swirling the leaves in the air and causing careful hairstyles to become tangled. I was glad I chose a low ponytail, demure enough to match my knee length gray skirt, light purple sleeveless blouse with a long cream-colored overcoat, and no jewelry besides my earrings.

I was surprised with how busy the mall was on a Friday afternoon. I assumed people would be working, but as I drove down the fourth section of parking spaces without finding one vacant, I was starting to sense the place was packed. "Hope you don't mind walking," I said to Cari, finally squeezing my Breeze into a tight spot between a Hummer and a convertible.

"No prob," she replied, even though she was wearing five inches of spiked stiletto'd glory. True to her word, she made it to the door without whining or limping. Impressive. I had heels on myself, but a more comfortable pair of two-inch purple sandals complete with an ankle strap. My version of comfortable mall-walking shoes.

"This shit is huge," Cari proclaimed, stopping in her tracks and staring at the expansive architecture that displayed before us once we were inside. I had to agree. It was actually somewhat overwhelming. Three levels of buyer's paradise stretched before us, with a waterfall starting on the third floor and crashing onto rocks on the first. A glass elevator stood beside the waterfall, its clear frame giving shoppers an up-close view of the water droplets rushing by. Looking up, part of the ceiling consisted of only skylights, the sun's rays shining on shoppers below. Everything was open and inviting, just waiting to lure us in with promotions and sales.

We started at Victoria's Secret, natch. I was on the hunt for something special to wear when Nate came to visit in two weeks. Cari didn't have a boyfriend but she was a fan of wearing lingerie under her clothing, something I found hot and sophisticated. Maybe I should try that. Seemed a little pointless, though, if no one was going to enjoy it.

"Yeah, but I enjoy it. Wearing it makes me feel sexy and more confident, like I have a secret no one else knows. Unless I feel like throwing hottie Mr. Gabrison on the table after Econ class." She wiggled her blonde eyebrows at me, smirking.

"Ew! You think Gabrison is hot?" I gave her a shove, picking up a demi-cup bra. "That is so wrong."

"Come on, he can't be that old!"

"He has gray hair!"

"Only at the temples. That's sexy, polished. A silver fox."

"Wrong, wrong, wrong."

Cari sighed. "I bet he could teach me a few things in the sack."

"You're going way too far. He's your teacher." I felt the need to remind her of that small fact.

"I like to call him professor. But speaking of lessons, you going to teach Nate a few moves when comes? Excuse my pun," Cari laughed at her own crude joke.

I felt my cheeks grow warm. "I don't know. Maybe." I started to smile. "Hopefully."

Cari squealed. "Oh, and you think I'm bad. You're going to steal your boyfriend's virginity the second he steps onto that campus, aren't you?"

I shrugged. "I wouldn't consider it stealing, exactly. We've talked about it and…"

"Really? You've, like, discussed different positions and if you should light candles?"

"No! Not those sorts of details. Just, like, if we're ready and stuff. You know." I shoved Cari with one shoulder. "Stop looking at me like a dope. I know guys' virginities aren't quite the same as girls but I still want Nate to know that I care."

"No, I get it. I really do. And that's nice of you. Thoughtful, as usual. But you really should get something spicy to wear for him. Amp up the excitement a bit more." She picked up a red lace…thing. It looked like an apron, except the sides were cut out and there was no back. Not even anything to cover my ass with.

"Right. I think that might be a little too, um, risqué for my taste. How about just a teddy?" I made a beeline for the other side of the store, where the not-so-naughty outfits were kept. I didn't want Nate to be questioning my integrity. He was an innocent farm boy virgin. The more revealing outfits could wait for later in the relationship.

As Cari and I continued to search for my perfect V-card stealing lingerie, I let myself fantasize about the big night. Would we light candles or was that too cliché? Would Nate want to be on top? How long would it last?

"When was your first time?" I asked Cari later in the day, while we were browsing through Lila's Boutique.

"What? Oh, it was, like, oh, whatever." Cari suddenly became very weird, not looking at me and stammering over her words.

I fingered a pair of skinny jeans, feeling the smooth denim on my skin and wondering how I would look with my skinny ankles on display. "Say what? You're first time was whatever? What does that even mean?"

Cari's pale face became unusually red. "It's a long, complicated story, J. One that I don't want to talk about. Sorry, it's just…complicated. Let's just forget it, okay?"

My confident friend, the one who always had a comeback, something snappy to say, suddenly was at a loss for words? Was red in the face and her hands were shaking? What the hell was going on?

"Cari, do you need to talk about something? You can tell me—whatever it is—you can tell me," I said, feeling a sudden sensation of worry for her. What could have happened to bring on that sort of reaction?

"Later, okay? Just, later. Not in a mall, not right now, just not…yet. Not yet."

And with that, Cari walked to the other end of the store and disappeared inside a fitting room. She didn't have any clothes in her hands to try on.

Chapter Four

MOM SURPRISED ME WITH THE NEWS OF HER impending move on a rainy Wednesday afternoon. Classes were over for the day and I was sitting at the kitchen table working on travel homework when she called.

"Hi, Jasmine, how's your day?" she started off with. My radar immediately went up. She rarely used my full name unless I was in trouble or something was wrong. And I was pretty sure there was no way Mom knew that I stayed up until three in the morning with Cari and Kiley having a movie marathon night, almost making me sleep through my alarm that morning.

"Just doing homework. What's up, Mom?" I asked, tapping my pencil against my notebook. Was it Jeremy? Grace? One of Grace's kids?

"Well, I wanted to let you know some big news that I have." Did she find a man? The landlord? Getting remarried?

"Okay."

"I'm moving to Kentucky."

"What? Why?" I blurted out. Not what I expected.

"You know that your sister is there. And my grandkids. And with you gone and Jeremy being, well, a teenage boy and living with his father most of the time, I don't have much going on up here anymore. I need something to do and Grace has been thinking about going back to work. I can move in with them and watch Megan and Elliott so they don't have to pay for daycare."

I was silent for a few moments, clicking my nails on the table. Mom was moving? Leaving Iowa for good? Where would my home be now? Where would I go for holidays? Where would I stay when I went to Julien to visit Nate?

Mom told me she was moving in two months. Her job as a phlebotomist couldn't get a replacement for her until then and since she had been at her job over ten years, Mom made the decision to stay on and not leave them high and dry. That would also give her time to plan and organize a garage sale since she would no longer need her furniture. I listened quietly while she chatted about her plans, trying to be excited for her. She was lonely in Julien. I tried to come home every other weekend but I was busy when I was back, visiting Nate or doing homework. And by moving she would be able to see her grandchildren grow, something she probably otherwise wouldn't have the privilege to.

My big sister married Roy Ramsey when they were both just eighteen, straight out of high school. Roy had enlisted in the Army and was getting stationed in Fort Lewis, Washington. They needed to be married in order for Grace to live with him on base, and since they had dated all throughout high school and were madly in love, they quickly tied the knot on a hot July afternoon. They boarded their plane to Washington just four weeks later.

That was six years ago, and Grace and Roy have been on the move ever since. Roy's career had moved him all over the United States, once to Cuba and once to Germany. I placed some of the blame for my intense love of traveling on my sister's lifestyle because I would often fly with Mom and Jeremy to visit them. I loved seeing the new places, the people, the different lifestyles. I was only allowed to travel within the US, though. Cuba and Germany were too dangerous to visit according to Mom. I actually made a list of all fifty states and placed check marks next to the twenty-six I had visited, all thanks to Grace and Roy. I still have the list, and I was determined to check each and every state.

I couldn't focus on my homework after that phone call. My thoughts were too jumbled with the idea that my mom was moving. She wouldn't be just a drive away—she would be a whole plane ride away. Big difference. But I tried to remind myself that she was going to be happy. Grace and Roy had two children—five-year-old Megan and two-year-old Elliott. They would bring joy in her life. It often upset me that I couldn't spend more time with my niece and nephew. Mom needed to go, she really did. And I was going to be happy for her.

Knock, knock. I threw my pencil down and walked towards the door, thankful for whatever distraction was beckoning. It was Kiley, asking if I wanted to hit up Irving's gym with her. Perfect timing. A workout could definitely help clear my head.

Kiley had become my workout buddy after we realized we both had the motivation and drive to visit the gym on a regular basis. Another reason why I should never judge someone by their looks: not only was Kiley not a snob just because she looked like a supermodel, but she loved sports. She played basketball all throughout high school and could be seen almost every day in the gym shooting hoops. She liked to stay fit and I loved a good workout to keep me a size two, so we teamed up and kept each other motivated to get on the treadmill or in the weight room.

"So where is your sister stationed now?" Kiley wanted to know after I told her the news about my mom. I began telling her about Grace and her jet-setting life on our walk to the AC. We stepped into the empty weight room, setting our water bottles on the floor, and got down to business.

"They actually just moved to Kentucky. Hawaii had been in the running, which would have been sweet. But no. Kentucky." I blew a breath out while lifting ten pound dumbbells above my head.

"Have you been to Kentucky yet?" Kiley sat next to me on a weight bench, doing bicep curls. Her brown hair was tied back in a ponytail with a thin sweatband holding back her bangs.

"Nope. So at least I get to see someplace new. But really, Kentucky? What's there even to see?"

"Hey, maybe you'll be surprised. You might fall in love with the, um, the…" Kiley struggled to come up with anything interesting to see in the great state of KY.

"Yeah, fall in love with all the great stuff, huh?" I chuckled, setting my dumbbells down for a quick rest.

"Ha, sorry. I was trying. Are you really upset your mom is moving down there? And why exactly is she moving?"

"I guess she figured with me so far away and my brother not really needing her she might as well go see her grandkids grow up. Which I totally understand. I mean, I'm sad about it, don't get me wrong. It'll be weird having no one close by. But I can still call." I felt a twinge in my heart. Calling sure wouldn't be the same as a face-to-face visit every other weekend.

"I would be devastated if my mom and sister moved away from me." Kiley's expression turned solemn.

"Yeah, but you've always been close to your sister, right? Grace is eight years older than me and we didn't get along the greatest when she was in high school and I was the annoying little sister trying to hang around her. Then she got married and left. I still love her, of course, but without that connection I'm never really sad about it."

"I understand. Kimmy and I were best friends growing up. But she's only two years older than me, and we had to team up against our younger brothers. They were awful."

"My brother's only four years younger than me, not too bad, but twelve years younger than Grace. They have absolutely nothing in common. But Jeremy's at that age now where he's too cool for family. Just entering high school, boys have to keep up that tough image or whatever. I can hardly get him away from his phone or his friends when I go back to Julien."

"He has a different dad than you, right?"

"Right. My mom married Thomas, Jeremy's dad, three years before Jeremy came along. They divorced five years ago."

Kiley nodded, digesting my complicated family business. I had yet to tell her the real story behind Stuart and his disappearing act. I simply told my new friends my parents divorced and he never cared to stick around. I wasn't really lying. Just withholding a bit of the truth. What would they think of me if I told them the real story? I already had a twisted life as it was. And all my friends at Irving had normal families, parents still married. It made me feel like an outcast at times. Now with my mom going to be living in Kentucky my life would just get more complicated. And I wanted to keep those complications away from Irving, from the new me. I was no longer the girl with the all family issues. No one whispered about me in the halls of college. Because they didn't know the truth. And I planned on keeping it that way.

Kiley opened her mouth to undoubtedly ask me another question about my confusing family, but the door to the weight room opened then. I saw Kiley's face turn a shade of bright pink as two guys walked in, the taller one flashing her a smile. He looked muscular, like he lifted weights daily and did a hundred push-ups before bed. The other had overly-gelled hair and too pale of skin. Not the most attractive guy but still cute. I continued on with my workout, not paying attention to the guys any further. Until I noticed a little spark between Kiley and Muscles.

"You like working out, girl?" he asked her, tossing his water bottle on the floor.

Kiley's face remained pink as she answered. "Yes, um, yes, I do."

"Kinda unusual for a girl, especially one who's already so in shape." His voice had an odd sound to it, overly cocky and self-assured. A drawl, maybe. I didn't like the way his beady eyes scaled Kiley's figure. It looked like he wanted to ravage her right there in the weight room. In front of me and Gel-boy.

"Oh, um, thanks. I play basketball, so I try to keep in shape for that."

"Basketball, eh? Me too. Of course, boxing is my sport of choice, but I dabble in the hoops when I can find the time between trainings and fights."

Ah, a boxer. No wonder the cockiness. And that explains the bulging biceps.

Kiley couldn't seem to find any more words, so she just bobbed her head in place, the blush beginning to fade.

"Well, I would like to invite both you ladies to a party this weekend if you're interested. Over on 33rd Street by Waxton Avenue. Buddy of ours just got his own place and we need to break it in right." He nodded towards his pale friend, who lifted a hand in greeting.

"Name's Logan," he said. "I don't think I've met either of you yet. Both first-years?"

We nodded in unison. "I'm Jasmine, and that's Kiley. And what was your name?" I directed my question to Muscles.

"John. John Raymond. Pleased to meet you, Jasmine." He drew my name out, now looking me up and down. I felt naked under his stare. "I've already met Ms. Kiley here a few nights ago. I sure hope you both can make it this weekend."

"Did you know that guy?" I asked later. Kiley and I finished our workout quickly after John and Logan showed up. Neither of us liked lifting weights in front of guys.

"Well, kind of. He lives on my floor, and I met him at our floor meeting a few days ago. And have seen him around campus." Her cheeks were back to that pink color just talking about him.

"So, I'm going to guess you have a thing for him?"

"I—I—I don't know. Maybe."

"Girlfriend, you are bright red. You have a thing for him." I decided I wasn't good enough friends with Kiley yet to tell her I got scum vibes from John Raymond. Probably too early to worry, anyways. She could barely get a word out around him, much less date the douche.

"Do you want to go to the party with me this weekend?"

"Can't, sorry. Going home with Abby after class tomorrow."

"How is Abby?"

Pausing outside Kiley's room, I considered the question. "Still the same. Missing classes, says she's sick, no social life. I'm sure this weekend she's going to run right into Jason's arms. Whatever." I took a deep breath, trying to push the negative vibes away. "It'll be fine. Keep me posted on what happens this weekend. I'll want details, girl."

And with a wink, I took off. Back to my apartment and my unhappy roommate. Joy.

₧℗₧℗

Abby was napping when I got back from the gym, so I decided to give Nate a call. I still needed to wrap my mind around the fact that my mom was moving away. Except for the year she bailed, she had always been there. The longest we'd ever been apart didn't happen until I made the move to Des Moines.

"I can't help but only think selfish thoughts. Which is terrible of me, right?" I asked Nate. I slipped on my cream-colored overcoat and opened the door to our balcony. A blast of cold air smacked me as I stepped outside, but I stayed on the balcony. I didn't want to wake Abby.

"It's normal to think that, babe. She's your mom, your best friend, and she's moving away from you. It will take some time to get used to that idea. But nothing wrong being upset by the news."

"You're right. Of course you're right. And I am happy. I am. If it will make Mom happy, I will be happy. And it will just mean more trips to see the family. That I can't complain about."

"Thinking positive, that's more like it. What are your plans for tonight?"

"None. Maybe have dinner with Abby if she's up for it. What about you?" I asked, watching two cars pull out of Irving's parking lot. I wondered briefly about Abby and how my mom moving would affect her. Obviously I wouldn't be going back to Julien as much without her there. Where would I stay? Abby would be pissed when she found out the news. She wouldn't be able to see Jason as much if I didn't go home. But maybe that was a good thing. Less time in Julien meant less time she was around Jason. The thought perked me up.

"More homework. My calculus teacher is an animal." I refocused my attention back to Nate. "And I want to make sure I have all that out of the way for when you visit."

I smiled, feeling special that Nate was excited to see me. I knew he was my boyfriend—why wouldn't he be excited—but it was still a new feeling. So different from Kameron and the way he treated me.

"Well, I should get going then so I can do the same. I have a paper I need to type up sometime tonight and I'm starting to get hungry for dinner. I'll call you before bed, though, okay?" I said. After our goodbyes, I retreated back into my apartment.

Abby was coming out of the bedroom, wearing jeans and a Washington High navy sweatshirt. "Hey, you have any plans for tonight?"

"I was just going to work on a paper so I don't have to worry about it over the weekend. Why, what's up?"

"I'm craving some Happy Joe's pasta. Want to grab a bite with me quick? I won't be long so you could get some work done still when we get back."

I checked my watch, seeing it was barely past seven. Plenty of time. And with Abby actually offering to eat with me, there was no way I could pass that up. "Sure! Let me just grab my purse and we can head."

The car ride was mostly silent, but not the uncomfortable type. I let a CD play while I drove through the residential areas, past the posh golf course and up the hill to get to Happy Joe's. Abby and I quickly ordered our food, pasta and orange soda for her and plain cheese pizza slices and Sprite for me, grabbed some bubblegum jelly beans, and took a seat in the high-backed red chairs.

"Thanks for driving me here. I just couldn't get gooey pasta noodles out of my head."

"Not a problem. I didn't have any plans tonight anyways, except for that paper. Have you finished yours?"

"Ah, which paper is that again?"

I stared Abby, who continued to shovel pink jellybeans in her mouth. "The paper declaring your selection for our final project. I've been up to my ears studying Dubai. Where did you choose?"

More jellybeans. A shoulder shrug. "Um, I don't remember right now. Somewhere warm. Yeah."

"Somewhere warm? Abby, please tell me you have at least chosen what you are studying? I've been researching Dubai for weeks!"

Our waiter came at that moment, placing steaming food in front of us. Abby used the opportunity to stop talking to me about our travel class but I didn't want to let up. This was important. This was her grades! "Can I help you decide? Do you have a few choices you were thinking of? What about somewhere in South America? I bet you can find all sorts of ideas and information. I can help you tonight with it. I can just type my paper on Sunday when we get back."

"Jas, it's cool. I'll figure out, please don't worry. I'll be fine. Promise," she added when she saw the skeptical look on my face. "Now please eat your pizza before it gets cold."

&ℭℜ&ℭℜ

I walked into my 10:40 economics class the next morning and saw Cari in our usual seats, third row from the front. Cari claimed that was the closest she had ever sat in class and it was because she had a huge crush on the teacher, Mr. Gabrison. I didn't like sitting that close because economics was a foreign language to me, but I tried to humor my friend.

"I brought you a coffee," Cari said when I sat down, handing me a Styrofoam mug from the gas station down the road. She had an identical one placed in front of her. "I had to get myself one this morning and I thought it would be rude if I didn't get you one too."

"Well, thanks, doll. I appreciate it. But I've been awake since seven and in classes. I take it you haven't?" Cari's eyes looked only half open and she still had a telltale pillow crease lining her left cheek. Her outfit was perfection as usual: black leggings, a pink fitted blouse under a black blazer and towering black stilettos. Her makeup was minimal, only a light dusting of pink eye shadow covered her lids and she had managed to put some lipstick on, but she still looked fantastic for just waking up.

"Yeah, I had a date last night," she said, pausing to take a swig of her coffee. Some of her lipstick stayed behind on the mug. "I didn't get home until late and then I still had some homework to finish. If we didn't have a test today I would not be here."

"You didn't tell me you had a date! With who?" A cluster of boys walked in the classroom, all wearing baggy pants and hooded sweatshirts. They sat in the very last row and started talking in low voices. And I'm sure they weren't discussing the upcoming test.

Cari waved her hand in the air with nonchalance. "Just some guy I met at a party a few weekends ago. His name is Jacob. He's a sophomore at Kaufmann College."

"Where's that at?" I asked, not recognizing the name.

"Just on the outside of Des Moines. Not far from here. Anyways, he took me to dinner and we went back to his place and watched some movies. His roommates weren't there, so we had the place to ourselves." She wiggled her pale eyebrows suggestively at me.

"Cari! You didn't sleep with him on the first date, did you?" I had to ask. Cari seemed like a free spirit and always had her eye on a guy (or two or three), but I didn't want my friend to put out so easily.

"No! Of course not," she scolded me. "But just because we didn't go all the way, doesn't mean we couldn't round some of the bases," she said, just as Mr. Gabrison stepped in the room. He wore a dark gray suit matched with a sleek red tie and carried a briefcase. He was tall, well past six feet, but walked with a grace that most guys lacked. Even though he was turning gray at the temples, I guess I could somewhat understand Cari's infatuation with our instructor.

"Are you going to see him again?" I asked, lowering my voice when Gabrison started writing on the white board, signaling class was about to begin.

Cari shrugged her bony shoulders. "Probably not. He was kind of boring."

Kind of boring, yet she still rounded bases with him? Or was the rounding the bases the part that was boring? I opened my mouth to ask that question, but Gabrison beat me. "All right, class, welcome, welcome. Happy Thursday to you all. Now, let's open our textbooks to page forty-seven, shall we, and have a quick review before I pass out the tests."

The classroom was silent as textbooks opened, pages were flipped and pens clicked. Gabrison went through the review and answered questions by the students, including a question of Cari's that had her batting her lashes throughout.

After class was dismissed, Cari and I walked back to Williams Hall together. "How's Abby?" she asked, repeating Kiley's question from the night before. My answer that time was different.

"Actually, I think she's getting better. She offered to go out to eat with me last night. It was her idea and everything. I think that's the first time she's left the apartment in two weeks, except one time getting groceries with me. And she went to our travel class this morning."

"Well, that's an improvement," Cari said. We walked down the stairwell, saying hello to a group of girls all toting large book bags that passed by us.

"Yeah, so maybe whatever was bugging her passed? I really don't even care, just as long as she's human again and willing to accept Des Moines and Irving. That's all I want."

"Well, good luck. And have fun this weekend at home. I'll talk to you Monday." We had made it to the fifth floor, standing outside our apartments.

"Yeah, you too," I said. "Until Monday."

 —————

I sat quietly on Saturday evening in my bedroom at home, my eyes trying to soak in the words of my Geography textbook. I could hear Mom and Jeremy in the kitchen figuring out what items Mom could sell, what she wanted to keep, and what she could pass off to me and Jeremy. Mom sounded content, happy. I imagined she was glad to have two of her children with her that night, even though I needed to get studying in before a Wednesday test.

Nate understood the situation with my mom and why I wanted to stay home that particular weekend, and we agreed to have brunch together the next morning before I got back in the car to head to Irving with Abby. I had more conversations the past few days with Nate trying to sort out how I felt about my mom's impending move. I often wondered if he got tired of me repeating myself, but he never showed any signs of disgust or irritability when talking with me. His soft voice with just a hint of a country drawl kept me calm and focused on the positives. I felt like I was in a real relationship, one where two people really cared for one another and weren't selfish and truly wanted to see the other person happy. It was thrilling.

Abby seemed to be in a better mood the past few days. She finally apologized for the snipe on my mom, and I forgave her. She hadn't locked herself in the bathroom lately and she even started eating more. No more soup and bread for her. We ordered pizza together and went out for ice cream at Sweet Stop and feasted on turkey and Doritos sandwiches while watching our favorite TV shows together. Just like old times.

I leaned my head back against my pillows, letting the silk pillowcases envelop me in a feeling of comfort. Everything was going to work out. Abby was finally coming around to college and opening her mind to new experiences. My relationship with Nate couldn't be better. He was so different from Kameron, so patient and understanding and so not abusive. I was making great friends at college in Cari and Kiley. I was concerned still with Cari after our conversation in the mall, but I figured she would tell me when the time was right. And maybe then I could tell my new friends my life story, all the twists and incidents that led me to the path I was on then. Maybe. Maybe not. And now my mom would be happy, moving to see her grandchildren and feeling important and needed once again in the lives of those she loved.

I wrapped my arms around myself, wanting to hold on to that feeling of contentment forever. I let my eyes drift close, suddenly feeling very sleepy for the clock reading only half past eight. My life was finally right, finally free of people who felt the need to contaminate my happiness, to the demons that once pushed me to despair.

If only I could have sensed that was just the calm before the storm.

Chapter Five

"JASMINE." ABBY SAT AT OUR KITCHEN TABLE, expression serious. I had just walked in from classes, which Abby missed. I was a little surprised she didn't go to any. She seemed to be getting better and after the weekend in Julien I just assumed she was really starting to change. But she was still sleeping while I was getting ready and I didn't even try to argue with her.

It also surprised me that she had real clothes on, not just pajamas like she usual lounged around in after skipping class. Instead, she dressed in a gauzy white skirt that skimmed her toes, a baggy green and blue peasant top and her hair twisted back into a neat bun. Looking closely, I saw she even had makeup on. Mascara fringed her lashes and her face and skin glowed. I wondered briefly what the occasion was.

"Hey, you feeling better? We're having taco night down in Kiley's room later if you want to come with me. We're going to start making it a tradition. Every Wednesday a different theme." I started rooting in our cupboards looking for the corn chips I knew I bought last week. Cari was making homemade salsa and Kiley bought a queso dip from an authentic Mexican restaurant.

"Jasmine," Abby said once again. "Could you please just sit down for a sec? I need to tell you something. Important."

My hands froze between a box of Rice Krispie Treats and a loaf of white bread. Abby sounded serious. Way too serious. I turned slowly on my heel until I faced her. She couldn't make eye contact with me. Something was definitely wrong. Very wrong.

I took a seat opposite of Abby at the table, wondering what bombshell she was about to lay on me that day. "Okay, you have my attention. What's up?"

Abby took a deep breath and let it out slowly, shifting her gaze from above my head, to the door, down to her phone between her hands, back above my head again. "I guess I just have to come right out and say it. I'm pregnant."

And there they were. The two little words that changed my relationship with Abby, changed all the plans we had made for our new lives together. All gone away with those two little words.

"You can't be serious." I knew that wasn't the best reaction to the announcement, but by far not the worst thing I wanted to say at that moment.

"I am. Sorry. I'm almost eight weeks now, and I had to make a decision about what to do."

"What to do?" I spoke slowly, still struggling to comprehend her first announcement.

"Well, yeah. I'm dropping out of Irving. I'm moving back home."

"You're leaving?" I shouted, getting up from the table so fast my chair fell backwards, slamming into the wall. My confusion was quickly turning to fury as I realized she was serious. "But we just got here!"

"I can't stay in school, be pregnant and have a baby!" Abby yelled back, standing as well. "I need to be at home, taking care of myself."

"You're going to keep this baby?" I could feel my eyebrows rise in shock.

"I am NOT having an abortion, Jasmine! No effing way."

"So adoption! Thousands, millions, of people would die to have children. Responsible, *married* people."

"So, because I'm not married I can't have this baby?"

"Let's just back up a second. Is it Jason's baby?"

"Who else do you think it would be? Of course it's Jason's."

Of course. It's not like Abby embraced the college experience at all. She didn't even bother saying hello to people, much less sleep with them. No, she was too busy getting impregnated by her ex.

"And what does Jason think of this?"

"He's happy about it. We're moving in together."

My head throbbed. "What the fuck are you talking about? You're not even dating and last time I checked—he *cheated on you!* Like a million times! With a million different girls! And don't think I can't see that bruise on your arm, either. That's who you want to live with, want to raise a child with? You're insane, Abby. You're insane."

"I don't have to justify anything to you. This is my life and my decisions. I only came to this stupid college because you wanted me to. I never wanted to come. I don't care about college! It's a waste of money."

"Is that what Jason told you? Just because he doesn't have a college education you don't think you need one, either? I'm sorry, but what does Jason do for a living? What? Works part-time at an auto shop. Real winner there!"

In our six years of friendship, Abby and I never engaged in a screaming match like we were then. We stood across the table from one another, posed for battle. I felt she was ruining her life, all her chances. Going back to that scumbag and life in crummy Julien to start popping out kids? I could not watch her do that. I tried to be understanding of her past mistakes. All the times she took Jason back after he cheated on her or hit her. But now, she wanted to talk about a child. A real human being. We'd moved past the high school behavior and right into adult land. I wouldn't—couldn't—stand for it.

"I don't care what you think, Jasmine. Jason loves me. We've been through hard times but we aren't going to give up."

"You mean *you* aren't going to give up. Jason's given up on you plenty of times. And he'll keep doing it because you keep letting him get away with it." I stalked into the bedroom we shared, needing to get away from Abby. But as I crossed through the doorway, I saw our bedroom looked very different.

Abby's bed had been stripped of its sheets and comforter. The closet door hung open, looking oddly empty, and Abby's small pink suitcase stood by the door along with a handful of cardboard boxes.

"What the hell! Are you leaving right now?" I ran back out in the kitchen, where Abby still stood.

"Yes, I'm leaving right now. Jason is downstairs in the parking lot. I've already told Irving my decision to go." Brushing past me, she slipped in the bedroom and grabbed the suitcase. Pushing past me once more, she walked towards the front door. "And I'd appreciate if you weren't here when I come back to get the rest of this stuff. Have a great life, J."

"You're making a huge mistake!" I screamed after her, watching her retreating form shuffle through the hallway and down the stairs. Bursting into tears, I flung myself down on our couch. Just my couch now. Abby left. Really left. Our friendship could be deemed over. I couldn't watch her keep repeating the same mistakes, making the same bad decisions over and over and over. It was too much. I could no longer play the role of the supporting best friend. I was past that.

I cried for a few more moments until I realized that Abby and Jason would soon return for the rest of Abby's belongings. I had to get out of there.

I blindly picked myself up and grabbed my purse from the table. I ran down the staircase with no destination in mind, just needing to get away. I completely forgot about taco night and my contributions to the dinner. Life had just thrown me another curveball, and I did not want to handle it alone.

ೞೞೞೞ

"Pregnant? No way! What are you going to do?" Cari stared at me, her crystal blue eyes alight with shock and concern. After running out of my room I took the stairs to Kiley's fourth floor apartment, but she didn't answer. I forgot she mentioned she was studying in the library before taco night. The next move was to try Cari, even though her room was just kitty-corner of mine. I didn't want to risk running into Abby and Jason but I had to go somewhere. Luckily, the hallway was deserted and Cari answered right after the first knock.

"Yeah, pretty ridiculous. Totally out of left field. I just don't even understand what she's thinking. Jason is such a bad guy, Cari. He's just…awful." I started to cry again, and Cari wrapped me up in a hug, patting my back and hair and making comforting noises.

Through my tears I managed to take a look around her apartment. We usually met in Kiley's room, and Cari's apartment gave me a shock. She had told me her roommate was on the goth side, and she wasn't kidding. Heavy black curtains covered the oversized window, shunning their view of Irving's parking lot. Strange artwork had been placed around the white walls, all showcasing angry splashes of reds, blacks, and deep blue's housed between black frames. The small kitchen table, wedged behind the couch and the south wall, was covered underneath a black cloth. The room not only depressed me, it frightened me. I wondered how Cari could stand living here.

"Wow, you weren't kidding about your roommate, huh?" I managed to crack a smile at Cari.

She rolled her eyes, looking around in disgust. "Yeah, no joke, huh? You wonder why I don't like you girls coming in here. The whole vibe just screams emo. Or death. Or both." She gave a little shudder. "What's this Jason guy like anyways? What did he do that's so terrible?"

We sat on the couch together, facing one another. I kept my eyes on the floor, wondering if the time to reveal some of my past to Cari was now. I worked so hard on building up the persona I wanted for college. A life that was drama free, where new friends didn't need to know my secrets. Could I really be willing to share my stories? But something was telling me I could trust Cari. She wouldn't judge me. I decided to go with my gut feeling.

I took a breath, finally raising my eyes to hers. "Jason was best friends with my ex-boyfriend, Kameron. Kam and I and Abby and Jason all started going out right around the same time, when Abby and I were in eighth grade. Kam and Jason are older than us by two years, so we thought it was a big deal to be going out with high school boys." I paused, thinking about the early days with Kameron. I thought he might be the one I would marry some day. Abby and I often talked about our weddings, how of course we would be the maids of honor for each other. That was a joke now.

I told Cari about the beginning, how everything was perfect and smooth. The double dates, losing virginities, family vacations, everything was a first for both me and Abby, and soon months turned into one year, then two with Kameron and Jason. But after two years, things started to change. Kam and Jason became distant, breaking plans with us and often disappearing in the night without answering our phone calls. We began to catch them in lies, and Abby even walked in on Jason in bed with another girl.

"When we would try to argue with them, it just got worse." I paused and shook my head, slowly running my finger across the scar on my forehead. My Harry Potter scar. I had gotten eight stitches right in the middle of my forehead, and people at my school jokingly referred to it as the Harry Potter scar, because the fictional character also had a scar on his forehead. But they laughed because they thought I fell. They didn't know the truth.

"The boys started to get physical with us. Like hitting and shoving. Abby got it pretty bad one night after she found Jason cheating on her. She had a black eye for weeks, and he broke two fingers on her right hand. He was twisting her arm around or something and pulled too hard on her hand."

Cari stared at me with eyes wide, completely entranced by the horror stories I was spilling onto her. "And what happened to you?" she asked, her voice just above a whisper.

I took a deep breath, trying to prepare myself for the hardest part of my story. "Well, Kameron was the same as

Jason. Hit me a few times, called me every name in the book. I don't know why I stayed. Why we stayed with them. But I guess I was young and naïve. I was hoping Kam really did love me and whatever. But one night, Kameron came over to the apartment I lived in with my mom. It was the night before homecoming and he said a girl from his class wanted to have dinner with him. I said no, I didn't think it was appropriate. He was going to be going on a date with another girl, you know?"

Cari nodded her head in agreement, eyes looking straight at me. She reached over and grabbed onto my hand, seeming to understand I was agitated reliving my past.

"Anyways, we started arguing and he slapped me once, right across the face." I touched my left cheek in memory. "Then he picked me up and threw me against my bedroom wall. Kam was pretty tall, like six-two, and I was just a scrawny thing in high school. It took him no effort, just picked me right up and threw me at the wall. My forehead smashed on a glass figurine I had hanging there, and then I blacked out." I shut my eyes, remembering waking up in a puddle of my own blood. "When I finally came to, Kameron was standing over me kicking me in the chest and stomach. I was bleeding from my forehead, my mouth, and my elbow had been cut on the glass. But he just kept kicking away." I started to cry, all the horrible memories rushing back to me. The taste of blood in my mouth. The pain in my body. The pain in my heart, watching someone I loved treat me that way. Tears ran down my cheeks and I couldn't stop them.

"Oh, my God, Jasmine." Cari pulled me into a hug, wrapping her thin arms around me and holding me close. I leaned into her, grateful for a friend. Besides my mom, Abby, and the police, the only other person I had told this story to was Nate. It hurt to talk about, hurt to think about.

"Luckily, my mom walked in shortly after I came to. She started screaming and Kameron just took off. He ran right past my mom and out the door. Mom called the cops and they caught him at home, watching TV and acting like nothing had happened. I had to stay in the hospital, get eight stitches in my forehead," I gestured to my scar, "and I had three cracked ribs. I missed homecoming, I couldn't cheer for months, it was one of the worst moments in my life. And I've had some crappy things happen to me, believe me." I paused again, thinking about my life and how I could never seem to catch a break. "But I learned. I learned about love, about power, about abuse. I obviously got out of that relationship, did some therapy. Moved on with my life."

"And Abby and Jason?" Cari wanted to know.

I shrugged my shoulders. "She sticks with him. She got beat up a lot more than I did, because she never really put up a fight. Jason knew he could do whatever and get away with it. And she would just turn a blind eye when she caught him cheating. It's like she doesn't want to believe it or something. I really don't know. She always says she can't find someone better, she doesn't think she's pretty or funny or anything, so she just sticks with him. I'm—I'm afraid for her. Every time she goes back to him, I'm afraid she's going to end up in the hospital—or worse. These guys are capable of doing terrible things and she just lets him get away with it. And now to be having a baby." I shrugged again, feeling hopeless.

"Wow, Jasmine, I—wow," Cari said, holding both my hands now. "That's just so, so, awful. And sick. And—just— I'm so sorry you had to deal with that."

"Yeah, it was bad. But I got better, got help. But I feel like if I can't convince Abby to get away from him, I'm failing as a friend. But how do I stick by her side now when she is willing to have a baby with him? And what if after the baby is born he does something to it? I can't handle it anymore!"

"Jasmine, you're not doing anything wrong. You've stayed by Abby's side for years now and you've tried to help her. Some people just refuse the assistance. You can't blame yourself. Abby needs to get her shit figured out. You've done all you can. It's up to her now."

I listened to Cari as she spoke, trying to settle my feelings. I had supported Abby for years. Helped cover her bruises, backed up her lies, comforted her while she cried. I didn't want to play that supporting role anymore. I wasn't going to help Abby by helping her live a lie. And that's why I tried so hard to pull her from Julien, away from Jason. I hoped that starting Irving would help her realize domestic abuse is not common, not okay, not legal. But no matter how hard I tried to get her to leave Jason, she wouldn't budge. But I tried. At the end of the day, I tried to help my best friend and she refused. Now, she was going back to Julien, going to have a baby. I couldn't support that, so I had to let her go.

"I have to let her go, don't I?" I asked Cari, resting my head on her shoulder.

"I think you do, honey. It's just like a break-up, only this is your best friend. But I think it's what you have to do. I hate seeing you crying and hurting. Sometimes, friendships just need to end."

I nodded slowly. "Will you stay with me tonight? I don't really want to be alone in that apartment. Not just yet."

"You know I will. Let's turn taco night into a sleepover. I'm sure Kiley will stay too."

I managed a smile. "Thanks. You're a really good friend."

"Ah, don't mention it. Just wait 'til I tell you some of my issues. You'll have to listen to me crying away. Payback." We laughed in unison.

"Will you do me a favor, though?"

"I'll do anything for money."

I cracked another smile. "Will you tell Kiley all that? I just hate telling the story. Just fill her in for me so she understands why I'm de-friending Abby."

"I sure will. Now, come on, let's get out of this creepy ass apartment. I can only stand being in the dark for so long."

And with that, I followed Cari out the door, breathing a sigh of relief. One life story down and my friendships were still intact. I still felt uncomfortable that my persona had been cracked. Maybe I was making a mistake telling my friends the whole truth about me. And what about the other complications in my life? Would my new friends still be as willing to comfort me? And what about Nate? I would have to tell him the story about my father sometime. What would he think of me then?

I didn't sleep easy that night, tossing and turning, my dreams haunting memories of my past. I was grateful once morning came, and I could put all my energy on classes and schoolwork. The emotional drain from the day before was exhausting, but at least I was only talking about my past. I had already lived it, survived it, and that was the toughest part.

যটফট

"Whose side are you on, Nate?"

"Jasmine, there are no sides. And you know if I had to choose one, it would be yours. I wasn't trying to upset you more."

"Well, that's exactly what you did!" I shouted into the phone, outraged at my boyfriend. I waited until the next afternoon to call Nate and let him know I was down a roommate and a best friend. He had been appropriately shocked at Abby's pregnancy, and everything seemed to be going fine with our conversation. Until I started talking about how Abby was going to miss out on so many things in her life––college at Irving and traveling to Amsterdam were just two of those examples—when Nate said that maybe that wasn't Abby's plans. Maybe we had different goals in life.

What was he talking about? Abby and I were two peas in a pod, had been since the seventh grade. We liked the same movies, we wore our hair the same way, we shared clothes and shoes, we picked the same college and the same major. Why would Abby not want to live in Des Moines and go to Irving? Des Moines was the capitol! It has more opportunity than crummy Julien. And Irving was a top business college! Not just some run-of-the mill community college. And traveling! Who wouldn't want to travel, especially to a place like Amsterdam? No, Nate was wrong. And I told him that.

I heard him sigh on the other end of the line. I wondered briefly if I was being too stubborn. But only briefly. "Look, Jasmine, babe, I know you are frustrated right now. I was just wondering—trying—to take a different angle. I didn't mean to upset you. I know how hard this must be for you already."

I sighed deeply. "You're right, Nate. I'm sorry if it seems I was taking it out on you. You don't deserve that." I rubbed a hand on my forehead. "I'm sorry," I repeated, feeling much calmer. "You make some good points. But I don't really know what to do about it. I can't talk to Abby right now. I just can't. She left me. *She* left *me*. I just can't handle it right now. Maybe in a few weeks or something I can try again."

"And I think that is just fine, babe. Don't let yourself get stressed out about it. I have a feeling something will change, and your friendship with Abby will be back to normal before you know it."

ഇരുഇരു

I trudged up the cement steps outside of William's Hall, on my way to the Administration building. I had a meeting with the head of financial aid and was going to figure out a payment plan to help cover the cost of tuition, books and housing that student loans didn't extend to. I hoped they would be understanding with me. I had a minimal amount in savings that I could put towards what I owed but without getting a job I knew it wasn't going to be enough. Could I get kicked out of school for that?

And to make everything worse, my best friend was gone. Stormed out of our apartment and college life because she was pregnant. That was just the cherry on top. I wondered if I would have to get a new roommate. What if I didn't get along with her? What if she liked country music or was a neat freak or refused to ever leave the apartment like Abby? I would be so uncomfortable in my own home if any of those scenarios applied. I tried to be calm like Nate had told me to be. Not stress yet. Things would turn around.

I barely felt the sun on my back as I walked. The warm days were numbered. Soon enough, the snow would come, the winter would arrive. The Midwest would be blanketed under snow, classes would be cancelled and everyone would complain about the weather and stock up on salt and shovels. The holidays would come, the Christmas lights would shine from houses and snowmen would be built in the yards. Life would go on as normal. And I would still be without my best friend.

I found the reception desk and checked in. The young woman, whose name badge read "Shelley" and had white blonde hair almost reaching her waist, crossed my name off her clipboard and told me to take a seat. I waited patiently, crossing my legs and pulling out my cell phone to help pass the time. I re-read some of my saved text messages from Nate. He often sent me quirky little messages throughout the day that would cheer me up. Little poems or song lyrics that reminded him of me, or just a few simple words saying he wished he could see me smile that day. Each message reminded me how much I missed him and how much I liked him as my boyfriend.

I was scrolling through the messages, smiling like a sap, when a voice said my name.

"Are you Jasmine Jones?"

I looked up at my greeter, expecting to see the heavy-set woman from financial aid. Instead, a trim brunette had her hand extended to me in welcome, her pinstriped gray suit looking polished and professional. An aquamarine ruffled blouse peeked through her suit jacket and she had matching earrings and a bracelet to go with the blouse. Her chestnut hair gleamed in a way I thought only celebrities could achieve, but her face was friendly and inviting. President Natalie Greer of Irving University.

I jumped up from my seat, throwing my cell phone inside my purse. The president! I had met her formally once, when Abby and I came down for our tour before classes started. I couldn't believe I had met her. I hadn't ever met the principal at my high school during my four years there. And here she was again, remembering my name and everything.

I stuck my hand out and hoped I gave a firm handshake. "Uh, yes. Yes, that's me," I said, stammering over my words. I cleared my throat awkwardly. "Nice to meet you again, President Greer."

She smiled at me, surely able to sense my nervousness. "I thought that was you I saw sitting here. I was just heading back to my office from lunch in the diner." The president ate lunch at the school diner? Like a normal student or teacher would? "I wanted to touch base with you this week anyways, make sure you're okay with your roommate situation."

I could feel my face fall into a frown. Of course President Greer would know if one of her students dropped out due to pregnancy. I wondered what she thought of Abby's situation. Of course, she didn't know Jason and that side of the story, but I could bet she still wasn't happy about it. "I'm okay," I answered, trying to force a smile back on my face. I doubted she would be impressed if I started crying in front of her. "It was surprising, and—and—and just not expected," I finally managed to spit out. *Get a grip, Jasmine!* I mentally shook myself out of my stupor. "I can only wish the best for my friend now," I swallowed down the word 'friend,' "and hope everything goes smoothly for her."

President Greer nodded, her pretty face etched in sympathy. "I know it must be hard for you. I remember meeting you girls on your tour and you said you were such good friends." She remembered that? "Please know if you ever just need someone to talk to about it, my door is always open. "

"Jasmine Jones?" The financial aid officer was in the hallway now, signaling the start of my meeting. But I didn't want to stop talking to President Greer. I couldn't believe how down to earth, easy to talk to she was. She was the president of the university! She sat on the board of the Greater Des Moines Committee and helped better the town. She donated thousands of dollars a year to charities and schools. And she was standing in front of me, remembering my name and my past and giving a damn about how I was doing. I was amazed. And shocked, to be honest.

"I'll let you get to your meeting. But please, feel free to stop up anytime or schedule a visit with my secretary, Sheila. That way you'll know I'll be in my office." She squeezed my shoulder gently. "Good luck with your first year. I hope you enjoy Irving." And with that, she took off down the hallway, waving at Shelley behind the desk and then disappearing around the corner.

I followed Marybeth Lewis into her office, ready to crunch numbers and devise a suitable plan for me. But I felt lighter than when I first entered the building. President Greer knew me by name, offered to let me chat with her when I needed it. I wondered if it would ever come in handy having a connection with President Greer. Like my mom always said, it's not what you know, it's who you know.

Chapter Six

NATE'S VISIT TO DES MOINES COULDN'T HAVE COME at a better time. Abby had been gone for a week, I had no roommate, and I was stressing out over my money situation. I needed my boyfriend to snuggle up with, to stroke my hair and tell me everything would work out. And maybe, just maybe, tell me he loved me.

I was in love. With Nate. Obviously. He consumed my thoughts throughout the day and night. Seeing his name on my caller ID gave me butterflies. I had never met someone who was so understanding, so willing to talk to me for hours when I was upset or angry. Even the tiny tiff we got into over Abby's situation hadn't deterred my loving thoughts towards him. The distance wasn't bothering me near as much as I thought it would. No other guy at college could turn my head. Nate was the only one I wanted. And I wanted to tell him I loved him. And then probably throw up if he didn't say it back.

"Are you excited Nate's coming down tomorrow?" Kiley asked me. Cari and I were in her room watching mindless television while we painted our nails and tried on a new face cream Cari made. Yes, made. She said she used avocados and milk and some other edible things to slather on our faces and hope for the pimples to stay away.

"Couldn't be more excited. I need to think about something than other than losing my best friend."

Kiley gave my shoulder a gentle squeeze. She looked beautiful as ever tonight, even though we were dressed casual, with gray sweatpants dotted with yellow hearts and a tight white tank top, her brunette locks tied back in a loose French braid. Cari looked casual but still flashy: hot pink shorts with the word CORONA splashed across the butt and a light pink zip-up with nothing underneath. The girl didn't even need a bra; she was that flat-chested.

"Could I ask you girls a question?" I picked at some invisible lint on my purple tank top. Though my friendships with Kiley and Cari were growing stronger by the day, I still felt slightly hesitant to start talking about deeper subjects than just shopping and crushes. But Abby was gone now, and I needed to learn to confide in my new friends.

"What up?" Cari asked, touching her fingertips to her avocado-filled face, checking the progress of the mask.

"Have either of you ever been in love?"

"I haven't," Kiley answered, looking over at Cari.

"I think I have," Cari responded. "My junior year. I dated Martin for a year but then we just kind of drifted apart. Didn't have much in common. No bad blood, it just fizzled. And I'm not really sure love can just fizzle, you know? I think if we really had been in love we would have tried harder. But I think it was definitely close to love."

"Why do you ask, J?" Kiley wanted to know.

I paused before answering. "I—I think I may be in love with Nate. And I want to tell him this weekend but…what if he doesn't love me back? And then breaks up with me or something?"

I explained to the girls my feelings, or tried to at least. It was difficult to describe. I just knew that there was something different about Nate, something special that we shared. I could feel the passion and yearning for him spread throughout my entire body, from scalp to toenails. The intensity frightened me in a way, but also comforted me. Nate was my best friend, maybe even my soul mate, if I decided I believed in such a thing.

"I say you go for it. Love is all about risk, which might sound crummy but I think it really pays off in the end. And by the way you talk, you and Nate do have a special relationship. You guys are such opposites, but I think that's what keeps your attraction interesting."

"I agree with Kiley. You'll never know until you say anything. And even if he doesn't love you back, that's nothing to break up over. We all know guys are stupid and slower to mature. He might just need some more time."

I sighed, taking in the advice. "This weekend is just making me so nervous. First time Nate is visiting campus. First time we are having sex. First time he is having sex, period. And now first time saying the "L"-word. It just feels like a lot of pressure."

The three of us sat in silence for a few minutes, thinking, until I couldn't take it anymore. "Okay, let's change the subject. I feel like I could throw up if I keep thinking about it any longer," I said, wanting to get away from my thoughts for a moment.

"Okay. What did Wanda say about your roommate situation?" Cari asked, shaking up a bottle of pink nail polish.

I sighed, remembering my conversation with Irving's housing coordinator. "Either I have to get a new roommate before next term starts or I have to pay double to live on my own." Another reason to be stressed about money. I couldn't afford double rent. I could barely afford rent as it was, but now trying to scrape together money for the Amsterdam deposit…it was getting to be too much.

"I wish the three of us could move in together," Kiley said.

I narrowed my eyes. The three of us. Roommates. It was a terrific idea! "Why can't we?" I blurted out.

Kiley paused, looking thoughtful. "I don't know. I guess I never actually considered it. It would just be fun."

My spirits bungeed back to the floor. "Oh, so you don't really want to then?"

"No, no. I do. I would. Definitely. I mean, I get along just fine with my roommate but she isn't here a whole lot and it gets kind of lonely. That's why I'm always inviting you two over. Do you think Wanda would approve?"

"She would have to approve!" Cari exclaimed. "We would be doing this to help a friend. It's not Jasmine's fault Abby dropped out. Let's go talk to her right now!" Forgetting about the plate of chips balanced on her lap, she jumped up, spraying Doritos all over Kiley's white carpet. "Whoops, I'll pick those up."

I started to laugh. "You guys, that is awesome. You really don't have to do it, though, if you don't want. I'm sure I can find somebody or maybe Wanda will help place me."

"Nope, we're doing it. We want to, right, Cari?" Kiley asked, looking from Cari's eager face to the Doritos still taking up residence on her floor.

"Right! Seriously, I'll pick those up."

"Well, let's sleep on it tonight and then we'll talk to Wanda tomorrow and see if she'll approve it. If you both still want to."

೮ාඥ೮ාඥ

"Excellent, babe! Do you think the school will let you?" I called Nate the minute I got back to my deserted room, excited to tell him my possible roommate news.

"I think so. I hope so. I'll just be relieved if I won't have to pay more rent money. I don't know how I planned on swinging that."

"You would've figured it out. You always do."

Nate's vote of confidence in me boosted my mood. He was right, I could do it. Even if something happened and Irving wouldn't let the three of us live together, I could still do it. Even if only one person believed in me, that was enough to make me believe in myself.

"Are you excited to see me tomorrow?" I asked, cradling the phone between my chin and shoulder so I could remove my contact lenses.

"You bet. And that you won't have any roommates yet to ruin our fun."

A thrilling shiver traveled down my spine. A little part of me kept wondering if he would possibly back out of doing the deed. It was his first time after all. I knew guys were different and didn't put the emphasis on virginity, but still. It was Nate.

"Unless you don't want to, of course." Nate mistook my silence for hesitance.

"No, no, I do. I mean, of course I do. Just caught me by surprise there, sir," I giggled into the phone like the teenage school girl I was.

"Good. I miss you, baby."

"I miss you too, babe." Tears poked at my eyes. I really did miss Nate. Sure, I was busy with classes and friends and parties and now the Abby crap, but I missed Nate every day. He was the last person I talked to at night and the first I thought about in the morning. I wished he could be here with me now, sitting in the dark where Abby once was.

Instead I sat alone, wondering what Abby was doing, how she was feeling and if Jason was there for her. I could bet he wasn't, and that made me sad. Even though we weren't friends anymore I hoped she would be okay. I was speaking the truth when I told President Greer I only wished her the best.

"Babe? You there?" I had gotten so wrapped up in my own thoughts, I almost forgot I was on the phone.

"Sorry. Yeah, I'm here. Just thinking about things."

"Like what we're going to do tomorrow?" Nate had that devilish tone to his voice again, immediately making me think of him. Naked. In my bed.

"Oh, you just wait, babe. Tomorrow can't come soon enough."

෨෪෪෨෪෪

I was never a culinary genius. Not even close. But I loved being the perfect hostess. Wearing the perfect outfit, having the carpets vacuumed, the end tables dusted and the centerpiece placed just right made me feel good. But I never caught on to the cooking/baking part of being a hostess. It was one of my secret wishes to host a fancy dinner party one day, where I make six courses and served everything on matching plates and had rings holding the napkins together.

But we all have to start somewhere and before I could get to that dinner party, I was going to attempt to bake cookies. Simple, chocolate chip cookies. And not from a box pre-prepared by Betty Crocker. Dough made from me, from scratch. I wanted to greet Nate with a plate of homemade cookies just for him when he arrived. The best way to a man's heart is through his stomach and all that. And hopefully his libido was included in that cliché.

I glanced at the clock, noting I had roughly two hours before Nate would be in Des Moines. I rolled up my sleeves—

because that's how I saw the cooks do it on their shows—and compiled the ingredients on the counter. I had bought flour, eggs, butter, baking soda, vanilla extract, chocolate chips, white sugar *and* brown sugar, and even some salt during my grocery run that morning. I didn't think salt belonged in a cookie recipe but I was determined to follow every last step.

I carefully measured out the flour, baking soda and salt, and dumped those ingredients in a small mixing bowl I borrowed from Kiley. I plugged in the electric mixer (also borrowed from Kiley) and added the butter, both sugars and vanilla in that mixing bowl, put the beaters in the bowl and turned them on. The ingredients started flying everywhere. Butter, sugar and vanilla went spraying out from the mixing bowl, hitting my face, my clothes and the walls. "What the fuck!" I shouted to the mixer, yanking the cord out of the wall. The whirring noise stopped.

"Great. That's just great," I looked around at the mess I had made. Vanilla-smelling butter and sugar was dripping down the wall and the side of my face. Just what I needed.

I took a break to clean up my mess and change my clothes, opting for an oversized white tunic (so I would still be able to roll up my sleeves) and casual black yoga pants. Just in case I made a mess again, I didn't want to be wearing nice clothes.

I turned the beaters on before slowly lowering them into the batter, which worked a lot better. No flying batter. I added all the ingredients together and made sure they were properly mixed. I even cracked my eggs in a separate bowl before adding them to the main ingredients. It was one of the few things I remembered from my junior high cooking class. It worked for me that day because I had to pick out a few shells. Nate didn't need crunchy cookies.

Once all my mixing was complete, I dropped spoonfuls of the batter onto a cookie sheet. The sheet filled quickly but I still had batter left in the mixing bowl. I assumed this meant I put the cookies too far apart, and rearranged them so the uncooked dough was practically touching. All the batter fit after that, so satisfied with my work, I slid the pan in the oven.

I was getting ready to set the timer on my cell phone when it rang. My sister was calling.

"Hey, Grace," I answered, abandoning the timer and starting to clean up my mess of mixing bowls and utensils.

"Hi, sister. What are you doing?"

"Making cookies for Nate."

"As in, baking them? Why?" Grace had as much culinary skills as I did. Possibly even less.

"I thought I would do something nice for him. It wasn't even that hard," I bragged, before reminding myself about the batter flying incident. I would keep that one to myself.

"Well, I hope he likes them. But I'm sure a bakery could have made them just as easily."

I rolled my eyes. "I know, I know, but I really want to start baking. And maybe try some cooking. It's just following a recipe. It can't seriously be that hard." *Flying batter.*

"You let me know how that works out. Are you sad Mom's moving away?" she asked, changing subjects.

I gave up trying to clean while on the phone and settled on the couch instead. "Well, yeah. But if she's going to be happier with you then that's all that matters."

"The kids will wear her out, that's for sure. I'm glad I get to go back to work full-time. We could use the extra money." Grace and her husband were not hurting for money, I knew that, but my sister had a slight shopping problem. Heavy on the slight.

We chatted for a few more minutes about how the living situation would work with our mom in their house before Grace abruptly changed the topic again. She had the attention span of a toddler.

"Did I tell you I got locked in the back storage room a few days ago at work?"

"No. What happened?" Grace worked part-time for the home goods store Bracken.

"I was back in storage to pull some items out to the front and the door somehow locked and I got stuck back there! I was trapped for almost half an hour banging on the door and waiting for someone to realize I wasn't on the floor." Grace sounded distressed reliving the story.

"Did someone finally come get you?"

"Yes, after awhile. But the storage room is tiny and I thought for sure I was going to pass out and then who knows how long it would have taken for someone to find me? It was horrible, sister!"

"Oh, I can imagine. Sounds bad." I tried to keep the laughter out of my voice. Grace could be slightly overdramatic when she wanted to be.

"It's not funny!" She must have detected the laugh. "That room is tiny and you know how claustrophobic I am! It's not my fault that our father used to lock me in sleazy hotel rooms so he could go off and do his drug deals. He's the reason I'm claustrophobic!"

"Grace, I know. I wasn't laughing at you. I'm claustrophobic, too. I would hate being locked in a room. But––" I sniffed the air suddenly. What was that smell? "Oh, shit. My cookies! I forgot to set the timer!" I jumped off the couch and ran to the oven. The burning smell was stronger.

"Did you burn the cookies? I told you to go to the bakery!" Grace was saying over the phone.

"Yes, they're burnt. I have to go. I'll call you later!" I dropped the phone and pulled on an oven mitt, throwing the oven door open. The smell intensified, and I grabbed the edge of the cookie sheet and pulled it out, setting it atop the burners.

"Oh, no!" I shouted, looking at my cookies in dismay. Or, just the one cookie. Not only were they burnt, the edges blackened and hard, but the little spoonfuls of dough had run together and now one massive cookie covered the pan. It looked like a cookie cake. That was definitely not what I had in mind.

After letting my creation cool down, I carefully cut away the black edges with a pizza cutter, disposing them in the garbage. I sliced off a middle section and gave it a taste. It really wasn't that bad. Not the best cookie I had ever tried, but certainly not the worse. I sliced up the rest of the middle, making do with square cookies instead of round ones. Hopefully Nate wouldn't ask too many questions, and I wouldn't provide the details on my baking fiasco.

§೦೦೪§೦೦೪

It was as if I put a magic love spell on my square cookies. It took only one hour and three cookies for Nate to hand over his V-card. One hour, and the weekend went from there. Our plans of touring Des Moines, seeing the capitol building, walking around the lake, meeting my new friends and seeing my classrooms, *poof!* Magically gone. Instead, Nate and I saw each other, and only each other. In the bedroom, in the living room, on the kitchen table, the shower, even the outdoor balcony with the chance my neighbors could step out onto their balcony at any given moment. I blamed the new lingerie Cari had convinced me to buy.

My muscles were sore, my legs felt like jell-o, but I was glowing. I loved Nate; the weekend had cemented that thought. The chemistry between us was unexplainable, something that just happened between two people who are so clearly meant to be together. My heart felt like it could burst with happiness, my body tingled all the way down to my toes. It was love.

"Jasmine," Nate whispered my name, his mouth next to my ear. Sunday morning had arrived, only a few more hours until Nate would have to pack up and drive back home to Julien. I didn't want to open my eyes and accept the day was beginning.

I snuggled deeper under the comforter, leaning my head against Nate's chest and tucking one leg under his. "Hmmm," I mumbled.

"I love you."

My eyes snapped open and my breath caught in my throat. Did he just say those words? Or did I imagine them? Was I dreaming? I lifted my head until I looked him in the eyes, wondering if the moment was for real.

"I love you, Jasmine," he said it again, this time reaching one hand out and placing his palm on my cheek. I felt his calloused hand against my skin, and knew I was wide awake. "I love you."

"I love you, Nate!" I cried, pushing my mouth firmly into his. I felt tears on my cheeks, happy tears, of course. Nate loved me. I couldn't believe somebody could really love me. Especially someone like Nate. I couldn't have asked for a better guy. My guard, once so high on the defensive, was now completely buried. I trusted Nate. I loved him with everything I had.

The moment grew intense, our kiss growing more passionate and deep by the second. Our tongues danced and twisted with urgency, almost like we were trying to outdo one another. Nate slipped the t-shirt off my body and threw it aside. I pulled at his boxers, tugging the material down past his ankles. My chin had already started to chafe against his two day stubble, but I ignored the scratches.

"Wait, wait, wait. We used the last condom last night," Nate tried to sit up, catching his breath.

"What? No," I started to say before realizing he was right. We laughed at that fact last night, but not today. Not when the electricity was flowing between us. The want was there. The desire. The love. It wasn't right to ruin the moment.

"You're on the Pill, right?"

I nodded quickly. Birth control! Of course! I had been taking that little blue pill from the time I lost my virginity and no pregnancy for me. It was ninety-nine percent effective or somewhere close to that. We would be fine!

"Do you think it would be okay then?" Nate asked, hovering above my body, poised and ready to enter.

"Yes, yes, yes. I'm sure it'll be fine," I said, reaching up and pulling him into me. But wait—had I taken the Pill yesterday? Or Friday? I usually took it around nine at night but with the excitement of Nate being in my apartment and all the, well, sex we'd been having, I couldn't remember if I had taken it. Oh, well, I would just take three that night. I was sure people didn't get pregnant only missing one pill. Or two.

Chapter Seven

"I NEED A JOB." I LOOKED DOWN AT MY CALCULATOR, double-checking the numeric figures. My savings account would be depleted in a few weeks, between buying books for the winter term, stocking up on groceries and having a social life. I started working events at the T&T Arena to help pay for my Amsterdam trip, but without securing a job there would be no way I could make the deposit. Even if I starved myself for the next two months and didn't leave my apartment except to attend classes.

"How far from your goal are you?" Kiley sat upright on the floor, back leaning against the couch. Cari perched behind her on the couch, twisting Kiley's hair into a stylish chignon.

"Couple hundred or so. Probably more if I want any spending money there."

"Ouch. That sucks, hon. When and where are you going to start job hunting?" Cari asked, blunt as usual.

"I don't even know." I cradled my head in my hands, desperate for a solution to pop out at me. "I still barely know my way around Des Moines and between classes, homework and the trip, I don't know how much time that leaves me to work."

"Well, you have to do something. There's got to be a way." Cari looked down at Kiley's hair, a thoughtful frown pushed across her face.

I appreciated my new roommates trying to help me come up with ideas. Yes, my new roommates. Irving approved the three of us living together, which meant moving to a brand new apartment. Nobody complained about moving because we got a bigger apartment with more space and double the bathroom size. There were two bedrooms, and Cari and I decided to share the larger one and let Kiley have the smaller bedroom to herself. Since she was officially dating John Raymond and Cari was single and Nate didn't frequent our apartment as much as John did, that seemed to be the practical plan.

I loved my new roommates and our new living arrangement, especially the décor. Both Cari and Kiley had a keen eye for fashion, which made up for my utter lack of anything creative. Black and pink were our main focus colors, with small blank and pink throw pillows sprucing up the drab couches, pink curtains with black polka dots covering the windows, even black and pink cooking utensils we found on sale at Wal-Mart. The boring wooden kitchen table now showcased a festive pink tablecloth, and Kiley found a dazzling centerpiece to place in the middle, a glass square vase which she filled with different colored stones. Vanilla candles were placed strategically around the apartment: on the oven, in the bathroom, and atop dressers. When we lit them the apartment smelled like a vanilla factory exploded. Chic wall decorations hung proudly around the living room, showcasing martinis and wine bottles and a fancy drink called a Cosmopolitan. But my favorite decoration of all was the eight-by-ten picture frame that housed a photo of me standing between my two roommates, arms encircling one another and bright smiles beaming at the camera. The frame was placed front and center on the entertainment stand, and people were always complimenting it when they stopped by.

"I know!" Kiley exclaimed suddenly, her head popping up so fast Cari dropped the section of hair she had been working on. "What about getting a job here on campus? John's old roommate, Logan, works in the Activities Center and he's always saying how they can do their homework on the clock and everything. And it's right downstairs. It would be perfect!"

"That's a fabulous idea! But are they hiring? Can first-years work there?"

"Don't know and don't know, but we can find out! I'll text Logan right now and ask him. He could probably help you get the job. He thinks you're hot."

My cheeks reddened. "No, he does not. You're crazy."

"Yes, he does. He told John that he thinks you're hot and he wants to watch you run on the treadmill every time you go to the gym." She winked at me.

"I have no idea what that is even supposed to mean."

"It means he likes your ta-tas!" Cari supplied helpfully.

"That's the dumbest thing I've ever heard. Just—just text him and ask him if they're hiring and *only* that, please. I don't need Nate thinking I'm trying to replace him."

"As if he would think that. You two are nauseatingly adorable," Cari said.

I smiled, deciding to take that as a compliment. Nate had been down once more for a weekend visit since the three of us moved, and both were smitten by his natural charm.

Kiley's phone beeped and she flipped open the screen. "Logan says they are hiring right now and they usually hire first-years. Stop down in the morning and fill out an app. Cool! That would be awesome if you got that job. Logan always seems to have a good time down there."

"I'll stop down before my first class and fill it out. Thanks for the suggestion, Kiley. Hopefully I get it." I looked back down at my numeric figures scratched on the page. "I hope that will be enough."

"Jas? If you don't mind me asking, why can't you just ask your parents, er, your mom for money?" Kiley asked.

My shoulders tensed. I tapped the pencil on my notebook, debating to tell my roommates about my mom's financial situation. My financial situation. I knew that Cari's adoptive parents were extremely wealthy and that both she and Kiley were having their school paid for by Mom and Dad. They didn't need to worry about jobs and tuition and books.

"J?" Cari questioned. "You know you can talk to us, right? Let it out, girl. We're here for you."

I nodded slowly. What the hell. They already knew about Kameron. Why not let them in on another part of my past? "Well, actually—you see—it's like this," I stuttered, trying to figure out exactly how to say the story. Another crack in my persona. I took a deep breath, gathering my thoughts. "My mom was a gambling addict when I was in high school."

Silence. I looked over at Cari and Kiley, both who were staring back at me with blank expressions. Not what I had anticipated. "You know, like she spent all her money at casinos and stuff?"

"I guess I didn't realize that there was such a thing as being addicted to gambling," Kiley spoke first. "I'm not really sure what that means."

"Yeah, why is that such a bad thing? It's not like she was addicted to drugs or alcohol or anything," Cari said.

I gave a wry smile, remembering back to how confused I had been when Grace had filled me in on Mom's condition. "I know, I said the same things. But actually, it's pretty devastating. With my mom, she just became addicted to thrill of possibly winning more—but obviously in order to win money, you have to spend money. And she spent money. Like, all of her money. Then my stepdad's money. Then my money." I paused, running my hands through my hair. "She was addicted. She thought she could win, win enough money to change our lives. She did change our lives, just not in a good way. She blew through all of her paychecks, not having enough money to pay the mortgage or groceries, anything. All of her money went to the casinos, lottery tickets, whatever."

Cari stopped working on Kiley's hair and both girls sat straight up, staring at me as I spilled family secrets. "Once Thomas, my stepdad, figured out what was going on, he tried to get her to stop. Get her help. But it was an addiction, a sickness. She couldn't stop, she didn't want to. Thomas threatened to leave her, because how could he support our family on just his paycheck? Mom wasn't contributing, she was only making things worse. So Thomas divorced her, and she…left."

"Left?" Kiley asked, reaching out to hold my hand.

I nodded. "Left. Vanished. I woke up one day to get ready for school and she was gone. Thomas didn't know where she had gone. Neither did my sister. My grandma. She simply just left." My tears came on fast and furious, like someone had flipped a switch inside of me. I was so frustrated with my mom for the past, for making me feel like she didn't love me enough to stay. That gambling was more important than family.

"How old were you?" Cari asked.

"Fifteen." I didn't speak for a few moments, trying to regain my composure to tell the rest of the story. Once I was able to calm myself, I finished telling Cari and Kiley that my mom disappeared for a year, appearing in my life once again at the end of my junior year of high school. I never asked for an explanation of where she had gone. I didn't think I wanted to know. She lived with Grace and Roy for awhile before she could get back on her feet again, and then we moved into the apartment we were in before she moved to Kentucky.

It wasn't all neat and tidy, though. Mom's credit score had taken a huge hit, one that would be nearly impossible to salvage. It was up to me to help support the apartment and buy my own clothes. I worked two jobs my senior year, all while preparing for college, being captain of the varsity squad, and still managing to graduate with honors.

It was worse, though. When Mom left the family, she had emptied my bank account. Since I was under eighteen, Mom's name was on the account as well, and she had full access to deposit and withdraw money. All the money I had saved throughout my fifteen years—from birthdays and holidays and part-time jobs—was gone in one day. I was hoping to put that money towards a car or my college tuition, but that wouldn't happen. I had to accept the fact that I would probably never see that money again.

"How the hell do you say your mom is your best friend?" Cari exclaimed. "Why don't you hate her?"

I shook my head, gratefully accepting the tissue Kiley held out to me. "Sometimes I wonder the same thing. It seems I always have to work so much harder than anyone else just to fit in. Just to wear stylish clothes or go to the movies. Out for lunch. But I can't hold her mistakes against her forever. She was sick. It took her some time, but she got help. And I'm proud of her for that. She had to accept that she had a problem, then get treatment. And it only took her a year. Some people waste half their lifetime on their addictions, never bothering to admit they are in the wrong. I—I'm just thankful she came back." Tears welled in my eyes again. "I used to think if only I was better, if only I was smarter, she would come back."

"Jasmine, you can't put that on you," Kiley said.

"I know. I know that now. But I threw myself into my schoolwork, trying to get the best grades possible. I made captain of my cheerleading squad two years in a row. I never went to parties or drank alcohol or touched drugs. I still don't. I thought maybe if she knew what a good kid I was, she would want to come back." I shook my head. "Silly now, I know, but—–I just wanted my mom back. I think that's why I still don't drink or anything. I guess deep down I still just want to always please my mom. I don't want to give her any reasons to leave me again."

Cari and Kiley wrapped me in a hug and my spirits lifted at their support. My mom's story wasn't one I repeated often. Nate knew, as well as Abby, but that was it. My family never mentioned that time anymore. It was like that one year was just erased from our lives. Everyone just wanted to forget it ever happened. But the financial struggles that I had to deal with, they would never go away. I didn't have anyone to turn to when I couldn't afford something, even something necessary such as food. I couldn't bear to ask anyone else in my family for fear that they would just assume I was irresponsible. I was on my own.

೫ಆ೫ಆ

"Jasmine? Jas, are you awake?"

I turned my head to one side, squinting in the midnight darkness of my bedroom. I could see the door slowly open, with the figure of Kiley being illuminated by the dim kitchen light.

"Kiles?" I asked, confused and sleepy. I thought I had the apartment to myself on that Friday night. Cari had gone back home for the weekend for her sister's birthday party and Kiley was staying at John's. I had to work events at T&T both Saturday and Sunday, so I was staying in Des Moines all weekend with no Nate to visit me.

"Hey, yeah, it's me. Um, sorry, are you awake?"

"Well, I am now. Come in, come in. What are you doing home?"

"I—I—I had to come home." I noticed then that Kiley's voice sounded like she had been crying.

"Hey, girl, what's wrong? Come here, come here. Flip on that light so we can actually see each other."

The light flickered on and I squinted in the sudden brightness. Looking at Kiley's face, my heart dropped. Mascara ran down her cheeks in rivers and her carefully done-up eyeliner now smudged above her eyelids. Her cheeks were a blotchy red but the rest of her face looked shiny and pale. She looked like hell.

The moment she sank down onto my mattress she started sobbing. Loud, painful sounds came from her mouth, and I was startled speechless. I had never seen Kiley cry like that, and we had been friends for two months, roommates for one. She couldn't even speak, just gasping sobs kept shaking her thin body as she hugged me tightly. I didn't know where to begin.

"It's okay, it's okay," I tried to be soothing, rocking her back and forth.

"I don't think it is," she sobbed into my shoulder. I could already feel my t-shirt sleeve getting soaked with her tears. "He can't take back those words."

Now I felt confused. I wasn't sure who she was talking about, but something told me I would only need one guess to figure it out. "Kiley, who can't take it back? You have to tell me what happened so we can fix it. Together."

After a few moments of hiccupping herself to a calmer state, Kiley explained to me that she and John had gotten into an argument. My guess would have been correct.

"He called me a bitch and said that I should expect other girls to hit on him. He said he doesn't spend five hours in the gym a day just to make himself feel better. He needs to look good for the ladies. But he has me—why would he need other girls to drool over him?"

"He called you a bitch?" I was immediately outraged. "Kiley, listen to me. That is *not* okay! You do not need to be called names. And who does he think he is, expecting to have girls drop at his feet? Girl, this guy is bad news. Dump his ass!"

Kiley immediately came to John's defense. "I know he shouldn't call me names but he really didn't do anything too terrible. I mean, he got some of their phone numbers but he promised me he wouldn't call them. He said sometimes the guys try to outdo one another at parties, see who can get the most numbers and stuff."

"And they also compete on who can bring home the most panties. Come on, you cannot believe that. Why else would he be getting multiple girls' numbers if he isn't going to call any of them? You should not be treated this way! He needs to treat you like a princess and not pay attention to other bitches when you're out with him! Even when you're not out with him! He is dating *you*, and you only."

"But it did look like the other girls were hitting on him first. They were the ones who approached him. Well, some of them approached him first. I think."

"It shouldn't matter! He should politely decline. Or just ignore them! You're a fucking beautiful girl who obviously cares about your relationship more than he does. You need to move on from this loser, like, yesterday." I knew John Raymond was a douche. I thought so the first time I saw him when I was in the weight room with Kiley. Just the way he talked and stared at my body gave me the creeps. I couldn't figure out what she saw in him.

"I don't know. I think he was just really drunk tonight and that's why things got out of control. I'll talk to him in the morning when he's sobered up. I'm sure he will apologize."

"No! He shouldn't be saying those things—or doing those things—in the first place. Whether he's drunk or stone sober. It will only get worse, trust me, if you let him think he can get away with that." Kiley and Cari knew about Kameron and Jason, and I hoped Kiley was remembering those stories now. She couldn't really want to stay with John?

"Maybe. I don't know. I'm just so confused. Can I sleep in here with you tonight? I don't think Cari would mind if I slept in her bed."

"Of course, it's fine. But Kiley, really, I think this John Raymond is bad news. You need to get rid of him."

"Yeah, okay. I'm just going to change into pj's real quick and I'll be back. Thanks for listening to me."

But had she listened to anything I said? A nagging feeling told me she hadn't.

৪০৫৪৩৫৪৩

The following Sunday, I awoke in the middle of the night feeling like a train ran me over—twice. Every muscle and bone in my body ached, making it difficult to swing my legs out of bed and stand up.

I immediately regretted the move. My vision swirled and head pounded, and I became so overcome with dizziness that I fell back on my comforter. *What the hell?* I squinted at the clock. 4:04 in the morning. Ugh. I needed to be up and awake in three hours to get ready for my first class.

As I stood in the middle of the room contemplating my next move, I realized Cari wasn't in her bed. I frowned in confusion. She fell asleep before me.

Just then my stomach did a flip, and I knew I was about to throw up. I rushed to the bathroom door and tried to pull it open. Locked. I tugged in panic, feeling the bile start to rise. I clamped one hand over my mouth, willing myself to keep it down until I could get over the toilet.

"Just a sec!" Cari's panicked voice wafted out from inside. I squeezed my eyes shut and listened to the odd noises coming from the bathroom. Something sharp seemed to be dropped, hitting with a small *ping* on the tiled floor. I heard Cari muttering under her breath and the sound of crumpled...paper? The cabinet door slamming shut. What was she doing in there?

"Cari!" I pleaded, desperately needing to get inside. Relief flooded through me when the door finally swung open, and I rushed past Cari and started heaving into the toilet.

"What the—? Jasmine, are you okay?" I heard her say, but I couldn't see her. I was too busy vomiting all my dinner of macaroni and cheese up and out of my system. I clutched my stomach and cried out in misery. Tears blurred my vision as the putrid smell reached my nostrils.

I felt Cari behind me, murmuring calming words in my ear. She scraped my hair, damp with a cold sweat, off my forehead and neck, holding it back so my sickness wouldn't get on it. What seemed like hours later but was probably only about ten minutes, I finally ran out. I leaned back against the wall, chest heaving. My throat felt raw, eyes burned with hot tears, and stomach still felt like it was doing flips. I felt exhausted, like I had just run a half marathon without any stretching or water breaks.

"You okay, girl?" Cari asked, peering at me with worried eyes.

"Water," I whispered.

She ran out to the kitchen, and I could hear the faucet turning on and cabinet doors slamming. She appeared just seconds later with a tall pink glass filled to the brim with tap water. I gulped a few grateful sips and tried to calm myself down.

"Now you okay?"

I gave a shaky nod. "Better. Thanks. For everything."

"No sweat. Are you sick? I know you're not wasted."

I let out a little laugh. My roommates knew that I didn't drink alcohol, and who gets wasted on a Sunday night before a school day? "No, definitely not drunk. Maybe a bug? Or food poisoning? But that doesn't make a whole lot of sense; I ate mac 'n' cheese with Kiley. Unless she wakes up tomorrow sick too. But I'm so frickin' dizzy." I paused, trying to focus on Cari and not the spinning room. "Ugh, maybe I just need to go back to bed." I put my head in between my knees, trying to find the strength to stand up. "All right, seriously, going to bed now." I went to stand, but as I did, I noticed Cari trying to discreetly slip a Band-Aid on her lower right leg. "Hey, you okay?" I asked, forgetting about my concerns for the moment.

"What? Me? Yeah, yeah, I'm fine. Just a little cut," Cari stammered, turning her body away so I couldn't see her face or leg.

"What did you cut yourself on?" I remembered then that I thought I heard something sharp drop earlier while I was waiting outside. I hoped I hadn't caused her to hurt herself.

"Oh, this cut? Oh, it's an old shaving scab that I scratched open. Just wanted to throw a Band-Aid over it so I wouldn't get blood on my sheets, you know? Yeah, just trying to patch it up a bit." Cari's voice had become high-pitched, and she kept stammering over her words, unusual for her.

"Okay." I didn't want to press further. It was almost five in the morning, we both had school the next day and I badly needed to brush my teeth. "Well, thanks again for your help. Appreciate it. Now go back to bed. I'll be in mine in a few."

After Cari left the bathroom, I took a few deep breaths and tried to get the dizzy feeling to pass. I eventually gave up and grabbed my toothbrush, squirting a generous portion of Colgate on the bristles. After I rinsed my mouth out, I reached above the toilet into the cabinet Cari and I shared. I opened the left side, Cari's side, to try to find a bottle of Ibuprofen or something to help my upset stomach. I ducked my head when something small, pink and sharp came flying out at me. The object landed with a small *ping* on the tiled floor. Stooping down, I picked up Cari's razor. I looked back up in the cabinet and then back down at the razor in my hand. Well, that was odd. Why would her razor be in the cabinet and not in the shower?

It hit me suddenly how tired I was. I needed to try to get a few hours of sleep if I hoped to make it through all my classes tomorrow. Shoving Cari's razor back in the cabinet, I flicked off the bathroom light and made my way to bed. I drifted off to sleep the moment my head hit the pillow, not giving another thought to Cari.

Chapter Eight

"NICE BOOBS."

I looked up from my current obsession, a Skye Mitchell romance novel, to find who else but Cari complimenting my girls. I was lounging on the couch in the living room after just completing a tough cardio DVD workout. I still had thick black sweatpants on, but my t-shirt lay discarded on the floor, so only a navy blue sports bra covered my chest.

"Ha, thanks. Yeah, I think this sports bra might be a bit too small for them, huh?" My breasts, which were already a small C, seemed to be growing nonstop lately. They now spilled over the top of the stretchy material, not supporting me with all the jumping and kicking I just completed. "Guess I'll need to have a little shopping trip here soon to get me some new ones. Or just borrow Kiley's."

"Please stop making me so jealous that you both have the biggest boobs and God granted me with pancake titties. It's just not fair."

"Well, God also granted you with a tiny body that I would kill for. I've tried cutting out fast food for the past two weeks and doubling up my workouts but I still seem to be gaining weight. Unlike you who never has to work out and won't go past a size zero jeans."

"We all want what we don't have," Cari said, opening the kitchen cabinets and staring inside them. "Speaking of what we don't have—we don't have anything to eat. Where the hell did all our groceries disappear too?"

"I think John Raymond might have something to do with that. Kiley said John had some friends up here the other night playing cards when I was at T&T and you were out of town. Kiles said they basically ate everything, which I totally don't get. This isn't their place, and John lives one floor down. Why the hell did they have to play cards up here?"

"Don't know. Don't like that John, though. Or his new douchy friend. What's his name?" Cari paused, pushing her lips together in a frown. "The big one. You know him. Damn, can't think of it. But he's a definite sleaze ball. Just like John."

Cari and I frequently discussed our dislike for our roommate's boyfriend. Kiley and John had been dating for the past month and she seemed head over heels for him. But whenever we went out, he acted like she was invisible and Kiley would get upset, but then John would take her out on a date and all was well. It was a tiring cycle.

"Well, whatever. Kiley said she would make him replace all the food. But you know what that means—Kiley will be the one replacing it all, which isn't fair. But it isn't fair if we have to buy it all, we didn't let our boyfriends eat us out of house and home."

Cari wrinkled her nose at me. "That's an old saying. Anyways, where is our third musketeer?"

"John's." We both groaned, but didn't say anything more on the bad boyfriend subject. We practically talked ourselves to death on the matter most days, and could only hope Kiley would come to her senses real quick and dump the douche.

We settled into a familiar pattern then, me laying on the couch reading, Cari at the kitchen table studying. Occasionally, one of us would get up and move around, going to the bathroom, getting a snack or a drink, but we didn't speak. I enjoyed the comfortable silence, one that could be shared easily with close friends.

I did not think I could have survived my first year in college without Kiley and Cari. They were my rocks, my biggest supporters and my best friends. I had been sick the last couple of weeks, some virus that I could not shake. My new roommates were always helping me out, whether it was making me soup, hot chocolate, or Doritos and pickle sandwiches, which I had developed a weird craving for. And I liked to think that I supported them as well. When Kiley came home dissolving in a fit of tears over something John had done, Cari and I were there with comforting words and a carton of Ben &Jerry's. And when Cari got in her depressed state, Kiley and I were there to cheer her up, offering to drive her to the mall or rent the latest comedies.

I worried about Cari sometimes. I lifted my eyes then to watch her, sitting with one leg propped up on the opposite chair, pen in her right hand. She jotted notes, every once in awhile dragging her pink highlighter across something in the textbook. She had recently cut her hair into a bob and put some streaks of red throughout the white-blonde locks. She was wearing a typical Cari outfit that day: tight blue jeans with sparkles on the back pockets, a long pink t-shirt that almost reached her knees and a white flower barrette tucked behind one ear. Her shoes, kicked off by the door, were four-inch tan sling-backs, with almost no wear or scratches showing. Her shoe collection was immaculate, her dedication of keeping each pair in fantastic condition obvious.

Cari's personality was outgoing, a bit loud and brash sometimes, but always friendly. It wasn't until we were alone, or she was with just me and Kiley, that she would reveal more of a different side. Our last serious conversation took place on Wednesday when were having a roommate dinner night. Kiley made some killer tater tot casserole and Cari worked her magic on brownies. I complimented their food and skills and helped set the tables and fill everyone's glasses. I still hadn't overcome my fear of the stove after my cookie-making fiasco.

The conversation had turned to our families after Kiley questioned my mom and her impending move to Kentucky.

"She's getting more and more antsy to go. I know the kids make it worth it to her," I said, sinking my fork into a cheesy tator tot and taking a bite. I had been feeling irritable and moody that night, probably because of the big test slated for the next day, and really didn't feel up to talking about my family. "What about you, Cari?" I changed subjects onto her. "Do you ever want to find your real parents?" We knew she had been adopted as a baby. She told us once but hadn't mentioned much of it again. I was curious about her situation. I never knew anyone else who was adopted.

"I would definitely want to meet my real parents. Biological parents, I mean."

"Is that possible to do?" Kiley asked, helping herself to seconds from the pan sitting on the stovetop.

Cari shrugged. "I'm not really sure. I think it would be. But every time I try to talk to my parents about it, they change the subject and get all upset. But they should let me. It should be my decision." Her voice tinged with anger at that last sentence, surprising me. Cari didn't get angry often.

"Do you think maybe they think that you think they weren't good enough parents? Or something? That maybe that's why you want to find your real parents. Biological parents, sorry," I corrected myself.

"Maybe. Don't know. But I just want to meet them, just shake their hands and understand their story. Why did they give me up? Could they not handle a little baby? Too young, not financially stable, what? I have no reasons. I have nothing to go on. I just sometimes feel like I don't even know who I am."

I looked up from my plate and saw the expression on Cari's face. Sadness, a longing that overpowered her constant smile. She craved to know where she came from, to know the people who made her. I could identify with her to an extent. Sometimes it would be nice to have just one conversation with Stuart, understand why he did what he did and why he never got to meet his second daughter. But that was impossible. It seemed it would be that way with Cari as well.

Since that conversation, I had seen that look on Cari's face from time to time. Sometimes she talked more about it, about wanting to know and how upset she would get with her adoptive parents for refusing to help or give any information out. But what concerned me the most was when she didn't talk. When Kiley and I would try to get her to tell us her feelings and she would simply pull away from us and hide in a shell, not saying a word. And what especially worried me is when I could hear her crying at night when she thought I was sleeping.

"Hi girls." Kiley walked into our apartment then, dragging my thoughts away from Cari and her adoption situation. She threw her oversized leather purse on a kitchen chair and shuffled into the living room.

"Why the long face, chica?" I asked, regretting the words the moment I said them. Of course, it would be something with John. And I really wanted to finish reading at least another two chapters before I called it a night.

"Oh, John and his friends are planning a ski trip to Colorado over Christmas break and John told me I couldn't go!"

Yep, I was correct. Grudgingly placing my bookmark between the pages, I sat up on the couch. "And what was his reasoning?" I asked, sounding like a judge in a courtroom.

"He said that nobody wants their girlfriends tagging along because then they won't have fun. But other girls are going—

Katie and Alicia. Just because they're not dating anybody in the group, even though they have sex with all of them! Except John, of course," she hastily tacked on.

"That's so bullshit." Cari twisted around in her chair, facing us. "What difference does it make if you're a girl or girlfriend? You both have vaginas."

"Thank you, Cari, for that highly informative insight," I quipped. "But seriously, Kiles, that's ridiculous. If this isn't an all male trip—which I could understand if that's what they wanted—but since there are other girls going along, you should be invited. And what's more—John should straight-up want you there. Isn't that what vacations are for, making memories with friends and loved ones?"

Kiley's eyes started to fill with tears. "That's what I think. But apparently, he doesn't agree. We got into a big argument about it and I just wanted to come home. You girls doing anything the rest of the night?"

Inward sigh. Now Cari and I would have to tend to Kiley's open wounds, reassuring her all night that she was beautiful and a great girlfriend and any man would be lucky to have her. I didn't mean to complain, because Kiley listened to me enough, but come on. When would she see that John Raymond was simply not boyfriend material?

At that moment, my cell phone started to ring. "Sorry, it's the mother," I said, slipping in the bedroom I shared with Cari. "Hey, Mom, what's up?" I asked after flipping open the screen.

"Heading over to the mall quick. Your Aunt Janet is meeting me there. Wilson's is having a big shoe sale," Mom crackled through the line. I could hear traffic noises in the background and worried briefly about my mother's driving abilities while talking on a cell phone.

"Ah, nice. Anything specific you need?" I threw myself down on my bed and started to examine my split ends. Note to self: schedule a hair appointment ASAP.

"Not really. Maybe a pair of tennis shoes for your brother. His look terrible, of course."

"Well, you know Jeremy. Doesn't want anything stylish because then he wouldn't fit in."

"Yeah, yeah. Weirdo. Anyways, I wanted to talk to you about something." Mom's tone sounded serious.

"Oh, yeah. What's wrong?"

"Nothing wrong, really. I saw Abby today."

I paused for a moment, the name of my former best friend taking me by surprise. Cari and Kiley stopped mentioning her around me because they knew I only got upset. "And?" I asked quietly, wondering where Mom was going with this.

"She came into the clinic today for a checkup. Alone."

"All alone? No Jason or her sister or even her mom?"

"No. All alone. And she looked, well, she looked sad, Jasmine."

"Well, that's certainly not my fault!" I exclaimed. I knew Jason wouldn't be there for her during the pregnancy, a monkey could have told her that.

"I know. I'm just passing along some information to you. She's all alone, no one to go to appointments with her. Who knows who she hangs out with up here, you were her only friend. Maybe it wouldn't hurt to just phone her quick and check in. Or do one of those text things you always talk about."

Not even my mother's limited technology skills could get me to smile. Why should I have to check in with Abby because she didn't have anyone else? That was why I didn't want her to go back to Julien—I knew that would be precisely what happened. But no, don't listen to Jasmine. I half wanted to call her just to say *I told you so.*

"I don't know. I'll think about it. How's that?" I told Mom, mostly just to satisfy her. I wasn't calling Abby. She could call me if she needed a friend to talk to. She was the one who stormed out like a bat out of hell on that final day.

"Do what you want. But if you were in that situation, you'd certainly need a friend to talk to. Just remember that."

"Ugh, Mom wants me to call Abby," I said a few moments later after I wrapped up the conversation with Mom. I walked back out into the living room to find both my roommates in the kitchen, pulling ingredients out for spaghetti. A bag of angel hair noodles, a can of tomato sauce and a block of meat sat on the counter, waiting to be made into our delicious supper.

"Grab the box of breadsticks out of the freezer," Cari called to Kiley while turning on the front burner. "Oh, yeah?" she said to me. "Why? You going to?"

"Probably not. She said she saw her today at the clinic for an appointment and no one was with her and she looked sad. Whatever, right? I tried telling Mom that I knew she would be in this alone, but Mom still thinks it's good if I check in. Dumb."

"Maybe you should. I mean, you have to miss her, right? You were best friends for how many years? It would be hard to just give that relationship up," Kiley said.

"Six years. And yes, I miss her sometimes, but I have you two now," I smiled at both girls. "And school, and Nate and all our new friends and going to Amsterdam. I don't want to get sucked back into that world."

"I would just think about it a bit before making a decision," Kiley advised before dumping the noodles in boiling water. "Who knows, something may change and you'll want to talk to her. "

Chapter Nine

SPLAT. VOMIT HIT THE WATER IN THE TOILET, landing with a sickening sound, splashing tiny droplets back up towards my face. I tried to lift my head farther from the stool, but my body felt so weak it didn't want to respond. I threw up until I was retching, heaving noises coming from somewhere deep in my stomach. Tears rolled down my cheeks and landed in the tainted toilet water.

I had thrown up almost every day for the past three weeks. Maybe longer, I was starting to lose track. I got sick mostly in the mornings, sometimes throughout the day, and even at nights. Certain smells seemed to trigger the virus—eggs Cari cooked in the morning or the cheap frozen steak meal Kiley frequented. The worst part of being sick was the body exhaustion and dizziness. Those symptoms made it hard to go to class and I had been missing more days than usual.

I also started my new job just two weeks prior, working in the Activities Center. John's friend Logan had put in a good word for me and I was overjoyed to be working on campus. But I had to ask Logan to cover for me twice because I was too sick to go in. That couldn't keep happening.

I had gone to the doctor after I missed the first day of work. My unfamiliar Des Moines doctor checked my throat and questioned my eating patterns, and sent me off with a prescription to help ease the symptoms of a particularly nasty flu virus that was going around school campuses and daycares. Swallowing horse pills twice a day did nothing to help.

Now I was alone in my college apartment on a Thursday night. Cari left for a house party and Kiley had gone back to her hometown to introduce John to her parents. After I finished vomiting, I leaned back against the bathroom wall, the cold tiles sending goosebumps down my arms. Sweat dripped down my temples, running a river down my chin. I didn't even sweat that much when I worked out. I grabbed a towel and dabbed at my forehead, willing myself to take deep breaths. I knew what I had to do.

Walking out into my bedroom, the tears unleashed with a vengeance. How silly, getting so upset. There was nothing to be worried about. But if I wasn't worried, why had I bought that stupid test from Laird's drugstore down the street?

I reached underneath my bed and grabbed out the plastic bag, pulling it towards me. I knew both my roommates were gone, but still felt the need to hide any evidence of what I was about to do. Nobody could know I was even paranoid about this matter; it was too sensitive after all the Abby bullshit.

Stepping back into the bathroom, I took in the familiar surroundings. Cari's dark pink towels hanging haphazardly from the towel rack. My light blue towel with deep navy strips hanging over the shower door, still damp from my last post-workout shower. The cabinet doors were closed, holding back a plethora of body lotions, makeup, hair accessories, nail polishes and more girly items of Cari's than I ever owned in my life.

I slowly tore open the box and read the directions twice. Aim, pee, wait. Simple. I followed through and set the stick atop the box it came in, checking the directions one more time. Minus sign, not pregnant. Plus sign…I couldn't even go there.

While I waited out the two longest minutes of my life, I paced back and forth on the tiled floor, wringing my hands, picking at my fingernails. I couldn't be. I had been with only Nate the past few months—obviously—and we'd always used condoms the few times we even had sex. Well, except that one time, on Nate's first visit down to Irving. That would have been, what, only six weeks ago? And that was just one time! And I took birth control, so that should have prevented everything. Though I did recall missing a few days of pills but I had made up for that, taking three pills in one day. I was fine!

But then why was I constantly throwing up? Why did certain foods make me sick? Why had my boobs ballooned up to almost a D cup? I had more than one classmate ask if I had a boob job done. Nothing my body was telling me made sense. Unless, of course, I was pregnant.

A sob escaped my throat then, shocking the still silence surrounding me. I had been so mad at Abby, so upset with her getting pregnant. And now what was I, a hypocrite? I was going to be in the same position as her—young and pregnant and poor and uneducated. No! That couldn't happen to me! I had goals, I had plans, I had a future.

Before I started to become absolutely out of my mind hysterical, I needed to check the test. Just make sure and see what exactly my future held. Though deep in my gut, I knew what it would say.

I sat in silence when I saw my answer. Stared at the tiny stick that was intent on ruining my life. When the tears finally started, I lay on the bathroom floor for almost an hour, sobbing. Feeling my hopes and dreams floating past me, brushing my fingertips but not letting me hold on. Taunting me, teasing me, knowing I could never reach them. Not now. One mistake, one moment of love, led to this. What would Nate say? Would he still love me? What about my mom? My friends? My school?

With shaking hands, I grabbed my cell phone off my bed, fumbling it once and dropping it to the floor. When I was finally able to get a steady grip, I dialed Nate's number before I could change my mind. I had to let him know. Hopefully, we would be in this together. *Please don't leave me*, I thought to myself as I heard the click of the dial tone. *I can't do this alone.*

‍80C880C8

I walked into the library on campus, unsure why I was even there. I had left two garbled voice messages for Nate, but I couldn't sit still in the apartment. I had to do something to get my mind off how my life had just changed. So I chose to go to the library, where I would have to be quiet. I couldn't shout and yell and cry and throw things there. It seemed like the most practical choice.

I shoved two of my textbooks in my book bag and remembered to grab my notebook at the last minute. Picking up my purse from the table and checking to be sure my cell phone was securely in place, I locked up the apartment and headed across campus. The library was a part of the Administration building on the lower east end. I swiped my student ID card to gain access, and heard the click of the door being unlocked.

The library was almost empty—not unusual for a Thursday night at Irving. Since we didn't have Friday classes, Thursday was technically the kick-off to our weekend. Two students sat at different tables, each with their nose in a textbook. The boy, who I didn't recognize, didn't even look up as the heavy door slammed shut behind me. But the girl glanced up and smiled when she saw me. It was Raine, the non-traditional student in my major.

"Hi, Jasmine!" she whispered, keeping her voice down for the other student. "How are you?"

"Good, thanks," I whispered back, trying to plaster a smile on my face. I hoped she wouldn't notice my red-rimmed eyes or the look of fear that I knew must be evident on my face. She looked perfect—as usual—wearing a fitted black skirt and purple blouse with ruffles on the cap sleeves. Her hair was stick straight with no hint of frizz, and her makeup looked flawless. I knew I must have looked shitty in comparison, wearing gray sweatpants and my red THP sweatshirt. I had tossed my hair up in a bun because I kept yanking on the ends in frustration.

Any makeup that I had on that day was worn off and I hadn't bothered to reapply any when I left.

"Everything okay with you, honey?" Raine asked, peering at my face with concern. Great, I must have looked really terrible if it took a stranger one second to figure out something was wrong.

I forced another fake smile. "Oh, yes, I'm okay. Just feeling a little under the weather." Which wasn't a complete lie.

"Why don't you come sit with me?" She patted the table, indicating she wanted me to sit across from her. "Are you working on travel? We could do it together."

I hesitated before responding. But her friendly face was just what I needed then and she would be able to distract me from my thoughts. I slid into the wooden chair, setting my book bag on the seat next to me. "Thank you. I appreciate it."

"Not a problem. I was just researching Amsterdam. Have you done any research yet?"

I shook my head. "Just a tiny bit after the announcement. I marked some places that I want to see but as far as our assignment goes, nothing."

Our trip to Amsterdam wasn't just a vacation for travel students, it was also homework. Each student had to put together a trip package—finding flights, hotels, transportation in Amsterdam and sites to visit once we were there. We would be graded, of course, but our actual package that we would be using for the trip would be decided on by the second-years and Reba.

"Well, here is a print-out of different flight combinations that I found for the dates. This is one that I like the best, with the first connection in Ohio." Raine showed me the highlighted flight. "But this is a good one too, the first connection in Minneapolis. You could use that one."

"That does look like a good one. The Columbus one is definitely better, not such a long layover, but Minneapolis isn't too bad." I scratched down the airline, times and flight numbers in my notebook.

"I'm hoping our actual connections won't be so bad. One time, I had a twelve-hour layover when I was going to Paris. Let me tell you about the torture," Raine said, rolling her perfectly made-up eyes. "It was an awful experience, but the tickets were cheap and I was just a poor starving artist at the time. In the end, it was all worth it."

I saw my opportunity to get more information about Raine. Her stories that I heard in class sounded fascinating, and I always wanted to ask more but never felt comfortable doing so. Now that we were sharing homework, I felt I could.

"Where all have you traveled to? I don't mean to sound nosy, but from what I've heard it sounds like you've been so lucky to go places," I said.

Raine sat back in her chair, rolling a pen between her fingers. A smile stretched across her face and her eyes had a faraway look in them. "I have been lucky. It wasn't necessarily easy, but I was very fortunate. I knew I wanted to travel since I was a young girl, and I wouldn't let anything get in my way. As soon as I graduated high school, I moved to New York City. I grew up just outside of St. Louis, in case I've never told you that," she added.

"No, I didn't know that. I kind of just assumed you were from Des Moines, I guess," I said.

"Nope. Good old St. Louis. It was a fun town, don't get me wrong, but there wasn't enough excitement there. Enough opportunity. I wanted to really live life, see everything there was to offer. And it doesn't get any bigger than New York City, does it?"

"It sure doesn't," I agreed.

"So I took my savings and found myself a dingy little studio apartment. It was terrible. It smelled bad and I had to climb ten stories up each day, but I was happy. I thought I was doing something. I worked as a waitress at nights, took art classes during the day. I realized the potential I had for art, and so did my teacher." Her cheeks blushed a deep red, and I realized what she was saying.

"You and your teacher…." I trailed off, still hesitant around her. I didn't want to offend her by assuming.

But her eyes sparkled and she seemed to take no offense to my assumption. "Yes. My teacher and I got along extraordinary well, and it didn't take long for me to fall in love. "But—" she noticed my unintentional blissful sigh at the mention of love— "it wasn't all great. He was in his thirties, I barely scratched eighteen. But I wanted to believe. Even when he told me he was married but leaving his wife I went along with our relationship."

I sat wide-eyed in my chair, all thoughts of homework and Amsterdam out of my mind. "What happened?" I asked, eager to know the story.

"Well, I continued working and saving money. I wanted to get a nicer apartment and buy more art supplies so I could start entering real shows. But one day, Fredrick came to me and said he was going to Paris. He had accepted a job as an art teacher in one of the universities and asked if I would go with him."

"But what about his wife? Did he really leave her?"

"I never asked why she wasn't going. I never questioned their marriage. He told me a few stories about how they lived together after the separation simply to pay the mortgage, but looking back, I'm sure that wasn't the truth. I believe that she caught him in our affair and kicked him out."

"Was the Paris offer real?"

"It was. Fredrick had great connections in the art world, which was how he secured the university job. I had no job lined up before we moved and had some difficulty finding one once we got there. Fredrick and I would have the worst fights—he would complain that I wasn't pulling my weight financially. We were renting a flat and I did have trouble coming up with rent payments. But I was young, jobless and had just moved to another country for this man. I thought he could take care of me for at least a bit." She sighed, looking wistful. "But it simply wasn't meant to be. The fights became out of control, and then I discovered he was cheating on me with one of his students."

"Oh, no! That's awful, Raine," I said, disgusted with the sleazy art teacher, yet still fascinated by her story.

"It was quite devastating at the time. But I decided I would take control of my life once again. I went back to my first love, traveling, and set out to see the world. I traveled for the next four years, visiting countries, experiencing new cultures and learning more than I could have ever imagined. It was the time of my life," she smiled at her memories.

"Wow. That's incredible." I was filled with jealousy at her story. I wished I was brave enough to pick up and move to a new country, all by myself, no plan in mind. How exhilarating, freeing. "But how did you end up in Des Moines? At Irving?"

"I went back to St. Louis to visit my family when I was twenty-three over the Christmas holidays. I was introduced to Mark Schallsberg, the son of my parents' new neighbors. Mark works in Des Moines as a financial advisor but he was back in St. Louis as well for the holidays. We met, hit it off immediately. I knew this was different from Fredrick, but I wanted to be sure. I started traveling again but kept in touch with Mark. I didn't even make it a full year away from him. I had to come back and be with him. That was three years ago, and we've been together ever since."

My eyes were moist when she finished her story. I knew I would never look at Raine the same way. She was so much braver than me, traveling the world by herself, taking a chance on a married man, getting burned and still being able to fall in love again. And to chance that love by leaving? That took strength. "I'm so happy for you," I told her. "That is really inspiring. I hope I have great stories to tell one day."

She reached over the table and patted my hand. "I know you will. I watch you in class. I think you have quite the future ahead of you. Remember, you can do anything you want to do. Cheesy, I know. But I believe it with all my heart."

We started concentrating on homework after that, comparing hotels in Amsterdam. But I couldn't keep my mind off Raine's story. Having a baby would change everything. I wouldn't be able to travel. I wouldn't have the time or money with raising a child. I wouldn't have the chance to go to Paris or Italy, my top travel destinations. I wouldn't be able to just pick up and decide to move. I would always have to be thinking of my child, putting their needs and wants in front of mine. For the rest of my life. I was nineteen. My real world was just starting. And now, it was ending before it even got a chance to begin.

℠℞℠℞

"Jassy's home!" My mother's jubilant voice rang throughout the small apartment. She wrapped her arms around me, having to extend her arms vertical as I had a good three inches on my petite mom.

"Hello, Mother Dear. Hey, Jeremy," I called to my younger brother, who sat with arms crossed on the loveseat. Dressed in ripped jeans, a tattered bright yellow skateboarding shirt and monstrous shoes that looked like they had been washed in mud, Jeremy looked like a poster child for the new grunge-wave rocking Julien.

Jeremy grunted out a greeting to me, not turning his head from whatever riveting MTV show played on the television. Jeremy had just started his freshman year of high school and instantly became too cool for all things family. I'm sure the only reason he made it to dinner that night was because it was a special occasion. Mom's last dinner in Julien. She was moving to Kentucky the following week.

"Jeremy, take your sister's bags to her room! You've been on that couch for almost an hour. You're starting to match the couch pattern for Christ's sake!" Mom started barking out orders, all while opening the fridge and piling ingredients for dinner on the countertops. A pound of meat, bag of noodles, cans of tomato sauce, three bags of shredded cheese and a bowl of grapes suddenly filled the once empty space.

"It'll probably be about two hours before dinner. Are you starving now? Did you stop anywhere on the ride home? I can whip up a salad for you if you're hungry now." Mom was in a tizzy, bustling around the kitchen and firing questions at me. I knew it was my fault—I hadn't been home for weeks and she was just excited to see me before she left. But I started to worry she might have a heart attack right there by the stove.

"No, Mom. I'm okay, thanks. I didn't stop anywhere on the ride, just wanted to get home. I'm going to unpack my bags and give Nate a call."

"Does Nate want to come over for dinner? He's invited, of course!"

"Yeah, thanks. Actually—I guess I forgot to tell you. He is coming over for dinner. Must have slipped my mind. Sorry."

"Not a problem! There will be enough food to go around," Mom called to me as I slung my purse over one arm and headed into my bedroom.

The apartment hadn't changed in the slightest since I left for college. Once Mom was able to get back on her feet and more financially stable after living with Grace, she rented her own apartment and I moved in with her. The apartment complex was just a few blocks from where Jeremy attended high school, and close enough to the mall and a slew of fast food restaurants. The landlord was a polite older gentleman, close to Mom's age, who came by instantly if there was ever a problem—from the plumbing to Mom's key breaking off in her mailbox (which she had done twice).

The two-bedroom apartment was tiny compared to the modern, four-bedroom sprawling home I once lived in with Mom and Thomas. But Mom made the space feel welcoming, covering every inch of bare wall or table space with pictures of me, Grace and Jeremy throughout the years. All the furniture Mom had bought at garage sales, but the deep green couches looked chic against the almond colored walls that Mom and I painted ourselves. The kitchen table was tiny but doable when it was just me and Mom—sometimes Jeremy and Nate—and Mom stashed the extra chairs in her room when they weren't needed to give the cramped kitchen more space. Mom excelled at baking and cooking, and treats could always be found on any free countertops. Her apple-themed kitchen was a fun cliché, with apple patterns covering her dish towels, washcloths, and even place settings, as well as apples on the curtain ruffle covering the one minuscule window in the kitchen and a bright red apple clock perched above the stove.

I took a right off the hallway and into my bedroom, untouched since I left. My bookshelf that had been in my possession since I was a young girl and found my fascination for reading stood proud against the center wall, holding the Baby-Sitter Club and Sweet Valley High series that I just couldn't part with. Grace's old desk that got handed down to me sat in one corner, the dark wood covered with stickers of Disney princesses that both Grace and I had tacked on the surface. And my tiny twin bed took up the middle of the room, the light pink lace comforter and pillowcase a Christmas gift back when I was fourteen and received a full canopy bed.

The canopy was now long gone but the pink lace remained, a reminder of my childhood, as well was the Disney stickers and books crammed between the shelves. A part of me never wanted to let these things go. They were a symbol of what I wanted so badly—a normal life, normal parents and a safe upbringing. Not what I had been dealt with. Not what I was dealing with now.

I took a deep breath to steady myself. I just needed Nate to be here with me, to hold me and say he would fix everything.

Nate was the calm one, the one who was good at making decisions. Me—I could never decide whether I felt like McDonald's or Wendy's for lunch that day. Nate was sensible. I was a wreck at the moment.

Just leaving my house. See you in 10. Love you JJ.

I stared at the text message on my phone. I must have texted Nate earlier from the car letting him know I got home. I didn't even remember doing it. And now he was coming here. On his way. Oh, God, I couldn't handle it. He hadn't flipped on the phone when I broke the news to him, or if he did, I was too hysterical myself to notice. What if he wanted to break up now? What if he told me he didn't want the baby? Or what if he told me he did? I wasn't sure which option sounded worse at the moment. I didn't think I could handle it if he broke up with me. I trusted him with all my heart. And now he was going to turn out like every other guy and run away at the first obstacle. It just wasn't fair!

My stomach did a flip, and for one tiny second I thought it might be the baby and an odd thrill passed through me. But of course, that was silly. The thing was just a tiny peanut. Not enough for me to notice it doing flips. And thankfully I would have some time to figure the whole situation out before my belly started to grow and I began to waddle like a penguin. Oh, God, I would make a horrendous looking pregnant woman.

As I stood in my room laced with crazy thoughts spinning round and round my mind, I didn't even hear the knock on the front door. "Jasmina! I think Nate's here!" Mom hollered from the kitchen, about five decibels louder than she needed to be given the small space. "Can you get it? I've got my hands full of lasagna and your brother is a lump of coal!"

I rushed out of the bedroom and pulled open the door. Seeing Nate for the first time in weeks and after giving him our horrible news was just too much emotion for my pregnant ass to handle right then. To the surprise of everyone, myself included, I burst into tears right there in the entryway.

Chapter Ten

"I DON'T KNOW WHAT TO DO, NATE. I JUST DON'T know," I cried into my boyfriend's shoulder for about the eighth time that night.

"It's okay, it's okay," Nate soothed me in a voice that could calm a child, gently stroking my hair. "We'll figure it out together. We just need to figure it out together." The way Nate's voice warbled showed me his lack of confidence. At least he tried. At least he still wanted to be my boyfriend. I felt foolish for my earlier thoughts. What happened to my trust in him? I was hanging him out to dry while he was still here, supporting me and holding my hand. I couldn't believe how fast I had jumped the gun, how fast I wanted to believe he would be the bad guy.

"I don't even know where to start. Where do we start? How do we decide? How can we possibly decide?" I continued to sob, my feelings overwhelming me. Exactly one week had passed since the pregnancy test. One week that I had to endure classes and chat normally with my fellow classmates about the Amsterdam trip that I probably could no longer go on. One week without telling my best friends what I was dealing with. And one week of not being able to see Nate, not having him hold me and tell me we'd figure everything out together like he was at that moment.

"Let's just think. Calmly. Are you sure you don't want me to run inside and grab you a blanket? It's starting to get cold out here." Nate and I had taken up residence on the lone picnic table that sat behind the apartment complex. I somehow made it through dinner with Mom, Jeremy and Nate, after calming everyone down and assuring them I was fine. My sudden tears had startled my family. I blamed it on being happy to see Nate.

"No, I'm okay," I shook off the offer and dried my tears. "But let's figure this out. Right now. I can't handle keeping secrets from Mom and my friends. So, what then? Adoption?"

Nate looked shocked for a moment at my sudden change of pace. "Uh, what? I mean, yeah. Well, no. Hold on, let me think for a minute." Nate looked down at the grass beneath his feet, running one sneakered foot back and forth through the blades. His curly hair had become disheveled from running his fingers through it, tugging in frustration at times. His green polo shirt was wrinkled, and there was a damp spot on his left shoulder from where my fresh tears had soaked through.

I took in a deep breath while Nate contemplated my words. The crisp air of autumn filled my senses, making me think of Halloween and Thanksgiving. The leaves had already begun to change colors to beautiful reds and oranges, littering the ground and flying in the breeze. The wooded area just to the south of the complex towered like a mystical land, with the heavily populated trees alive with color, holding back the deer we often saw in the mornings on our lawn. I could faintly hear the drizzle of the small creek that ran through the trees, which would soon be frozen once the snow started falling.

"Is that what you really want, Jasmine?" I almost didn't hear Nate, his voice a whisper.

I turned back so we were face to face. "I don't know, do you? We can't keep it, can we? We're too young, not married, not ready, not anything. I certainly can't afford raising a child. You're not even out of high school. We need to be realistic."

Nate looked like a bobble head, nodding up and down. "Yes, yes, I see your point. But, uh," he cleared his throat uncomfortably, "have you ever thought of maybe our other option?"

"You want to keep it? I thought you just agreed with me! I mean, if you want to keep it, that's your opinion. We can give every option some deep thought," I stumbled over my words. Maybe deep down he secretly wanted to be a young dad. He had never mentioned it before, but maybe.

"No, not keep it, J," Nate interrupted my babbles. "Abortion."

The word hung in the air like a foul smell. I was so surprised that Nate—sweet endearing little Nate—had actually said that aloud. The shock wrote on my face, not allowing me to hide any emotions. Nate saw it.

"I'm sorry for thinking it. For saying it. It's just, well, how do we tell our parents? And our friends? And school and your big trip? You would be pregnant when you're supposed to be in

Amsterdam and you have been dying to travel there. Have you considered the fact that you probably wouldn't be able to fly? I thought I've heard somewhere that pregnant women can't fly. I mean, there are just so many things to think about. It would be—well, let me sound evil here— but it would just be easier if we didn't have to go through all those hurdles. Just be Nate and Jasmine again."

I still stayed silent, thoughts buzzing. Nate picked up my hand and held it tightly. "Let's not make any rash decisions. We can think about this. Take some time. But pretty soon, it's going to be obvious what situation we're in."

I just nodded, my face burning red with shame. I didn't want to admit to Nate that I already thought about abortion. I quickly erased the thought from my mind, though, because I told myself a nice Catholic boy like Nate would never have such crass thoughts. But now—it would be so much easier to make this go away. It might not be the best decision, or the right decision, but if it was a decision we came to together, as a couple, then maybe it would work.

"I thought about it," I choked on my words, holding back a sob trying to escape my lips.

"Thought about what?"

"Abortion."

Nate's face looked even more surprised than when I mentioned adoption. "Really? Well, okay. And you thought you would want to? Or no?"

"I'm not sure. I didn't think you would go for it. At all."

"Maybe we should see someone, a doctor. Get some information on what steps we can take. That's what doctors are there for, to help. And we need help."

"We need help," I repeated back, suddenly feeling exhausted. The emotions of the last week—keeping everything bottled inside and now talking so openly—was an odd feeling. I felt relieved, a little sick to my stomach, but mostly calm. I wasn't going to be Abby and have to make all the decisions myself. Nate would stand beside me and hold my hand, helping me every step of the way.

As I sagged my tired body onto his, letting his arms encircle me, I wondered for a brief moment what our baby would look like. Would it have Nate's curly hair? My green eyes?

That's ridiculous, I scolded myself. There would be no keeping the baby. Whatever decision we came to, raising a child was not in our future.

ഇരുന്നു

I learned to master my fake smile by the next day. I survived brunch with Mom, Aunt Janet and my cousin Elaine, not breaking down once in tears. I ran into some high school friends when I went to the mall by myself and got through a twenty-minute conversation in the food court with the girls. I was relieved when I could just go home, lock myself in my bedroom for awhile and be alone with my thoughts.

Mom was out for the night, her last night out with her four sisters before her move. Aunt Janet had picked Mom up before

I got home from the mall, and the group was out for pedicures, dinner and a show at the Julien Theatre. I knew Mom would have a good time, and I had plans to attend Nate's football game. Jeremy was accompanying me, along with the rest of the city. It was the championship game, Washington versus Jefferson, the high school across town. It was the Superbowl of high school games in Julien.

I got ready slowly, taking time to add leggings underneath my jeans for added warmth. I put two t-shirts on, then a long-sleeved tunic, then my navy cheerleading sweatshirt. I pulled my hair into a high bun, threading a red ribbon through the elastic band. The ribbon was an old cheerleading staple, and I surprised myself by breaking down in tears once I saw my reflection in the mirror. I looked like my high school self, getting ready to cheer for the big game. How had I become young and pregnant? What would the other cheerleaders think of me when they found out I was having a baby?

But you're not having a baby, my inner voice reminded me. Right. Abortion. That disgusting eight letter word gave me chills. I didn't feel confident in the decision we made, but the more I thought about it, the more it seemed to be the only way. I couldn't imagine coming back to Julien with a baby bump, running into my girlfriends at the mall. I could feel their judging stares, the questions they would ask. The whispers that would be about me, about my baby. What would my old teachers say, my former cheerleading coach? It would be humiliating having to endure that.

My phone rang, snapping me from my thoughts. I released it from the charger, checking the caller ID before flipping it open. "Hey, bro," I said, giving myself a shake to force the baby thoughts from my mind.

"Hey. What time you picking me up?" Jeremy didn't sound excited to be attending the game, even though it was the hottest event in town.

"Give me half an hour and I'll be over. Are you wearing school colors?" I had to ask, though I knew the answer.

"Hell no! I'm only going to this thing because Mom pretty much forced me."

"Jeremy, what else would you do on a Saturday night? Everyone from both schools is going to be at the game."

"My friends are going down to the river to drag race."

"Drag race? Sounds like a thrilling way to get arrested. Or killed." I was protective over my little brother even though he didn't like it. But drag racing? Next, he'll be coming home saying he knocked up a girl. Just what the family needed, another screw-up like me.

"Whatever," he sighed, sounding completely uninterested in our conversation.

I heard a bark in the background, and could feel my spirits lift at the sound. "Is that Dodger? How is my puppy?" Dodger was the Yorkshire terrier the family had bought seven years ago. He stayed with Jeremy and Thomas because Mom's apartment hadn't allowed pets. I missed that little dog.

"Yeah, he's going crazy right now. He can see a squirrel in the tree from out the window." Jeremy's voice had a laugh in it. Dodger was the only thing that seemed to perk my brother up since he became too cool for anything else.

"Aw, my Dodgers. Maybe I can come in for a bit and play with him before we leave?"

"Well, um," Jeremy cleared his throat before answering. "Actually, Bart is here tonight."

My good mood dropped to my toes. "Oh, well. Never mind, I guess." I couldn't suck all the venom out of my words, and I know Jeremy noticed.

"Maybe I can bring him outside, though. We can play in the yard for a little bit."

My heart broke at my brother's optimistic words. He sounded like his old self again. He was the little brother trying to protect his sister. I hated that he got thrown in the middle that way. It wasn't fair to him.

"Thanks, but that's okay. We probably won't have much time, anyways. Another time. No worries," I said, trying to escape the sadness that had settled over my heart. "I'll just finish getting ready and text you when I'm outside. Be sure to bring gloves." I hung up before he could whine about me babying him. He didn't deserve what his stepbrother had put the family through. Jeremy was young when it happened, too young to understand, but now he knew. He knew the truth, and I wished I could protect him from all the harsh realities of life.

I would bring an extra pair of gloves for him just in case.

ഇൻൻഅൻ

The following Monday I was back at school, hiding my secret from my friends and classmates. I hoped I was acting normal in class, not giving anything away, but nobody questioned me. I told Cari and Kiley that I was feeling a little ill and made up a story about Jeremy being sick with the flu over the weekend. They believed me, which only made me feel worse.

After classes dismissed Monday afternoon, I decided to take a walk around campus. I had too much on my mind to sit in the apartment with my roommates. I just needed to get away from everyone, everything, for just a minute.

But my plan didn't work. No sooner had I reached the top of the hill by the Administration building when I heard a voice calling my name. I turned around, looking for the culprit, and realized with a start that it was none other than President Greer waving at me. How could I face the president at a time like this?

"Hi there, Jasmine. I thought that was you. Were you coming to see me?" she asked, her face friendly as always, slightly red in the cheeks from the cold wind. She wore another business suit, this one deep red with a matching jacket and skirt. She wore delicate black heels on her feet that made me wonder how she could walk in them, and her dark hair was pulled back into a bun. As always, she looked elegant and in charge, while I was a pregnant screw-up in a baggy sweatshirt and a wrinkled pair of jeans.

"Oh, hello there," I managed out, wondering what to say to her. "I was just going for a little walk. Getting some fresh air." I breathed in deeply, trying to show my appreciation for the outdoors, but the cold wind sliced through my throat and caused me to cough like a maniac. I felt like a fool.

"Yeah, it's chilly out here. Why don't you come into my office? I would love to hear how your new roommates are working out."

I looked toward the Admin doors, wondering how I could possibly talk to the woman and not blurt out my secret. There was just no way. "I really can't right now. Thank you so much for the offer," I tried to decline respectfully. "I work in Activities and have to get down there for my shift soon." That was a lie. I didn't work until later that night.

"Oh, that's okay then. Work first!" She gave a little chuckle, patting me lightly on the shoulder. "But know that my door is always open for you, for any of my students. If you ever need anything, you can come to me." With another wave, she was off, climbing the stairs and disappearing through the double doors.

I stayed put for another minute, thinking her words over. What did she mean? Did she somehow guess I was pregnant? That would be impossible! Did she know I would need help in the future? How could she though without being physic? I shook my head to clear my thoughts, turning around and heading back to Williams Hall. I was starving, even though I had eaten a big lunch over break hour. I guessed that was something I needed to get used to. Until the abortion.

ഇരുഇരു

Later that night, I reported to work in Activities from five until ten, closing time. I didn't mind the nightshift—most students came down to the gym during that time and I got to socialize. But on that night, socializing was the last thing I wanted to do. I stayed in my chair, behind the desk, working on my travel project. I was researching transportation modes in Amsterdam. From what I could tell, there was something called a tram that seemed to be the most convenient way to get from point A to point B. The pictures of a tram looked like a cross between a subway and a train, but it ran on tracks in the middle of the road. A little dicey, in my opinion.

"Hey, Jasmine, how's it going tonight?" I looked up when a voice got my attention. It was Logan, John Raymond's pale friend and my Activities co-worker. He was dressed in blue basketball shorts and a white t-shirt with the sleeves torn off. He came around to the side door and let himself in the office, placing one foot on the desk to tie his shoe. Logan had tried hitting on me the first few times we worked together, but quickly got the point that I was with a boyfriend and not going to stray.

"Fine, fine. Busy night," I answered, hoping he wouldn't want to stay for a chat. He was a nice enough guy, even with being friends with John Raymond and after hitting on me, but I didn't want to talk to anyone that night. Or for the next nine months.

"Are the hoops lowered?"

"The west end is lowered. Some girls are playing volleyball on the east, so I raised the hoops for them." Irving had a full-size gym, and basketball and volleyball were the favorites among students. One of the biggest jobs of a student worker was raising and lowering basketball hoops accordingly.

"Sweet, we'll take the west end. Did you get that memo about the work meeting being moved up?"

"I did, and I can still make it," I said, pausing to smile at a group of guys that signed in and headed off to the gym.

"Be there in a minute," Logan called to them, indicating those were who he was playing with. "Good, glad you can make it. We need to go over preparations for the variety show we're putting on in a few months. And you and Ben need to learn the concession stand still for when we host high school basketball games. It's simple, you'll catch on fast."

I opened my mouth to respond when another voice caught my attention. "What up, man? Ready for some hoops? I feel a domination creeping in these muscles." John Raymond.

I turned my chair so I was facing my roommate's boyfriend. The Activities Center office reminded me of a garage, with a large open window that closes by lowering a metal cage across it. The window is open during business hours and students sign in whenever they use the gym. Inside the office are two desks, one facing the main window and one facing the door to the gym. On busy nights, two student workers are assigned but usually one can handle the duties. Those include making sure students sign in, answering the phones, dealing with any requests from the gym, general cleaning duties and clearing everyone out at ten p.m. and locking the doors.

John Raymond stood outside the window, flexing his muscles to me and Logan. Douche bag. I didn't say anything to him, just looked down at my notebook in front of me and pretended to jot down some notes. Logan stood behind me, stretching his arms over his head. "The other guys just got here and the hoops are down."

"Money. Hey, Jasmine ,baby, how you doing?"

I looked up in disgust, not trying to hide my emotions from him. "Great, thanks for asking," I said sarcastically before looking back down. What did Kiley see in that guy?

"Well, you don't seem to be all that friendly for being on the clock. Come on now. What's wrong, princess? You can tell me." John placed his muscled arms on the window ledge, still flexing.

I shot Logan a look, telepathically telling him to get John away from me. "Nothing, but I'm studying. Big project coming up."

"Yeah, let's let her stay focused. Come on, the guys are waiting. Collin wants to be back in his room by nine for some wresting match on TV." Logan saved me from any further conversation with John *Douche*-mond, and the office was quiet again after their departure.

I researched Amsterdam for the next hour, learning about tram fares and other modes of transportation. I learned that bicycles could be rented, but that idea wouldn't work because I never actually rode a bike before. But they seemed mighty popular with the Dutch.

At 9:30, I finally quit my Amsterdam plans. I had worked on only homework for the past four hours, not letting my mind wander into other topics. But I needed a break, and decided to start making my shift-ending rounds. I slid my flip-flops back onto my feet and stood up. Even though it was only in the low forties that day, I still wore my flips to work. And why not? I didn't have to go outside for any reason once my Econ class was dismissed.

I headed upstairs into the cardio room first. The lights were on and the TV was playing the local late night news, but nobody was in the room. I squeezed some liquid cleaner onto a handful of paper towels and set to work wiping down the ellipticals, treadmills and stationary bikes. I stacked the yoga mats neatly in one corner and placed all the dumbbells back on their stands. I shut the TV off, then crossed through the room and opened the door that led to the full indoor track, right above the gym. The sounds of tennis shoes on the hard floor and a basketball being dribbled met my ears.

I took the stairs down slowly, biding my time. I couldn't see who was left in the gym because a concrete wall was blocking my view, but I hadn't seen Logan or John leave yet. More John Raymond, just what I wanted.

I turned the corner from the staircase and gasped when I saw the scene in the gym. John stood at center court, his arms wrapped around a petite brunette with hot pink volleyball shorts on. The tiny spandex kind that left nothing to the imagination. I couldn't see her face because she was too busy whispering into John's ear, but I knew it wasn't Kiley. He grinned at whatever she said, then slid his hands down until both palms were placed over the ass barely covered by the scrap of hot pants.

My mouth dropped open and I quickly stepped back so I was hidden by the wall. What the hell was John Raymond doing? Who was that girl? Didn't she know John was dating Kiley? Wouldn't John have told her he had a girlfriend?

Of course not, I told myself bitterly. John didn't strike me as the faithful type, I could sense that the moment I met him. But now to see it with my own eyes—what was I supposed to do? Tell Kiley? Confront John and Miss Hot Pants? I paused for another second, weighing my options. I stuck my head out from the wall to see if they were having sex on the gym floor, but no one was there. John and the girl were gone, the gym was empty.

Later that night, I waited for the right time to approach Kiley about John's disgusting behavior in the gym. I was uncomfortable talking about what I had seen, but Kiley deserved to know that her boyfriend was probably cheating on her.

Cari, Kiley and I were sitting on the couches, watching TV. Except none of us were really watching. Cari was painting her nails hot pink—the same shade as the bimbo's hot pants—Kiley was flipping through a Shape magazine and I was fretting over my John Raymond knowledge. Curse him for putting me in an awkward situation.

"Hey, um, Kiles, could I talk to you for a second?" I blurted out when Kiley stood up from the couch. If I didn't do it before we went to bed, I was afraid I would have lost the courage by the next morning.

"Yeah, what's up?" She sat back down, tucking her long legs underneath her. I still couldn't get over how pretty Kiley was, her flawless face and deep blue eyes and shiny perfect brown hair. I tried buying the same shampoo and conditioner that she used and my hair still looked dull.

"Um, I saw something tonight that, um, makes me feel really awkward. And that you should know about. You need to know about," I fumbled through my words.

"Okay. What is it?" Kiley smiled at me with patience in her eyes, surely not assuming I was going to tell her that her boyfriend was two-timing her. Who would cheat on Kiley? She was tall and beautiful and had huge boobs and was perfect. And could cook.

"Well, it's like this. You see, um, okay. Here it is." I told her the whole story, from when I came down the stairs, what I saw, the placement of hands, everything. By the time I finished my story, I had Cari's full attention. She wasn't a fan of John Raymond, either, and I could see the fury on her face as I spoke.

"You're sure it was John?" Kiley asked immediately after I wrapped up my story. I stared at her in bewilderment. What was she asking? That I needed a new contact lens prescription?

"Yes, I'm sure it was John. John Raymond," I added for good measure. "I could see him clearly, and he was wearing the same clothes as when he checked into the AC. It was him, Kiley, I know it."

"But he didn't actually do anything with this girl, right? They were just talking."

I looked at Cari, not understanding what Kiley wasn't understanding. Did I tell my story wrong? "Kiley," Cari spoke up. "Your boyfriend was grabbing another girl's ass. Are you seriously okay with that?"

Kiley jumped to defend herself. "I'm not saying it's okay. But is that really what you saw, Jasmine? He grabbed her, um, backside? But did he kiss her or do anything else? Maybe his hands just slipped."

"They did not slip, Kiley. He deliberately put them there. Look, I'll show you. Stand up, Cari." Cari stood and I walked over to her, putting my hands around her waist. "This is exactly what it looked like." I slid my hands down Cari's back and slipped them to rest on Cari's tiny butt.

"I bet so many guys are wishing they could see us right now," Cari attempted humor. "I've always wondered what it felt like to be a lesbian. Are your nipples hard, Jasmine?"

I stepped away from her, hands on my hips. "Haha, and no, thanks, they're not. Perv. Jokes aside, Kiley, don't you get it? John shouldn't be grabbing other girls that way. It's not right!"

Kiley was on her feet, squaring off across from me. "You're wrong, Jasmine. John wouldn't cheat on me. And you probably are taking some act that meant nothing and blowing it out of proportion because you don't like John. Well, I do, so get used to it!" She stomped off to her bedroom, swinging the door shut behind her but catching it before it slammed. Even when she was angry, Kiley wouldn't get out of control.

I shook my head, looking at Cari. "You believe me, right?"

"Of course, I do. No doubt in my mind," she reassured me. "Don't worry, babe. We'll catch him. Or she'll catch him. One way or another, the relationship won't last. Trust me. He'll fuck up, and we'll make sure he takes the fall."

ഔരുഔര

I had to wait another week until Nate could come down to Des Moines and we could see a doctor. I scheduled our appointment on Friday afternoon at a Planned Parenthood. Nate somehow convinced his parents that I had a school dance Friday night, and they allowed him to take school off that day to drive the four hours so we could get ready and go to the dance on time.

Only we weren't going to a dance. There was obviously no said dance occurring at Irving. Instead, we were going to the doctor, to learn all our options. Even though one option seemed to be our front runner.

So that week I suffered through, painfully dragging myself to each class, methodically taking notes and highlighting my textbooks. I learned about airport codes for different countries, how to manage a five star resort in the Bahamas and how to input mathematical codes into an Excel spreadsheet. I didn't learn how to handle a pregnancy, or how to explain to a professional doctor that I would rather abort a baby than give it up for adoption because I was too ashamed to admit my situation to anyone except for the one other person along for the ride with me.

Everyone on campus acted the same around me. No one knew my dreadful secret, what I was keeping hidden under baggy t-shirts and long sweaters. I wasn't visibly showing yet, but I felt my stomach had a pudge to it, making me enormously self-conscious. I usually frequented the gym with Kiley in the evenings when I wasn't working in Activities, but instead I started to stay in, pigging out on items such as ice cream and donuts bought by the dozen. I didn't care, I was pregnant. Pregnant ladies were supposed to eat junk.

"Are you working at T&T this weekend?" Raine asked me on Tuesday before geography class started.

I had signed up to work that weekend, and it was for a great event—a concert by the rock band Balthazar. I had been looking forward to that concert since I signed up four weeks ago, but there was no way I could work it now with Nate coming down and our baby appointment. I couldn't believe I let it slip my mind.

I told Raine I wasn't working without letting her know I originally planned to, and made a mental note to tell Reba after class I couldn't make it. Hopefully, a few backups had been scheduled.

It may have been my imagination, but as I stuttered my way through excuses when letting Reba know I couldn't make it on Friday, I swear she knew I was lying. And was it me or did she keep glancing at my stomach, which was safely tucked away under my red THP sweatshirt? I couldn't be sure.

When Friday morning finally arrived, I was a wreck. Nate texted me at exactly 8:01 saying he was pulling out of his driveway. Which should have put him in Des Moines at 12:01. Well, give or a take a minute or two. Our appointment was scheduled for two o'clock, the latest the doctors took new patients on a Friday. That gave us plenty of time to grab some lunch and act like a normal couple on a date, not a paranoid couple afraid to face the future.

I kept glancing at my phone, anxiously awaiting Nate's call to say he was downstairs. Even when the clock read nine o'clock and I knew there was no possible way he could be in Des Moines yet, I still checked. Kiley and Cari, who were lounging around the apartment that day, quickly picked up on my unusual behavior.

"Jasmine, no offense, but you look like you're on crack or speed or something. Will you just sit down and hold still for, like, a minute?"

I shot Cari a dirty look, but before I could retaliate, she threw up her hands and said, "I said, no offense!"

"That's like calling someone fugly, then following up with no offense," Kiley chimed in, shooting Cari a disapproving look. "But really, J, what's the matter? Are you and Nate in a fight? We could tell you haven't been yourself all week."

I looked between Kiley and Cari's faces, their friendly expressions, willing to help me sort out whatever drama I was going through. A strange sensation floated through me as I looked at my two roommates, one of longing and sadness. They had been so good to me, moving in when I needed a roommate, supporting me when I bitched about all my family drama, buying me McDonald's when they knew I really couldn't afford a ninety-nine cent cheeseburger with a small chocolate shake. We were best friends, the Three Musketeers.

But looking at my friends at that moment, I couldn't help but think there was only one other person besides Nate that I could tell my story to. And they weren't the girls sitting in front of me at that moment, wanting to help. No, it was only Abby, who sat miles away from me, also pregnant, but accepting of her situation. Wanting her situation. We were so different, yet I knew she would want to help me. She was my best friend. She would listen.

At least I thought she would. But we weren't friends anymore. She didn't need to do any of those things. I turned my back on her when she told me was pregnant but I thought she would come running to my side when I told her I was? There was just no way.

I suddenly felt so alone, so confused and hurt and full of pain that the emotions took my breath away. I started to cry, trying to will the tears back in my eyes but they stubbornly insisted to fall. Immediately, Kiley and Cari flanked my sides, stroking my hair and caressing my arms. Their soft voices told me everything would be okay, but I knew it wouldn't. They didn't know what they were talking about, couldn't begin to understand the situation I was in. And I couldn't tell them. I couldn't tell anyone.

"I told you it was Nate. It's always a stupid guy," Kiley was muttering under her breath to Cari, like I couldn't hear her though her mouth was inches from my ears.

"I thought he was coming down? I'll kill him the second he walks in the door. That guy better hold onto his balls because they are about to be castrated!" Cari exclaimed, not bothering to whisper her threats.

"Just stop it, both of you!" I shrieked, wrestling away from their grasps. How could they say those things about Nate? They knew how good of a guy he was. What did he do to deserve them turning their backs so quickly and threatening his manhood? It was absurd. He had proved himself to be the good guy. Why were they being this way?

"Jasmine, it's okay. Guys will be guys. We're here for you, though, sweetie. We'll help you get through it. Do you want some more ice cream?" Kiley looked at me with those warm blue eyes alight with concern, but I just wanted to slap her.

"Just because your boyfriend cheats on you every other day and doesn't like to admit the fact that he's dating you in public doesn't mean my boyfriend is the same way," I heard myself yelling. I saw Kiley recoil like someone slapped her, and tears immediately started to flood her eyes. I had to stop, say I was sorry. But I couldn't. "So don't you dare try to pin anything on him! Nate is a great guy, a terrific boyfriend, but you wouldn't know the meaning of one because you let John walk all over you. Get your head out of your ass and realize you're dating a jerk-off! For fuck's sake!" I hollered for good measure, stalking toward the bedroom and slamming the door behind me in my glorious hormonal rage.

Chapter Eleven

NATE FINALLY ARRIVED TO DES MOINES JUST AFTER noon. I crept out of my bedroom and down to the parking lot, not bothering to have him come up. I was embarrassed about what I had said to Kiley, how I let myself get so agitated over her stupid boyfriend. I never spoke to my friends like that. I figured I could probably blame the pregnancy hormones, but I obviously couldn't tell Kiley that. She probably just thought I was still mad at her over the John Raymond/bitch with hot pants situation. She had apologized to me that next morning and promised she would ask John about it, but I hadn't heard anything else on the situation. I could only imagine what lies John told her—if she even asked him at all. But I was too tired to be mad at her. I made a promise to myself to plead my case to her later that night, tell her I wasn't feeling well and was too stressed over money. Hopefully she would forgive me and all could be well again.

After Nate and I had a nice lunch at Alfie's, carefully dancing around the subject of our impending appointment, we headed to the Planned Parenthood clinic. I checked us in and filled out the necessary paperwork, then returned to my seat to wait. Nate reached over and grabbed my hand, giving it a reassuring squeeze. I tried to smile at him, but I knew it didn't reach my eyes. I wasn't happy and even though my palm was encased in Nate's warm (though a little sweaty) hand, I didn't feel reassured.

I tapped my fingertips with my free hand on the hard plastic chair, trying to ignore my surroundings. The white walls were bare except for two posters, one a picture of a baby sleeping on what looked to be a gigantic flower, and another a pregnant girl holding her stomach. The caption above the second poster read, "Not ready? Need help? Planned Parenthood is here for you." I guessed that was reassuring. The brown carpet beneath the chairs looked worn and dirty, like it had been there for decades and someone continually forgot to vacuum. Parenting magazines littered the one coffee table that stood in the center of the room, the covers wrinkled with age and use.

The waiting room was busy, filled with mostly teenagers, some girls alone, others with a boy. One couple arrested my attention, a girl who couldn't be older than sixteen and a boyfriend with an even younger face, as they spoke in hushed tones with one another. The girl held a bundle of pink blankets and when she leaned back in her chair, I saw a tiny face peeking out. The boyfriend rubbed the girl's back, smoothing her long black braid in a loving way. They looked like such a serene little family.

Suddenly, the baby girl opened her perfect tiny mouth and let out an ear-splitting scream. The couple snapped to attention, grabbing the diaper bag, pulling out a bottle, then a pacifier, then a rattle. The baby kept on screaming, her face so red I wondered if she could breathe. Everyone in the waiting room stared at the couple until the girl got up and rushed outside, cooing at her baby in hopes of quieting her.

After the door swung shut, the room fell back to silence. My heart pounded in my chest, a bead of sweat escaped down my forehead. My thoughts had been so jumbled lately, but sometimes I wondered if we should keep the baby. Make it work. But that scene in the waiting room snapped my senses back to reality. How could I handle a baby who cried like that? Could I go in public with it? What about sleeping and going to school?

My thoughts slammed around my head like a tennis match in full force. I couldn't decide which side could be the winner. Right when I thought I might start screaming just as loud as the baby girl, the double doors swung open to reveal a blonde nurse dressed in all pink scrubs. "Jasmine and Nate?" her voice asked for us, all light and bubbles. Sure, she didn't have to wait in agony and make terrible decisions about the fate of a human life. Her hardest choice that day was probably picking between dark pink lipstick and light pink lip gloss.

Nate and I walked down the hallway with the nurse, who introduced herself as Tiffany. She looked like a Tiffany. We settled in room eight, Nate sitting on yet another plastic chair, Tiffany on a swivel chair at the desk and me on the bed. The thin sheet of paper crinkled as I sat down, the only noise at the moment besides Tiffany's pen scratching down notes.

"So we need to do a pregnancy test. Is that correct?" She flashed a smile at us, her teeth glowing like oversized Chiclets in her mouth.

I nodded at the same time Nate said, "That's correct."

"Well, sweetie, first we'll need you to urinate in this cup." A clear plastic cup with a bright orange lid appeared in Tiffany's hand. Where did that come from? Tiffany could do magic? I really needed to stop hating on the nurse. "And then come back here and your doctor will be in shortly."

With that Tiffany was gone, out to call another name, administer another test. Why did she keep smiling at us? She could see our ages on the paperwork we filled out. It obviously was not a happy or proud moment.

"Welp, be right back." I slid off the table and grabbed the cup, quickly did my thing in the bathroom, then returned to room eight to wait. And wait. And wait. After almost twenty minutes of waiting in agonizing silence, the door handle turned and in walked a tall, slender woman, wearing form-fitting dark pants and the standard white lab coat. Dr. Romera introduced herself and shook both our hands, then opened our files and became serious.

"Your pregnancy test did come back positive," she said, her dark eyes alight with concern. She looked almost Indian, maybe Armenian, with black hair reaching her waist and creamy dark skin. I stared at her earrings, oversized black crosses with a diamond piercing the middle, as she continued talking. "If you want to lie back on the table, we can do an ultrasound and I can see how far along you are. Then we can discuss your options."

Options. We needed to discuss our options. Because I was pregnant. Nate and I were going to have a baby. There was a human growing inside me. I was going to be a mom.

I scooted my body down until I was flat on the table, my eyes gazing at the ceiling. Pregnant. A baby. Pregnant. Dr. Romera squeezed some cold gel onto my stomach and swirled it around with a wand.

"Okay, Jasmine, we are getting a picture of your pelvic area. This probe will send me sound waves to this screen here," she gestured towards the right side of the bed where a small screen stood on a thick steel pole, "and we can determine how far along you are." A few moments of silence ticked by. Nate and I were quiet, eyes focused on the same screen as Dr. Romera. "Ah, here we are," she said suddenly.

The room filled with a strange noise, like a whooshing sound happening over and over and over again. Then a beat started, pounding alongside the whooshing waves. Our own strange little musical production.

"There's your uterus and if you look right there," Dr. Romera pointed at the middle of the screen, "that is your baby."

Nate and I both craned our heads to look at the screen. I saw a black and white image that wouldn't stop moving with some strange lines running across it. Where was my baby? Why couldn't I see it? Not wanting to seem like a total dunce, I just nodded my head. "And what's all that noise?" I couldn't help but ask.

"Well, that is the baby's heartbeat."

My own heart stopped beating. "It has a heartbeat? Already?" I croaked out. The thuds resounded off the walls, closing in on me. I feared I might pass out on the table.

"Looks like you are about seven weeks along right now. Seven weeks and five days." Seven weeks. I had been pregnant for seven weeks. That seemed like a lifetime.

Dr. Romera handed me a towel to wipe the gel off my stomach. I sat up, still trying to comprehend the new direction my life had taken. Seven weeks.

"I know you both are very young, and I see you marked that this was not a planned pregnancy," the doctor said, taking a quick glance at our files.

I spoke first. "That's correct. I missed a few days of the Pill and we had unprotected sex. *Once.*" I emphasized that last word, not wanting the nice doctor to think we always acted irresponsible.

She nodded. "Yes, but one time is enough. What options were you thinking of exploring?"

Silence. I knew Nate didn't want to say the word. I didn't want to say the word. I tried to telepathically tell the doc what we wanted, but she continued to stare at us with non-judgmental eyes.

I blew my breath out. "We are highly considering an abortion." Said it.

"I see." Did she sound less friendly or was my imagination playing with me? "I want to give you some information, a few different brochures and handouts. I want you to read these closely before making any decisions." She bundled up a packet for us, stapling a few papers and highlighting others. "Read through all your options, then I want to see you both again and we will discuss more in depth how we shall proceed. If you do choose abortion, we typically perform those before the nine-week mark. Eight weeks if we can. If you feel comfortable doing so, please schedule with the receptionist out front to come back on Tuesday or Wednesday of next week."

"But, Nate, he won't be able to come," I said before I could stop myself.

"I'll find a way to be here. Don't worry about that," Nate said, placing a hand protectively on my knee. "I'll figure it out."

"There is no way your parents will allow you to come down here on a regular weekday. They'll know something is up. Doctor," I turned my attention back to her, "Nate lives four hours away. Can we just make our decision today? We've done our research together and we've decided. We know what we have to do."

Dr. Romera looked between my face and Nate's. She sighed, stacking her papers against the desk. "I understand. It is not recommended, but I understand. You are at seven weeks now. This procedure needs to be done quickly."

"Today?" I gasped, my heart thudding to my toes. I couldn't handle it today. No, not today. I wasn't prepared. I wasn't ready.

"No, not today, not today," she shook her head. "But within the next two weeks. I still want you to read this information. If you change your mind before your appointment, that is always acceptable. If you do choose to have an abortion, you have two options. The abortion pill or an in-clinic abortion. There are two types of in-clinic abortions, aspiration or dilation and evacuation. Read carefully before deciding and if you have any questions at all about the procedures, please call me." She secured her business card on the front brochure with a paper clip. "I am always here to help."

Later that night, I couldn't fall asleep. All the information Nate and I had read about abortions zipped through my mind and I was feeling more confused and overwhelmed than before the appointment. Was this the best choice? Which abortion route would we take? Would I be able to have children in the future—when I was ready to have them?

I tossed and turned underneath the comforter, willing sleep to come to me. Nate had passed out hours ago next to me, his breathing deep and even. He flipped onto his side suddenly, facing me. I smiled looking at his full lips, thinking how much I loved the man lying next to me. He would protect me, stick with me through the difficult situation. He mumbled something incoherent under his breath and reached his left arm around until he placed his palm on my stomach.

I held my breath as tingles shot through my body. Nate's touch on my stomach felt incredible. Warmth radiated throughout me, from my scalp down to my toes. I let my breath go and placed my hand over Nate's, at last falling asleep.

☙୧৭৩☙୧

Nate and I were busy making breakfast on Saturday morning, and we hadn't uttered a word yet about the pregnancy news. We were acting like everything was normal. Nate was really the one making the breakfast. I was watching and making positive comments. He scrambled half a dozen eggs together in a large bowl and poured in some milk, and I let him know how sexy he looked while doing so. When he poured the egg mix into a frying pan and started flipping it around to make them scrambled, I let him know how sexy he looked while doing so.

"J! I need you!" Cari shouted when she burst through the front door. Nate was standing at the stove, spatula in hand, wearing gray sweatpants and a plain black t-shirt. I had thrown on my comfy blue robe over Nate's boxer shorts that I was wearing, and only had a sports bra on underneath the robe. Since our fight on Friday, Kiley had been staying with John, which I felt bad about. I knew I would have to apologize immediately once she got home. Cari had gone out last night to some party and said she wouldn't be back until the afternoon. That's why I was scantily clad at ten in the morning. Good thing I had been chilly and shrugged my robe on after waking.

"What do you need me for?" I asked. Cari was wearing her clothes from the night before, a beaded halter dress cut just above the knee and creamy tan boots that almost reached the hem of the dress. Her makeup was barely smeared, but her hair looked disheveled and flat.

"I agreed to go on a date tonight with this guy I met at the party but when he gave me a ride home this morning, I decided I'm pretty sure he might be a serial killer."

"A serial killer? And you agreed to a date with him *and* let him drive you home?" I questioned my friend's decisions.

"Well, I didn't realize it until the car ride. My beer goggles must have been working overtime last night for me to miss the signs."

"Why don't you just not go on the date?" I suggested, opening a cupboard to get plates out for our breakfast. "Do you want any eggs?" I offered to her.

"No, I'm cool. Thanks, though," she said, unzipping her boots and lining them up on the shoe rug. "I feel bad saying no now. He asked me last night and then confirmed again in the car this morning. I can't just back out. Plus, he's got a bunch of other hot friends and a couple of them have a house together on the west side. It even has a hot tub!"

Nate shoveled a spatula full of steaming eggs onto my plate. "That does sound like a conflict. You can't pass up a decent hot tub." I hoped he was joking. "Maybe Jasmine and I should go with you as your bodyguards."

Cari's face lit up. "That's exactly what I was thinking! We could make it a double date and then I could fake food poisoning or something and you guys could take me away. What do you say?"

I stared at Nate, trying to figure out why he offered up our Saturday night. We had planned to stay in and rent movies, though we really needed to talk about our doctor's appointment yesterday and how we were handling the news.

"Well, I mean, sure. If that's really okay with you, Nate," I said, trying to get my boyfriend to look at me so I could give him *the look*. The one that said, 'no way am I going on a date with a serial killer when we need to talk about the baby growing inside me.' But he didn't turn around, instead he kept piling his plate full.

"Sure. It could be fun," he said, his voice cheerful, not giving away that we were hiding a secret.

"Fun," I echoed. Oh, well. The date could be entertaining, and what if the guy really was a serial killer? Better off saving my friend and escaping my thoughts for the night. "Count us in."

෨ଔ෨ଔ

"Okay, that guy is definitely a serial killer. I don't feel comfortable leaving Nate out there alone with him." Cari and I were in the bathroom of Demetri's, a popular fondue restaurant in Des Moines. Cari was faking her food poisoning and I was fretting about Alan, the guy who wore a trench coat to the double date.

"I know! Let's not stay in here long. Just long enough for him to believe I'm puking, then we can grab Nate and go."

"Was he wearing the trench coat last night?" I had to know.

"I don't remember! I was drinking. Beer goggles, remember?" Cari made little circles around her eyes with her fists. "Though I think I would remember a trench coat," she mused.

I rolled my eyes. "Where do you even find these guys?"

"At parties. They're really fun. You should come sometime."

Cari was a social butterfly in Des Moines because one of her high school friends attended a neighboring college. Kiley preferred sticking to Irving parties—probably to keep an eye on John—and I just simply didn't like to party. I didn't drink alcohol so the crazy drunken party scene wasn't my style. The seldom parties I went to I was often pressured to drink or take shots or do a keg stand. I knew in my condition that parties weren't a choice I had anymore. I would have to stay home. Maybe I should have gone out more and attempted to enjoy the taste of alcohol. Now I didn't have the chance.

"I think I'll pass, but thanks. Come on, I want to make sure your date hasn't dismembered my poor boyfriend." I started to grab her wrist, but paused. "Wait. Here, take a piece of a gum." I pulled out a pack from my purse. "Makes the whole throwing up seem more believable."

"Genius. Covering up the stench. You're going places, Ms. Jones," Cari joked, folding some Big Red in her mouth and quickly chewing.

Demetri's was a unique place, with low lighting, candles on the tables, the ambience just right. I loved the cheese fondue and using a giant metal stick to poke the bread and dip it into the cheese. And the marshmallows dipped in chocolate? Out of this world. Nate and I would have to go back there for a real date some night.

I tried to force the image out of my mind, the one where I was pregnant with a huge belly and couldn't fit into the booths at Demetri's. And where everyone stared at me with disapproving eyes because I was young, unwed and knocked up. I didn't want to think about it. The double date night had been just what I needed to take my mind off what was happening to my life. But I knew I wouldn't be able to avoid it for much longer.

Chapter Twelve

"HEY, KILEY?" I RAPPED MY KNUCKLES AGAINST MY roommate's door, hoping she was in so I could finally apologize after my rude comments I made on Friday. It was now Sunday, just before lunchtime, and Nate had left for Julien minutes earlier. We finally got a few minutes to ourselves after Cari fell asleep Saturday night to look over all the information from Dr. Romera, trying to make sense of what we were about to do.

But I didn't want to think about my impending abortion. I wanted to see my friend and make things right. Kiley had been out with John all day Saturday but I thought I heard her bedroom door shut early that morning. "Kiley, you in? I need to talk to you. Please. Pretty please," I said through the door. Was she that mad at me that she wasn't going to let me in?

"Kiley, please! I'm pretty sure you're in there. I'm coming to apologize. I said some really awful things and I'm really sorry. I was just having an off day—no excuse I know—but I truly didn't mean to hurt your feelings. I love you, girl, please open the door and talk to me."

I finally heard the click of the lock and the door slowly swung open. My feelings went from euphoric that Kiley wasn't going to shut me out forever to horror when I saw her face. A deep purplish bruise was forming under her right eye and her bottom lip was cut and swollen. She wasn't wearing a stitch of makeup and it was evident she had been crying for some time.

I just stared at her, mouth agape, eyes unblinking, frozen to my spot on the floor. I was in shock. Beautiful Kiley. Kindhearted Kiley. Who could have done this to her? *John Raymond*. Kiley had been out with her scumbag boyfriend all weekend. I knew John was less than a decent guy, but this?

"Oh, Kiley," was all I was able to say. It was enough to make her burst into tears, crying her heart out while lowering her head to the floor. My heart broke looking at her. I wrapped my arms around her shaking body and held her close, starting to cry myself. I remembered back to the Kameron days, when I looked just like how Kiley did now. Beat up, abused, broken. It wasn't fair. Kiley didn't deserve that.

We stayed embraced for some time, Kiley clinging to me as her tears stained my t-shirt. I didn't say anything—couldn't say anything—just held her close. When she eventually broke away from me, she walked over to her bed and shuffled beneath the covers. I followed suit, laying next to her, and noticed a box of tissues on the ground, several of them bloody. I winced looking at them, imagining Kiley cleaning herself up. I wished I would have been in the kitchen or living room when she came home so I could have helped her straight away.

"Jasmine," she whispered my name, her eyes closed. I hated looking at the purple eye. I could feel the pain radiating from her body and the bruises.

"I'm here, honey. What can I do?"

"It hurts so bad."

Tears flooded my eyes once again. My God, it wasn't right. I felt so helpless just sitting next to her. I needed to be doing something, getting some sort of plan together. Call the police? Take her to the hospital? What if she had internal injuries, broken ribs or something?

"Kiley, I need you to tell me what happened, okay? Does anything hurt inside? Do you want me to take you somewhere, call someone?" I wanted to ask a million more questions, but fell silent as she spoke.

"We got into a fight. Over that Colorado trip I was telling you about. I was saying that it wasn't right Katie and Alicia can go but I can't. He started yelling at me about how I was being paranoid and I was just jealous of the other girls. And he's right. I am jealous. But he always shows other girls so much attention, how can I not be? So I told him that and he just flipped. Asked if I was accusing him of cheating. I said I didn't think so but how would I know for sure? He's so shady sometimes that I have to wonder. I went through his phone a few times. When he was in the shower and stuff. He's got a bunch of text messages from names like 'D' and 'S.' Not full names, just initials and shit."

I grimaced as she spoke. Kiley rarely uttered a cuss word.

"But I could tell they were girls and they were really flirty messages. I confronted him about those and he went off. Said I didn't have a right to go through his things and I was just a

psycho bitch that didn't deserve him or any man. And then...."
She trailed off, looking down at her hands.

"And then?" I prodded gently, not wanting to upset her.

"He hit me. He actually made a fist and hit me in the eye.
The pain came right away. He's a boxer, you know, he's trained
how to hit and hurt. I don't think he hit me full strength but it
still hurt. Knocked me off my feet. So I was laying there,
confused and hurt, when he started yelling at me to get up.
Called me a pussy," she spat the ugly word out," and said if I
can't handle him I needed to get the fuck out. I tried to get up
off the floor but stumbled and bumped into him. I swear I
wasn't trying to fight back. I was just dizzy and just bumped
into him. Promise. But he raged, asked if I thought I was
tougher than him and then slapped me in the mouth. I spit
some blood out, that's how hard he hit me, and then just ran
for the door. I was afraid for my life."

She fell silent, not making eye contact with me. *Thank God
she got away,* was all I could think. Imagine what he could have
done to her. What if he was outside our door at that moment,
just waiting to get in and hurt her more? How could I get her
help and keep her safe?

"Kiley, we have to go to the police. They can help you."

She was already shaking her head before I finished my
words. "No, no. I can't. I don't want to. It was a mistake, just a
mistake. He won't do it again. He already texted me a bunch of
times. He's sorry." She held her phone out to me like she
wanted me to read his pathetic texts.

"Kiley, no! Don't do this," I begged. "You have to turn him in. He's just going to keep doing it because he knows you'll let him. Please, Kiley, listen to me. As someone who's been in your situation before, please listen."

"I love John. And he loves me. He might have a temper, but he's a boxer. That comes with the territory."

"But it doesn't give him the right to use you as target practice when he feels the need! You will be making a huge mistake if you don't turn him in. Huge," I warned her. If she didn't go to the authorities, make John pay for what he did, I could only imagine what would happen the next time he got out of control. Broken ribs, broken limbs—or worse.

"I need to think about it. Going to the police, turning him in, would be ruining our relationship," Kiley said.

My fuse was running short. I was having flashbacks of my last argument with Abby. "Sweetheart, I think your relationship is already ruined. You have a black eye and a swollen lip. Your boyfriend is going on a trip out of state with other girls and won't allow you to go, and you're finding text messages from other girls on his phone. Your relationship is a joke. I'm sorry, I know this is why we got into a fight in the first place, but, Kiley, wake up! You are not in a good place right now. You're not safe. I'm scared. I'm scared for you. You don't know what else he is capable of doing."

I wasn't sure Kiley listened to anything I said. She laid her head on her pillow and closed her eyes. "Okay, J. I think I'm just going to take a little nap now. My head hurts. But I'll think about it, okay? I'll think about it."

I stared down at my friend, watching her breathing become deep and even. She wasn't going to tell. That was plain to see. I was going to have to figure out a way on my own to help her. Get her out of this mess. But how? If she wouldn't turn him in to the police, how could I possibly do it?

৪৩৪৩

"Jasmine?"

I lifted my head off my pillow at the sound of Cari's stricken voice. It was Sunday evening, just after six according to my alarm clock, and I had fallen asleep almost two hours ago. My body was exhausted, too tired to stay awake and focus on Kiley and her domestic abuse issues. I was grateful Cari had returned home and woke me up. Who knows how long I would have slept? I still had travel homework to get done before class the next day.

"Cari. What up, girl?" I asked sleepily, letting my head fall back to the comfort of my warm pillow. "How was your weekend?"

"It was fine. Great. But, Jasmine, I just saw Kiley. What the fuck?"

I sat up in bed, fighting off the wave of dizziness that threatened to knock me down. "So you saw her too? I know, it's bad. But she told me she won't turn him in."

"That guy is such an asshole!" Cari exploded, throwing her purse down on the worn carpeted floor. "He cannot get away with this, we can't let him. What do we do?"

I shrugged my shoulders, that helpless feeling returning. "If she won't turn him in, what can we do? The police would need proof—and Kiley's face is enough proof—but without her there we really have nothing."

Cari's eyes narrowed as she thought. "Can we take her picture then? What if we take photos of her to the police and let them know she's too afraid to come forward? They would have to help then, wouldn't they?"

I frowned, thinking that idea over. "Maybe. Always worth a shot. The police take pictures anyways once a girl does come forward." My own situation pierced through my mind. The snapshots the detectives took of me lying in that hospital bed. My bruised face, my battered spirit. I couldn't let Kiley make the same mistakes I did. Couldn't let her situation become out of control. "But how do we get her to let us take pictures? I doubt she's going to just smile for the camera."

Cari was silent for a few moments, her lips twisting in concentration. I stared down at my hands, trying to think of a plan but still fighting through the dizziness. Was it normal to be dizzy? Was something wrong? I instinctively put my hands over my stomach.

"I got it!" Cari shouted suddenly. "Right before I came to college, I got all four wisdom teeth removed. They put me under and everything but I was in pain for days. Could only eat pudding and ice cream. That shit hurts."

"Point, Cari, the point," I tried to urge her story along.

"Right. Well, after the procedure the doctors prescribed me Vicodin, a pain pill, to help me sleep and take the pain away. It knocks me out right away and I sleep like a rock the whole night. I still have, like, eight pills leftover. What if we give Kiley one to help with her pain, because I know she's in a frick ton, and once she's passed out we'll take some quick pictures of her!"

"Okay, I get it," I spoke slowly, not sure how comfortable I felt with drugging my friend.

"You don't like it?"

I shook my head. "It's not that I don't like it. It's just, well, a little uncomfortable, I guess. Drugging Kiley? And what is she going to do when we show her pictures to the police and they come to interview her? What if she's mad at us?"

"Jasmine, you've been through this situation before," Cari reminded me, her voice soft. "What if we do nothing and let him keep hitting Kiley? What if she ends up in the hospital like you did—or worse? We're being good friends here. Best friends."

Her words clicked with me. She was right. Of course she was. Kiley may not understand what we were about to do, but it was for her safety. Because we loved her and we were her best friends. "Okay. Let's do it."

₧₧₧₧₧

"Are you sure we're doing the right thing?"

"Of course, I'm sure. Now come on, just take the picture."

"What if she wakes up? How do we explain ourselves?"

"She won't! These pills knock you out, trust me. Couldn't you tell she was getting drowsy when she was doing her homework? She's out cold, seriously."

Cari and I were speaking in hushed tones over Kiley's sleeping body. We had given her the Vicodin just over an hour ago, telling her it would help lessen the pain and let her sleep through the night. Those were both truths. We just omitted the reason why we wanted her to sleep through the night.

Click, click. Click. I snapped Cari's digital camera, once, twice, then a third for good measure. The pictures of Kiley's face glowed on the display, the purple shining under her eye, her bottom lip swollen twice the size of her top lip. She looked peaceful in the pictures, like a little girl sleeping. If the little girl had just fallen off her bike, maybe.

"Got 'em. Let's get out of here."

Cari and I swiftly exited our roommate's room and slipped into our own bedroom. We examined the pictures together, deciding they would be enough to take to the police station tomorrow.

"We'll go right after class. Let's plan to meet by the doors so we don't risk running into Kiley here. Hey, are you bleeding?" I noticed a dark stain seeping through Cari's thin pink pajama pants near the ankle.

"What? Oh, shit," Cari jumped up and ran into the bathroom. I followed quickly behind her.

Cari stuck her right leg over the bathtub, rolling up the hem of her pants. I opened the cabinet door and pulled out a package of Band-Aids.

"Here, here's a Band-Aid," I said, ripping the packaging off one and handing it to her. I looked down at the blood in the bathtub, the water flowing from the tap trying to catch it. The crimson sight made my stomach a bit queasy, so I focused on Cari's leg instead. And realized quickly that a single Band-Aid wasn't going to do the trick.

"What happened to your leg?" I exclaimed, grabbing three more Band-Aids out of the box. It looked like a clean cut had been slashed across Cari's ankle. I estimated it to be at least five inches long and three inches wide.

"I had a cut and must have been picking at the scab when we were talking. Sometimes I do that when I get antsy," Cari tried to explain, holding a washcloth over the open sore.

"How did you get that cut, though?" I wanted to know.

"I—I don't even remember. I've had it for a long time. It just won't seem to heal. But it's fine. I'll just stick a Band-Aid on it and pay attention so I don't pick at it anymore." Cari refused to make eye contact with me when she spoke.

"Are you sure? I mean, it looks pretty bad…" I trailed off, watching my friend as she slapped multiple Band-Aids on her leg. I didn't have the faintest idea how she could get a cut like that.

"It's fine. Please, just don't worry about it. Come on, let's get some sleep. We have a big day tomorrow." And with that Cari marched back out into the bedroom, leaving me alone still holding the Band-Aid box. I stayed for a beat in the bathroom, puzzled over her actions. I wished Cari would open up to me. I could tell something was bugging her, but I couldn't figure out what it could be. I would just have to try harder to find out.

ഔൽഔൽ

"I just really hope Kiles won't hate us for doing this," I said later that night. After the whole bleeding debacle we had silently changed into sweatpants and washed our makeup off. We were snuggled in our beds, Cari lying on her stomach, me on my back with my hands over my stomach. It seemed that was the only place my hands wanted to go lately. I wanted to talk to Cari before we fell asleep, make sure nothing was awkward between us.

"She won't. Believe me, she will love us for this. Can I ask you a question?" she followed up with.

I rolled my head to the left so I was facing her. "Sure."

"How did you get out of your relationship with Kameron? What told you it was enough?"

I paused, thinking over her question. A loaded question. "I guess I just realized I deserved more. I've had some hard times in my life. I used to joke that I was born with a bad luck stick at birth," I gave short laugh. "Or that my path had already been planned out for me, that I was just destined to fail. But the day I was laying in that hospital bed, I just thought, this couldn't be it. The other things that have happened, none of those I had control over. But this, this situation, I could do something about. I could take the wheel and make my own decisions. It was such a powerful feeling, knowing I could control my own destiny. That bad luck stick can follow me my whole life but if I keep pushing to the positive, keep pushing myself to achieve, the bad luck stick won't matter."

Silence. I glanced over at Cari's bed, wondering if she had fallen asleep during that little speech. I had never been that vocal about my past to my new friends. She probably thought I was crazy, going on about bad luck sticks.

"Wow. That's—wow. You should be a public speaker," Cari said after a few moments. So she hadn't fallen asleep. "That was actually really inspiring." Her words sounded funny and when I heard a sniffle, I realized she was crying.

"Hey, what's wrong?" I asked, concerned. Cari wasn't a crier. "Why so sad?"

"It's nothing," she choked out. "Nothing."

"It can't be nothing if it's got you this upset." I shuffled my body to the very edge of my bed, poking my arm out from the comforter to touch her shoulder. "Talk to me, Cari. Please."

"Not tonight. It's late and we have class and have to go to the police. But this week. This week."

I returned to my normal sleeping position, hands over my stomach, my mind deep in thought. That was the second time Cari had become strange when talking about deep subjects. The second time she turned away from me citing bad timing. What could have happened to her? And how could I get her to confide in me?

I wasn't sure if I believed in things such as destiny and fate. But maybe all the events that had happened were for a reason. Abby getting pregnant and leaving Irving. Meeting Kiley and Cari. Having them move in with me. Maybe it was to help my new friends. They obviously were both troubled, Kiley in the present and from the sounds of it, Cari in the past. Maybe my own crappy experiences could be good for something—for helping others. Helping my friends get the help they needed, to deal with their problems and work past the difficult issues.

I fell asleep that night at peace, ready for a new chapter in my life. Ready to help. If only someone could help with the problem growing inside me.

Chapter Thirteen

I COULDN'T CONCENTRATE THE FOLLOWING DAY IN any of my classes. I was lucky there weren't any tests because I surely would have failed them. All I could think about was the pictures on Cari's digital camera and hoping the police would intervene. And that Kiley wouldn't hate us for what we were about to do.

After my last class dismissed for the day, I shot up the stairs, eager to find Cari and get our plan over with. The temperature outside was dropping by the day, so we bundled in our winter coats and stocking caps before climbing into Cari's red Toyota.

The sky was overcast, the first snow of the year threatening at any moment. Trees had been stripped of their colorful leaves, desolate and bare creatures preparing for the cold. A flock of black birds flew overhead, heading south for the winter. I couldn't blame them. The Farmer's Almanac had predicted one of the roughest winters in the Midwest that year.

We drove through the south side of Des Moines, not speaking to one another. My thoughts were focused on how to get the police to take us seriously, to help Kiley right away. I didn't want to risk her getting hit again. Thankfully, we had the pictures to back us up. They would have to be enough proof for the law to step in. I refused to think otherwise.

The police department looked like how I had imagined it in my mind. Square, gray, drab, intimidating. A wire fence ran across the property and surveillance cameras focused on each section of the parking lot. I swallowed hard as I exited Cari's car, and we walked towards the front door, shoulders back and heads high. We were friends on a mission.

Once we explained our situation to the woman sitting behind the front desk, who was surprisingly friendly for a cop, we took a seat in the waiting area. Cari clutched her camera between her hands; I rested mine on my stomach. It was hard to imagine that by the end of the week I would no longer be pregnant. Our abortion had been scheduled for Friday.

Less than ten minutes later we were ushered into a back room. We had two detectives listening to us, Detective Brown and Detective Tilson. Both were male, Detective Brown being much older with graying hair and plenty of wrinkles covering his face. Detective Tilson looked to be in his young thirties, with a head full of thick blond hair and broad linebacker shoulders. I could see Cari eyeing him up and down, then flicking her eyes to his bare ring finger. I had to chuckle to myself. Even a detective would get scrutinized by her.

"So, Miss Jones, Miss Ryan, we understand you have concerns about your friend, a Miss Kiley Miars, and a possible domestic abuse case?" Detective Tilson had a nice baritone voice, causing Cari to flutter her eyelashes even more at him.

"That's correct," I spoke up, not wanting Cari to ask the man on a date before we explained our situation. "We both saw her on Sunday with bruises on her face and she told me that he hit her in the eye and slapped her in the mouth when they got into a fight."

"Do either of you ladies know Mr. John Raymond well? Does he seem to have a volatile temper?" Detective Brown asked, scratching notes down on our file.

"We don't know him real well, but he's a boxer. He fights for a living," Cari said. "I've never seen him get violent before, but Kiley has told us many stories where he yells at her for no good reason."

More note taking. "What made you decide to come forward on behalf of your friend?" Brown asked.

I nudged Cari, knowing we needed to show our proof, the pictures. "Kiley doesn't want to come forward. She says she's in love with John and turning him in would ruin their relationship," I said as Cari handed the camera over. "But I've been a victim of domestic abuse before, and I understand how hard it can be to do something like this on your own. Cari and I decided together we would come forward before another incident occurs."

"We got some pictures of Kiley's face when she was asleep last night," Cari jumped in. "We just want to help our friend. Who knows what John will do next to her? We're scared." Cari spoke honestly, and it again clicked with me that we were doing the right thing for Kiley.

The detectives scanned through the pictures, murmuring to one another and taking even more notes. They asked a few more questions, but mainly spoke amongst themselves. Cari and I held hands, anxiously awaiting to hear them say they would go arrest John Raymond and take him away with sirens blaring.

"Okay, ladies. I think we have all we need," Tilson said, standing from the table.

Cari and I scrambled to our feet, confused. "What? Aren't you going to go get him? Charge him with assault? Throw him jail?" Cari asked.

Tilson smiled, showing a row of perfectly even white teeth. "It's not quite that simple. We'll be keeping your camera as evidence but we need to question both the victim and Mr. Raymond before we can start pressing any charges."

"What if Kiley protects him?" I was outraged. We showed them the pictures, the proof. That was enough, wasn't it? "What if she says she just fell down the stairs or something? We can't let him get away with this!"

"Don't worry, young ladies," Brown chimed in. "You did the right thing by coming forward, by protecting your friend. Now it's up to us to protect her and you can count on us. We're here to help."

Cari and I left the police station, defeated. The detectives weren't promising anything, just that they would talk to them. But Kiley already said she didn't want the help. If they didn't arrest John the matter would only be worse. Kiley would be upset because we went behind her back and John would be furious. What if he came after us next? Or took it out on Kiley?

"We have to make sure Kiley tells the detectives the truth. She can't protect him," I said as we drove back to campus.

"Then we'll have to tell her what we did, that we went to the police," Cari reminded me.

"I don't care. She needs to protect herself. She needs to know she has to tell the truth."

An idea began to form in my mind, a way that could possibly convince Kiley to turn John in. But it meant telling another part of sordid past to my friends. I knew instantly it didn't matter. Kiley's safety was the top priority now.

ഔങ്ങഔങ്ങ

Kiley was in the apartment when we got home, and thankfully she was alone. Her lip was still badly swollen, and she had done her best to layer on cover-up under her eye but I could still see the bruise shining through. I wondered how many people questioned her. How many people she lied to.

"There you guys are. Where have you been?" she asked the minute we walked in the door. She was curled up on the love seat, reading one of the Skye Mitchell novels I let her borrow. Her skinny body was drowning under an oversized wool sweater, but the patterned leggings and flower headband she had slipped in her hair made her look chic.

"We went to the police." Cari didn't bother to beat around the bush. "We told them what happened."

Kiley's mouth dropped open, and she looked from Cari's face to mine. "Why did you guys do that? I told you I would handle things!"

"No, Kiley. You didn't," I spoke up. "You never said you would handle things. You said that John was sorry and you didn't want to ruin the relationship. If you aren't going to help yourself, Cari and I will. Because we're your friends."

"We won't stand by and watch you do this to yourself," Cari spoke again. "The detectives will be coming to talk to both you and John. And you have to tell the truth, Kiley. You just have to."

Kiley slammed the book shut, getting to her feet. "You should not have done this! I'm nineteen; I can take care of myself! To get the police involved? What were you thinking? What if they want me to press charges? What will my parents say?" Kiley started to cry, and my heart broke watching her.

I knew how she felt—the shame, the defeat. Telling the police, pressing charges, filing reports made everything seem real. Not something you could just push under the mat and have it disappear. Kiley was terrified to face the truth, that her boyfriend hit her. That he had an anger problem.

"Kiley, I need to tell you something," I said, my heart pounding in my chest. "Another thing from my past. Something that might help you realize why you need to turn him in."

"More about Kameron?" she asked me, looking confused. "I thought you told us everything."

I shook my head. "Not about Kameron. About my stepbrother, Bart." I took a deep breath, thinking about how I could get through that story, one I rarely spoke about. Hated to think about. "Let's sit, okay? Cari, you come sit too."

The three of us sat together on the love seat, hips and shoulders touching on the cramped space. I sat in between my best friends, ready to relive a nightmare from my past. Hoping it would help my friend in the present. And giving away the last detail of my past. After this, my new friends would know all my secrets.

I launched into my story, not looking at Cari or Kiley. I spoke quietly, trying not to let my emotions get in the way. I wanted Kiley to understand that some people in the world are just truly awful—beasts—and if you continue to let them get away with their animalistic actions, real danger could be imminent.

At only eleven years old, I enjoyed the last days of summer vacation before starting sixth grade, playing with friends, going to the pool, just being outdoors. I had no idea what predators could be lurking in my home. Had no idea yet that someone who you trusted could take your naive vision of a happy home life and smash that to pieces, forever altering your view on men, sex, love, trust and family.

Bart was my stepbrother, Thomas's son from his first marriage. He was six years older than me, had just turned seventeen and starting his senior year in high school. He was a large boy, overweight by about one hundred and fifty pounds, with meaty hands, dark curly hair and a sprinkle of freckles across his nose, making him look younger for his age. Mom and Thomas had been married for about four years and Bart had become like a real brother to me. I relished in the fact that I now had a father figure and a big brother.

When did the first incident happen? I actually can't remember. During one therapy session with my fantastic counselor, Ann, I vented my frustration on not being able to recall that first time. I wanted to know what my emotions were, what thoughts were running through my mind, even what I was wearing so I could destroy those clothes. But no matter how hard I searched my memory banks, I came up blank. Ann told me that was common, that the mind can actually block out specific memories that are too painful for one to handle. A coping mechanism, she called it.

From what I could remember, I tried to explain it the best to the detectives. Bart would come into my bed after I had fallen asleep and start to perform sexual acts on me. I would always wake up and I could remember feeling scared, trapped, dirty, but most of all, confused. I was too young to understand all what was happening to me, but I knew enough to know it was wrong. Bart was doing bad things.

One night, I remember trying to wriggle away from his grasp, kicking my legs on his back and wanting to scream for my mom. Before I knew what was happening, Bart had all his weight on my small body, pressing one hand over my mouth. If I refused him, and if I told anyone, he would kill me. Then my mom. He whispered those threats in my ear, then moved back down my body.

That night was the clearest of all my memories. Hot tears drenched my cheeks and swam down my chin while I endured the abuse. I think I remember that night so well because of the fear Bart instilled in me. And I knew that night I had to make a choice.

Only four days after that particular incident, I confided in my cousin Katherine on our walk to school. She immediately took my hand and rushed me to the guidance counselor and from that moment, everything changed. Cops and detectives showed up, then Thomas and Mom.

I'll never forget the look on Mom's face when she came to the office. A terrifying mixture of fear, shock, horror and too many others that I can't describe were on display. I didn't want to talk to her, so the guidance counselor pulled her aside and explained what I had told her. Mom started crying, the first time I had ever seen my no-nonsense mother cry. And not just some tears fell, but they poured down her face and odd gagging noises came from her mouth like she was choking. I wanted to make her feel better but I didn't know how. I felt like I was the one who was making her sad, making her cry.

Bart was eventually arrested at his school and confessed to sexual abuse of a minor. What happened to him? I'm really not sure. I never asked those questions. Whether he paid fines, did probation, went to juvie, I don't know. I do know that because he was only seventeen it didn't stay on his record. Bart was able to get jobs at Wal-Marts and gas stations that had plenty of children at stake. He didn't go on the registered sex offender list and was able to live at a house just three blocks from an elementary school. And my little brother was able to live under the same roof as him. That sickened me the most. Thomas assured Mom and me that Bart took classes for his "problem" and Jeremy wasn't in any danger, but how could he be sure?

The incident with Bart scarred me for life, without a doubt. Even seven years later I still have nightmares where he is chasing me, always with some sort of weapon in his hands. I jump when Nate kisses me while I'm sleeping, because for one moment I am transported back to my eleven-year-old self, vulnerable and afraid of this monster in my house, in my bed.

I don't blame myself for the sexual abuse. I went to therapy for almost four years after, but I didn't need Ann to tell me it wasn't my fault. I knew that. People make choices every day. People set their own paths. It's when certain people decide to take the fate of others and dangle it so carelessly, so recklessly, that those choices are ripped away.

"Kiley, I am begging you to understand," I said, once I had finished with my story. At some point the tears had started falling down my cheeks. "I get that sexual abuse and physical abuse are different, but they are still abuse. I credit myself for getting away from Kameron so quickly because I knew it was wrong because of my experience with Bart. But I wasn't quick enough and still ended up in the hospital. But you—you have a chance to be brave, to stand up for yourself and show everyone you will not pushed around. You will not back down because you are a woman. It takes true strength and courage, Kiley, the kind I think you are capable of. You can do this."

When Kiley finally lifted her head to look at me, I knew she had gotten my message. A different light shone in her blue eyes, a glint of determination was peering through the veil of tears. "I'm so sorry, Jasmine," she whispered, turning sideways to hug me. "I can't imagine some of the things you've been through in your life. It's so unfair. But look at you." She pulled back and looked me directly in the eyes. "You've learned from each situation. You've become a better person in so many ways because of it. You're inspiring. An inspiration."

I could feel myself blushing, and ducked my head. I wasn't trying to make myself seem like a saint, I was simply trying to help my friend understand. I didn't want to see her go through whatever crap John was willing to do. "All I'm asking you, Kiley, if you can understand why I share my stories with you, my nightmares with you, is that you tell the detectives the truth. Don't protect someone who doesn't deserve it. Do it for me, do it for Cari, do it for all the other women who suffered in silence for too long. But please, do it for yourself."

When the detectives showed up just an hour later, Cari and I slipped out of the apartment and down to the computer lab to give them the needed privacy. I could hear Kiley's voice begin to speak as we shut the door, brave and bold, starting to rehash her story. I trusted Detectives Brown and Tilson to take care of the situation now that Kiley was finally ready to face the truth.

ᏸᎧᏣᏸᎧᏇ

Cari and I sat quietly in the computer lab. I focused on Kiley, how she was reliving her story. How the detectives would be taking their notes, possibly recording her words. I didn't want to focus on Bart and that part of my past.

Something was wrong with Cari, though. All three of us had cried during my Bart story. but I was able to pull myself together once I saw all the students in the lab. I recognized many classmates hunched over the keyboards and pounding out homework assignments. I dried my tears and put a smile on my face, but Cari let silent tears keep streaming even after we had been sitting for a good five minutes. Other students had started to look and whisper, so I grabbed Cari's arm and dragged her away to a more secluded area—the first-floor bathroom.

"Cari! What's wrong, girl? Why are you still crying? I think the other students are starting to worry about you," I said, once I confirmed the bathroom was empty.

Cari hoisted her body so she was sitting on the long granite counter, her feet inches from touching the floor. I leaned on the counter, touching my hand to her knee. "I'm sorry if I upset you. I just wanted Kiley to know she had to turn John in. I thought that story would help her understand."

"My uncle raped me," Cari suddenly blurted out through her tears.

Her words shocked me, forced me into silence. That was the last thing I expected to hear from my friend's mouth.

"What? Cari, no. Oh, no," I said, trying to recover and will coherent thoughts to my brain. I wrapped my arms around her as she sobbed into my shoulder, feeling her hidden pain and anguish being let loose.

I let her cry for—I don't know how long—an hour, it seemed like. When I finally felt I could talk, I started asking questions. "Who is your uncle? Does your family know?"

Cari stared down at the floor. "My Uncle Brian. He's my dad's brother. I've never told anyone—ever. Not my parents or my sister or boyfriends or friends. I've always been too ashamed. Embarrassed. Who wants to be known as the girl who's had sex with their uncle?"

I grabbed her hand and held tight. "Listen to me, Cari. No one can judge you. No one *will* judge you. Your uncle was going against your will and abusing you. When was the last time this happened? Or the first time?"

"I was thirteen the first time it happened." Cari let out a shaky breath. "He stopped by the house when my parents were out and I was home alone. He was dropping off something for my dad. At least, that was his story. I don't know if he had the intentions the whole time or what, but whatever. Guess it doesn't matter."

I nodded silently, recognizing that she was about to spill her story. I shouldn't interrupt.

"He was normal at first but after just a few minutes, something changed in him. His face got a weird look to it and he started pacing all over the house. He asked when my parents were due back. They had gone into town for groceries and to visit my grandma so I knew it could be hours before they were back. And told him that. I shouldn't have told him that." She started to cry, and I grabbed a fistful of paper towels from the dispenser.

"He told me he thought I was beautiful, was growing up to be a great girl. Asked about boys and boyfriends. And then started asking if I had been sexual with anyone yet. I thought it was an odd question but I told him no. That was the truth. I hadn't done anything but kissed a boy a few times. Brian said I needed to be prepared, that no boyfriend would want an inexperienced girlfriend. That he would offer to help me, teach me. Like he was doing me a big favor or something," she laughed wryly, flinging a soggy paper towel in the garbage can.

"I didn't feel right about that, so I said no, I would figure it out on my own. But he wouldn't take no for an answer. He picked me up and carried me to my bed, ripped off all my clothes and started doing…things to me." Cari started choking on her tears again, and I felt myself welling up. The sick, sick people that existed in the world. "He forced me to touch him, and then he had sex with me. My first time, with my uncle. My fucking uncle."

I remembered our conversation a few months back while shopping. I had asked her about her first time and she immediately got weird. No wonder. I felt like a terrible friend.

"When it was over he patted me on the head. Like I was a dog. Said I did a good job, but that I still needed more work.

He started finding out when my parents were gone and would come over. It went on for two years, until his wife got a job transfer and they moved to Seattle. I saw him at our family Christmas last year, though, and was terrified he was going to get me again. But he didn't touch me, just stared at me a lot with a little smirk on his fucking face, like he was imagining me naked the whole time or something."

I shuddered, thinking about the pain and suffering Cari had been through. At the hand of a family member, someone she trusted. Someone her parents trusted. An *adult*. Bart was only seventeen, not young enough to make it okay, obviously. But her uncle was a grown man, a man with a wife and family! I felt sick and disgusted and terrified of the world. So many predators in all shapes and sizes.

"Cari, I am so unbelievably sorry that happened to you. No one deserves that. Your uncle is a piece of shit. Worthless. Vile. But you did the right thing telling me. We can do something about it now, turn him in and help you get help. Are you willing? Are you willing to fight, to tell police your story and get him arrested and charged?" I knew it was a big step I was asking her to take. She had been living in silence for five years; asking a victim to come forward after so much time could be a difficult task.

"I am so ready, Jasmine." Her words relieved me. "Listening to you, seeing Kiley stick up for herself—you girls are so strong. And I want to be strong. Fuck Uncle Brian. Fuck

Bart and John Raymond and Kameron and any other scumbag that thinks they can get away this."

My heart swelled listening to her talk. So much conviction was behind her words. She may have stayed silent the past few years but she was going to come out a fighter. "Come on," I reached my hand out to her to help her get off the counter. "Let's go see if the detectives are still upstairs. They should be able to help point us in the right direction."

We walked out of the bathroom hand in hand, ready to face the fight. I was ready to bring another monster down, take another predator off the streets.

As we climbed the stairs, I wondered if maybe I hadn't found my calling in life. I loved helping my friends. I wanted to help more girls. But as I placed one hand on my belly and remembered the life growing inside me—the life I planned on ending before it ever got a chance— I felt sick. I was a predator. I was a monster. I was the one dangling the fate of someone's life so carelessly in my hands. I couldn't help others if I went through with the abortion. No, I just couldn't go through with it.

Chapter Fourteen

WHEN IT RAINS, IT POURS.

The first week of November was unforgettable. I wanted to tattoo that cliché on my forehead, just to see what else life would decide to throw at me. The events of that week weren't terrible—that's not it. But there were so many profound, unexpected and life-changing occurrences.

It all started with Cari's confession to me about her Uncle Brian. We ran back up to the apartment and waited impatiently while Kiley wrapped up her story. The detectives then took down Cari's words and put a call through to the police in Cari's hometown of Ridgefield. An investigation would be launched and the detectives told Cari if she wanted to press charges she more than likely would have to appear in court. She took in the news with a brave face, then got on her cell phone and excused herself into our bedroom to call her parents in private and deliver the heart-breaking news.

Detectives Brown and Tilson were heading to John Raymond's room, armed with Kiley's facts and our photo proof of her battered face. They took more pictures of her that day as well, just in case. Hopefully, John would confess and not make the situation any more difficult than it would already be.

I was sitting by myself at the kitchen table after the detectives left. My roommates were alone in their rooms, talking to their parents over the phone. I couldn't imagine what each parent was going through as they listened to their daughters. A few years after the Bart incident, my mom told me how she felt she failed as a parent because she thought she didn't protect me. I told her she couldn't feel that way, couldn't feel guilty over Bart's actions. No one could have seen it coming, no one could have protected me. But she loved me, she cared for me, and she made sure Bart never came in contact with me again. That was all I needed. The support. The love. The understanding when I didn't want to sleep alone at night and crawled into bed with her at two in the morning. That was all.

As I was sitting at the table trying to sort all my thoughts, my phone began to ring. I blinked heavily, trying to force the Bart thoughts out of my head. My brain was so foggy that I forgot to check the caller ID before flipping open the phone and placing it to my ear. "Hello?"

"Jasmine?" Abby's voice rang through the other end. She sounded just like she did the last time I saw her, walking away from me and Irving and our new life. Was that really just three months ago?

"Abby?" I was confused. Why was she calling me? I thought she wanted a fresh new life in Julien with trashy Jason. What could she want from me?

"Jasmine," she said again, sounding relieved. "I'm so glad you answered. I didn't think you would. I thought you hated me, and we could never be friends again, and…" Her voice trailed off when she started sobbing in the phone.

How much more could I handle that day? I had two friends crying in the other room. I wanted to cry myself for the shit in my life and the shit my friends were going through. What the hell was Abby's deal, and why did she have to pick that day to call me?

"Abby, what's wrong?" I couldn't just brush her off, the girl had been my best friend for six years. I owed her whatever conversation she wanted to have.

"I'm just sorry! I'm so sorry I left you. I know how excited you were, and—and—I'm sorry!" She hiccupped into the phone a few times before continuing. "And I'm sorry to call you like this but I don't know what else to do. I have no one here. No one! I'm almost five months pregnant and starting to get fat and Jason won't come with me to my appointments and my mom is pissed I dropped out of college. I don't have anyone to talk to and I'm alone and scared and I want my best friend back!"

I started doing the trend of the day—crying. Crying for my friends, crying for myself and the baby growing inside of me, crying for all the injustices in the world. Abby and I were two blubbering fools, crying hysterically into our phones. It took almost twenty minutes for us to calm ourselves and be able to speak normally. She apologized for storming out of Irving, and

I apologized for not being as supportive as I could. I also apologized for not always listening to her and assuming she would always go along with whatever plan I had. It wasn't fair to treat her that way, Nate helped me realize that. So she didn't love traveling like I did—so what? It was good that she had her own interests and ideas. She also talked about her problems with Jason (when would she ever learn) and I told her I had a secret I needed to share with her.

"Just tell me now, babe. How bad could it be?" she asked when I refused to tell her at that moment. Kiley and Cari were just a few feet away from me in their bedrooms; I didn't want to risk them overhearing me.

"I can't right now, but it's big, dude. Huge. And I really need someone to talk to about it. I've wanted to call you, but I thought you were still mad at me and would just go tell me to fly a kite or something."

"Fly a kite?"

"It's an expression. Take a hike, fly a kite. Basically like saying fuck off."

"Right. Well, anyways, call me as soon as you can with your news. I'll try to help, or if I can't, I'll just listen, okay? Like best friends do."

I smiled. Our friendship might not be back to normal with the snap of the fingers, but we were working on it. "Like best friends do. Love you, Abs."

"Love you more, Jas. Talk to you soon."

෨෬෨෬

By Tuesday evening, a lot had changed. John Raymond confessed to hitting Kiley after being questioned for over three hours by the detectives. Irving dropped him from classes and he was ordered to stay fifty feet away from campus. He also had a restraining order from Kiley that her parents insisted on putting in place. Becky and David Miars came to Des Moines and were staying at the Best Western down the road for the time being. Kiley said they weren't leaving until they felt their little girl would be safe.

Cari's case was a tad more complicated. Detective Tilson put in a call to the police in Ridgefield, who took a statement from Cari over the phone, then put in a call to the police in Seattle. The police there would be paying Uncle Brian a visit, and it sounded like hopefully bringing him back to Iowa to stand a trial if it went to court.

Cari's parents, especially her father, were completely devastated. Cari went home early Tuesday morning and would miss class the rest of the week. Her mom and dad were unable to leave Ridgefield for so many days due to their work, but wanted Cari close by. I could only imagine the unnecessary guilt they were feeling. They were Cari's adoptive parents, set out to provide their child with a good life that maybe she wouldn't have had with her birth parents. Hopefully, the family would find a great therapist to help them deal with the issues. Cari's parents, just like my mother and Thomas, could not be held to blame for the pervasive and evil acts that their family members committed. They could only support and love unconditionally after it was brought to the light.

As for me, I finally got to tell Abby what was going on in my life. I told her about the pregnancy, about our doctor's appointment and impending abortion. Abby just listened in silence, not interrupting, not making judgments, just listening. Like best friends do. We weren't one hundred percent again, but our friendship was slowly being repaired. I told her about helping Kiley and Cari and how I really wanted to help more girls. And how that feeling of wanting to help solidified my decision on not going through with the abortion.

"That's tough, Jas. Have you talked to Nate about it?"

"Not yet. I really just came to this conclusion about twenty-three hours ago. I wasn't even sure exactly if that's what I was going to do but after saying it aloud, I'm sure. I can't do it."

"And what do you think Nate will think about it?"

I paused, trying to imagine my boyfriend's reaction. I spoke honestly. "I don't think he's going to be very happy. I think he is going to be really ashamed to tell his parents. I feel like I'm being unfair to him too. We made a decision together, and now I'm going back on that."

"Well, it's your body. Your life. Your future. I think it's really great that you have goals. Ambitions. Helping girls like— well, like me." I could hear Abby sigh over the phone. "I've screwed up so many times. Let Jason treat me like shit. And then turned my back on the one person that was always trying to help me." I stayed silent. My sixth sense was telling me Abby was holding something back. "Jason's a bad guy. The worst. An asshole. He hit me in the stomach, tried to get me to lose the baby."

I dropped my head at that confession, my eyes heavy with unshed tears. How could Jason do that to her? Did he have no heart? That man was a monster.

"Oh, Abby. I'm so sorry. You don't deserve that."

"You don't have to apologize. You've been hounding me for years. I didn't want to listen. And now here I am—pregnant, living at home, being abused, nowhere to go, no life to look forward to." My heart was breaking for my best friend. "I made bad choices, the worst choices, but I want to get better. I need help."

Finally. Finally, finally, finally, Abby had admitted she needed help. She understood the path she was on was going to lead her nowhere and put her unborn child into danger. And she wanted to get help. That was the first time she had said that in all our years of friendship.

"I'm really proud of you, girl," I told her. "We'll get you help. I promise. But you promise me this—stay away from Jason. I mean it. Until we get this figured out, don't answer your phone, don't let him in if he comes to your place, don't have any contact with him. That's important, okay? Promise me."

"I—I promise," Abby's voice warbled as she spoke, and I worried that she wouldn't follow through. I would have to move quickly.

"If you can, if you feel up to it, I would let your mom know what's going on. She can help protect you and that baby. She will find out eventually and there's no time like the present to fill her in, okay? Just let her know and let her know you're scared. I'm going to call my detective friends and see what they can do to help me. And I'm going to call the therapist I went to in Julien after the Bart thing. She was great, and hopefully she's still working and can get you in." My thoughts were clicking in place, swiftly making a plan of action.

"Okay. I think I will tell Mom. I don't think I'm strong enough to turn Jason away on my own. I'm so pathetic." Abby started to cry again, her pain radiating through the phone line, stinging my skin.

"You are not pathetic," I said firmly. "It is not pathetic to ask for help. It is not pathetic to see that you were wrong about someone you loved. You are standing up for yourself, for your baby, and that is strong. That takes courage."

Abby sniffed, and I could picture her trying to pull herself together. "Right. Okay then. I'm going to tell Mom. Thank you. Thank you times a million. I'm lucky to have you as a friend. You're going to do good things, I know you are."

I smiled through my own tears that were now falling. That was the second person to tell me that. Raine, now Abby. If only I could really believe them. "Thank *you* for listening to me about my issues. Now I have to somehow find the strength and courage to talk to Nate, then our families about this baby. I'll be truthful—I'm scared out of my mind."

"You can do it," Abby encouraged. "If anyone can get through a tough time, it's you. You're stronger than anyone I know. And Nate loves you, he'll understand. Just talk to him."

"I will. Now go, tell your mom. Be safe, good luck and I love you. Call me if you need me, and I'll let you know what I hear from the detectives and the therapist. Be safe," I said again, saying a little prayer for my friend.

By the time I got off the phone with Abby, my emotions were exhausted. It was nearing ten at night, and I still had a few chapters to read about Microsoft Word for my computer class. I would talk to Nate the next day. I was just too tired then. I wasn't scared. Just too tired.

&)(%&)(%

"You want to what?" Nate's voice sounded…different. Leveled but angry. Confused but angry. All angry. Nothing like the loving voice he usually used with me.

I swallowed hard, tightening my grip around the cell phone between my hands. It was Wednesday during break hour, and while Kiley was in the computer lab studying and Cari still at home in Ridgefield, I called Nate to finally tell him my revised decision.

"I want to keep the baby, Nate. Or at least just have it. Let someone adopt it. I just don't think I can go through with an abortion. I just can't." I tried to keep my voice strong and firm, but I could hear it break at a few points. The decision was not easy. I was now going to have to face my mom, Nate's parents, my teachers, my friends. Get criticized in public and behind my back. I wasn't making this decision to be selfish or ruin Nate's life. It was simply the right choice.

"I don't understand what changed your mind. Our appointment is in two days, Jasmine. Two days! I just—I don't. Why?" Nate sounded miserable. The guilt crept in around me, suffocating me. But the pregnancy was bigger than the two of us. It was a life. A human life that we were discussing. I had to find a way to make Nate understand the severity of what we were doing if we went through that appointment on Friday. We would become murderers, ending a life before it even got a chance to succeed. Who knows what the baby inside me could do? Become a surgeon, a NFL player, the President, find a cure for cancer? Who were we—two teenagers—to be able to decide to end that life? It wasn't right.

"I understand why you're so upset, Nate. I really, really do. So much has happened these last few days and it really made me think about our situation. I told you about Cari and Kiley and how I was able to help them. I want to help more people, more girls, who are in difficult situations. I want to help girls who are abused. Who find themselves pregnant at a young age or alone like Abby. I want to do something good with my life. After all the bad that's happened to me—I refuse to just let that go. There has to be a reason for all the bad luck I've been through. All the 'why me' situations. I have to believe there is a way I can take all that negativity and turn it into something positive." I had started to cry now, thinking of all the crap life had given me. All the crap life had given other girls like my friends. It just wasn't fair.

"I don't know what I'm going to do or how I'm going to do it, but I will," I continued. "I will start a foundation or a charity or a club, just something to get started and find a way to help. I have to believe I can do that, Nate. And I can't do anything knowing I killed a baby. I ended a life because I was too selfish to admit I made a mistake. To stand up and take the consequences. So I'm sorry. I will not be having this abortion. I will have the baby and probably put it up for adoption. And if you don't want to be a part of it, then fine. I'll do it myself. No one even has to know you're the father. I'll tell everyone I cheated on you or something with a random dude down here. I don't think anyone will buy that story and it will make me look like a cheap hooker, but so be it. I don't care."

I exhaled, twenty pounds of anxiety being swept off my shoulders. I told Nate. I admitted my mistakes and wanted to stand by them. I knew what I wanted to do with my life, even though I didn't have a clue where to start. I just knew I was going to be okay. Raine and Abby's words resounded through my mind. I was going to do good things. I could get through everything, even if it meant going through it on my own. I was strong. I was independent. Nothing more could tear me down.

"Jasmine, don't be ridiculous," Nate said after a few moments of silence. "I will not let you do this on your own. I'm a part of it too. We'll get through this together."

My tears flowed harder hearing him say those words. I really wasn't sure he was going to stick by me. Why would he need to? Jason didn't stick by Abby. Nate could have easily turned the other cheek and went along with my cheap hooker story. How lucky I was to have found him.

"I'll still come down on Friday and we'll tell Dr. Romera that we've changed our minds. She can help us decide what to do about adoption. I really think that's better than us trying to raise a baby. I hope you can agree with me on that. We still have school to figure out, and moneywise—I just don't think it's in our cards to start a family. Yet."

I smiled, feeling all fluttery that he wanted to start a family with me someday. Preferably after we were married. And older. "I think that sounds great, babe. God, thank you so much for understanding. I've been working myself into a panic these past few days thinking about how you were going to freak out when I told you."

"Well, I did want to freak out there for a second," Nate admitted. "But I get what you're saying and I'm proud of you. You are a bigger person than me, that's for sure. I was being selfish and not wanting to own up to our mistake. And I could never lose you. I love you, JJ."

"I love you too, Nate," I said, finally lying on the bed after minutes of pacing the bedroom. I stretched deeply, resting my free hand on my belly. How surreal it was going to be to carry a child. I was going to need to get maternity clothes. And groceries. I was starving.

"JJ?" Nate spoke softly, and I expected him to start saying more about how he loved me and wanted to be with me forever. I didn't expect his next question. "Please tell me about your father. The real story, not just that he left. I want to understand."

I knew I would have to tell Nate the story someday. He had been curious the whole time dating me and it wouldn't be fair to keep holding back. But it was a story I was ashamed of, embarrassed to admit the truth behind my father. Abby was the only person outside of my family that I spoke to about him.

"Please, Jasmine," Nate said when I didn't respond right away. "I think your father has had a big impact on your life, and I want to understand what he did. Whatever it was, it made you who you are. It's probably where you got your independence from and why you never learned to ride a bicycle." I swallowed a laugh. Nate loved making fun of the fact that I couldn't ride a bike. "But I'm going to be a father now too, in a way," he continued. "And when I am a true dad one day, I want to understand your father's mistakes and make sure I avoid them. I want to be the best dad to our children someday. Please, help me understand your past."

Chapter Fifteen

I CHEWED ON THE TIP OF A FINGERNAIL, WONDERING how to get out of this phone conversation. I could simply hang up—but Nate probably wouldn't be too thrilled with me if I went that route. I could just tell him the truth. Nate and I were about to do something life-changing together—bring a baby into the world—and we shouldn't keep secrets between us. He had been patient enough with me up until that point and I realized I would have to tell him eventually.

"All right, I'll tell you," I finally said, halting the debate inside my mind. "But please don't think less of me, or my mom, or anyone in my family. Please. It would kill me to know you are constantly judging us whenever you are around."

"JJ, I won't judge you. Or your mom," Nate's voice sounded confident, and I knew in my heart he wouldn't judge. But I had become so paranoid of my family story throughout the years, feeling I was just giving people more fuel for the fire in passing judgments on my complicated family life.

"Okay. Well, um, I guess the easiest thing to say is that my father might possibly be dead." No gasps or shrieks or any sort of comment from Nate. I plunged ahead. "Stuart Romney— that was his name—was a bad guy back in the day. He was a drug addict. Mom said he wasn't one when they met and married, but it was a few years after they had Grace that he sort of fell into a bad crowd or something. Which sounds ridiculous. Grown adults don't fall into bad crowds, high school students do, you know?"

"Yes, that does sound strange," Nate confirmed. No other response.

"Right. Anyways, so he falls into this bad crowd and starts doing drugs. By the time Mom figured out what he was doing, he was way past help. She said it was some hardcore stuff he was doing. She wanted him to get help but he refused. Said nothing was wrong with him. But when he tried to sell Grace in exchange for drugs, Mom knew she needed to get out."

"What? Sell your sister for drugs? His own daughter?" Nate finally sounded outraged.

"Yeah. It was bad, Nate. Well, from what I'm told and what I can picture in my mind. Grace has told me the story herself before, how Stuart took her to a grungy motel and offered her up in exchange for the drugs. He didn't have the money to cover what he needed, so he thought the dealers would take a seven-year-old girl instead." The taste of bile formed in my mouth. That was the part of the story that sickened me the most. I couldn't imagine what would have happened to my beautiful sister if the dealers had taken her. It was too horrifying.

"So what happened? They didn't take her, right? I mean, obviously."

"Right, they wouldn't take her. Even the drug dealers knew how dumb that would be. There were cameras in the hotel that would show Grace there, and they figured my mom would report Grace missing in a heartbeat. It could get tracked to Stuart then back to these guys. It never would have worked, thank God."

"Thank God. Poor Grace. I wonder what the hell she was thinking while at that motel."

"She doesn't talk about it a whole lot, but I believe it's scarred her for life. I mean, how could it not?"

"Right," Nate agreed again. "So Stuart sounds like an awful man. Not fit to be a father or a husband, obviously. But why did you say he might be dead? Did your mom…" The question trailed off, and I started when I realized what Nate was asking.

"No! Oh, Nate, no my mom did not kill him! Sorry if I was making it sound like Mom offed him or something." That would really be a twist in the story.

"Okay, okay, good. I mean, I wouldn't judge your mom or nothing if Stuart was doing something like that, putting her or Grace in harm's way again. But I really wasn't wanting to think of your mom as a killer."

"No, thankfully. The story doesn't go that way," I said. "What happened is simply a mystery. When Mom was pregnant with me, about five months along, Stuart just disappeared. Mom said that Stuart never came home one Thursday night, but sometimes that would happen so Mom didn't think to be worried. Grace had a dance recital the following night and Mom and Stuart were supposed to go. But Stuart never showed. The plan was to go out for dinner at some diner they all loved afterwards but Stuart never showed there, either. Mom assumed he was still with his friends, probably too doped up to know what was happening. But when he still hadn't showed by Saturday afternoon, Mom called his friends. When they said they hadn't seen him since Thursday night, Mom got worried and called the police."

"So his friends hadn't seen him since Thursday, but he never showed up anywhere on Friday?" Nate was trying to piece the puzzle together.

"Right. Mom said she knew he hadn't been home Thursday night or any time on Friday. His closet was untouched, the side of his bathroom was untouched. There were no signs of anyone being in the house."

"So what did the police do?"

"Well, Mom filed a missing persons report. The police searched the town, interviewed his friends, my Mom and even Grace. I guess Mom was a suspect for awhile—they always blame the spouse—but she had witnesses that saw her at work Thursday night and my grandma spent the night at our house the night he went missing. She was in town for a long weekend for Grace's recital. So everyone vouched for Mom and she was never arrested. It's obvious that Mom has nothing to do with it but the police had to cover all their bases. So the search went on but he was never found. The missing person case was eventually closed and seven years later they confirmed Stuart as dead. But who knows? Maybe he ran off to Mexico or something. Maybe he had a whole other family on the other side of the country. It's all so confusing. How could someone just vanish? Leave his pregnant wife and young daughter?"

"Man, that's a story. So he was never heard from again? Ever? And after so long, the police just assume he's dead?"

"Yep. I guess that's pretty standard. Mom has his death certificate and everything. It's our own unsolved mystery episode. We'll never know if he left, if he was murdered or just died from the drugs or what. We'll never know." My voice reflected my emotions. It was tough growing up without a father. I knew that Stuart wouldn't have won any dad-of-the-year awards, but just to know who he was or what happened to him would be more settling than the unsolved case.

"That's plain awful. I wish for you and your family's sake that it wasn't an unsolved case," Nate said. "But maybe everything does happen for a reason. Maybe your mom wouldn't have left him and he would eventually sell off Grace one day and do who knows what to you?"

"Yeah, I guess so. Sometimes I think it's karma, but I feel terrible thinking karma needs to kill someone."

"Right, that's no good way of thinking. And I'm sorry to hear that story. That's something that nobody should have to live through. Not you or your sister or your mom. No father should act that way."

We were silent for a few beats, Nate still sinking in my story, me feeling grateful that I let him in on that part of my life. But there was another emotion bubbling up, and that was anger. I was tired of all the bullshit life handed to me. Why couldn't I just be normal? Have normal parents? If Stuart hadn't done drugs and disappeared maybe Mom would have never of met Thomas and the Bart incident wouldn't have happened. That would be two huge chunks of my life that I wouldn't have to feel embarrassed about. I wouldn't have to carry the burden of those situations around in my heart.

"It's just not fair," I muttered under my breath. I knew Nate could probably still hear me and I wasn't looking for a pity party, really. I hated when I would start to self-destruct, to criticize my life and ask 'why me?' But seriously—*why me?* What would be the next thing that could wrong?

"JJ," Nate's voice was soft, gentle. He was pitying me. He had the perfect home life. Mom and Dad still married. Successful. Nate didn't need to go to college next year. He could take over the farming company his dad operated and make just as much without having a degree. He had options in his life. He had support. He could grow up and be somebody. I would always be falling behind, trying to pick up the pieces that insisted on falling. I would never amount to anything. All the words and advice and support I had been receiving were shattering around me. Raine was wrong. So was Abby. I wouldn't be able to do anything good in life because something would always be holding me back. The bad luck stick was laughing in my face.

"It's not fair, Nate!" I practically screamed into the phone, feeling something inside me snap. "Why do some people get everything and others get nothing? Why don't I have anything? Why can't I be normal? Have normal issues like normal people. Your biggest concern is getting too sunburned when you work outdoors all day. Boo-hoo! Mine is being able to stay afloat financially and hope I don't have to live on the streets one day. I work so goddamn hard and nobody notices! I won't ever be ahead. I will always be struggling. Always be drowning. I hate my fucking life!"

I resembled a two-year-old throwing a temper tantrum, but with foul words. I lay face down on my bed, hot tears creating an ocean down my cheeks and seeping into my pillowcase. My legs flailed behind me like I was literally drowning in water, trying to kick myself to the top. My free hand had formed a fist and was pounding at my mattress, wishing it was the face of Stuart Romney, or Bart, or my mom's gambling addiction, or anything, anyone, else that had my life hell.

"Jasmine, baby," Nate's voice no longer sounded soft and gentle. He sounded panicked. "You have to calm down, okay? Just calm down, relax, talk to me. You don't hate your life, I don't believe that. You have a mother and sister and brother who love you. A boyfriend who loves you more than he could ever describe. You have great friends at school and you're getting an education. But look—look what you're doing with

Cari, Kiley and especially Abby. You're helping your friends. Getting them out of a bad place. Helping them find happiness. You want to do big things with your life and I believe that you will do it."

His voice was so strong, I could maybe start to believe him. The tears started to slow. My chest heaved as I took in deep breaths, forcing myself to listen to Nate, focus only on his words.

"Maybe all those shitty things happened to you for a reason. If you hadn't gone through those things, you might not know how to help your friends. Help all the others you plan on helping. Maybe you might not even be at Irving and in the position to meet your roommates and they would just go on suffering. You said it best yourself—you will find a way to turn these negatives into a positive. I know you can do that."

My tears halted completely. I suddenly felt deeply ashamed of my meltdown. And especially that Nate had to hear it all. There were other people in this world that had it worse than me. People that really were living on the streets, with no friends to help buy them McDonald's or rent the latest movies. People who couldn't shower everyday and go to the gym and get an education.

What was my problem? I did say just a few days ago that I wasn't going to let the negatives affect me. I would make them a positive part of my life. I would help people, help girls, like myself. I didn't have time for pity parties. I needed to get a plan in action, start the ball rolling on setting up a club or charity or foundation. Maybe talk to the detectives. My old therapist. The president of Irving. She was a powerful woman in Des Moines, maybe she could offer some insight on where I should start.

"I'm so sorry, Nate," I said, feeling chastened that I took out all those emotions on him. I sniffled the rest of the tears away. "And I'm really sorry for saying you only worry about sunburns. I know there's a whole lot more that concerns you and that wasn't fair of me to say."

"No worries, baby. You're allowed to feel down sometimes. It keeps you human. And I'll always be right here for you to help pick up those pieces. Always."

A could feel a soft glow permeate from my belly but as I went to put my hand in its usual spot, an abnormal pain shot across my stomach. I doubled over and gasped, the pain taking my breath away.

"Jasmine? You okay?" Nate asked, sounding worried again.

"I'm—I'm all right," I managed to say through the pain. "Just got a bit of a stomachache suddenly. Ouch, that really hurts." I pressed my fingers into my right side, trying to find the exact spot of the pain. It felt like menstrual cramps, but of course that couldn't be. I was pregnant. I didn't get my period.

"Do you think it's something to do with the baby?"

I shook my head, surprised to feel a drip of sweat running down my temple. "How could it be? It's not like I'm going into labor or anything. The baby's the size of a jelly bean. I bet this is just a normal part of it. Ooooh!" I cried out when another cramp hit me. Was it going to be that way for the next seven months? I needed some medicine to avoid the pain. Stat.

"I'm scared, Jasmine. Are you sure you're okay? Maybe we should call Dr. Romera."

"No, no. I'll be okay," I insisted. "But I'm going to get off the phone for right now. I— um—kind of feel like I have to go to the bathroom." That was embarrassing to say to Nate, but I really felt like I had to go, and I surely didn't want him on the phone with me for that.

"Okay, but please call me later. Let me know you're okay. Is Kiley coming home soon?"

"She's just down in the computer lab studying. She'll probably be up soon. Anyways, I'm sure I'm fine. Look it up online or something so you can be sure. But I've got to go. I'll call you later!"

I quickly snapped my phone shut and rushed into the bathroom. I rolled my sweatpants and underwear down my legs, bending to sit on the stool. I dropped my head in my hands, wishing the pain in my abdomen to go away. It was when I finally opened my eyes that I saw the blood. My underwear was soaked through with red and there was blood on my inner thighs.

"What the fuck?" I spoke aloud. I tore toilet paper off the roll and wiped, and when the white paper turned crimson, I knew I was in trouble. Bleeding couldn't be a part of a normal pregnancy. Something was wrong with my baby.

I pulled my underwear and pants back up, not even caring they were covered in blood. I ran out to the kitchen, where my purse was slung over a chair back. I dumped the contents out, spilling chapsticks, pens, my checkbook and a stray bracelet I had been hunting for. I finally found what I needed—Dr. Romera's business card.

My cell phone. Where the hell was my cell phone? I ran back into the bedroom where my phone still lay on my bed. I had just flipped it open and started dialing when I heard the front door open and Kiley's voice met my ears.

"Thanks for taking me out for lunch, Mom! That was nice of you to drop by."

"Well, your father and I will be leaving at the end of the week and I just wanted to squeeze in a few extra minutes," Kiley's mom spoke. Kiley's mom! Maybe she could help me. *Kiley doesn't even know you're pregnant,* my inner voice was quick to remind me. Word could get out if I even told one person on campus. *Your baby needs you.* My newfound maturity knew I needed help and the faster the better.

Without wasting another second, I stepped out of the bedroom and faced Kiley and her mom.

"Jasmine! What's wrong? What's happened?" Kiley took in my tear-streaked face and started firing questions. Her mom grabbed me by the arm and led me gently over to the couch, giving me a slight nudge so I would finally sit.

"I need help. Please, I need help," I cried out, struggling to stand again on wobbly legs. My stomach felt like there was a fire burning inside, incinerating my organs and leaving them to die.

"Jasmine, sweetheart, we are here for you," Becky Miars said, wiping the sweat off my forehead with a handkerchief she pulled from her purse. "Let us know what happened. Did someone hurt you?"

I shook my head, standing now and trying to pull Becky up from the couch. "I think I'm having a miscarriage," I finally said, halting Kiley and her mom in their tracks. Kiley's face went pale and she sank heavily to the love seat. Becky's grip on my hand loosened for just a fraction of a second, then she regained control and shot up from the couch.

"Let's get into the bathroom, sweetheart, and tell me what's going on," she spoke in hushed tones, leading me back into the bathroom. Kiley didn't move from the couch.

"I'm just over eight weeks pregnant and I just started having these horrible stomach cramps, almost like period cramps," I spoke through my tears, doubled over while trying to walk. "I came into the bathroom and there's so much blood in my underwear. I think something could be really wrong."

"Have you had any other pains? Maybe pain in your back, the lower back especially?" Becky wanted to know. We finally reached the bathroom, and Becky indicated she wanted me to pull my pants off. I didn't feel any embarrassment or shame for letting Kiley's mom see me half naked. I just wanted help.

"Yes, lower back pain. But I always have pain in my back. I didn't think that was a problem," I replied truthfully, sliding my sweatpants off my legs and past my feet.

"Do you have a doctor in Des Moines?"

"Yes, Dr. Romera at Planned Parenthood. I was just holding her card. It might be on my bed."

"Kiley, I need you!" Her mom spoke loudly, and Kiley came charging in the bathroom. Her face somehow turned whiter when she me, sans pants with blood in between my legs, standing over a dark blue towel Becky had spread on the floor.

"Get the business card off the bed and bring me a cell phone." Kiley stood frozen. "Now, Kiley, this is an emergency!" I hadn't heard Becky raise her voice like that since she arrived in town. That couldn't be a good sign. The word 'emergency' shook fear through me.

"Okay, sweetheart, just lie down, okay, nice and easy. Just lay back on the towel, why don't you prop your head on the bathtub here. Just like that. How is the pain in your stomach?"

"Not so bad," I whispered, feeling so ashamed that her nice cream linen suit now had splotches of my blood covering it. I shut my eyes again and tried to focus on breathing. In and out. In and out. I wondered if that would be what they would teach me in Lamaze classes. I hoped Nate would be able to go to those with me. If not, maybe Kiley could come now that she knew I was pregnant. My thoughts raced around, not making any sense to me.

Very suddenly, I started to get light-headed, like when the dentist slips a gas mask over my nose. With each breath my thoughts got hazier, and Becky and Kiley's voices started to overlap. I tried to hang on and listen to what was being said, but it was becoming increasingly difficult not to fall asleep. I needed the gas mask to come off.

"Tell her a sac," I thought I heard Becky say.

"There's a sac. Blood. Cramps." Kiley's words spun in front of my face, blurring together and I wasn't able to comprehend what was happening to me.

The last thing I heard before I finally let the gas pull me under was Becky's words. "I believe she lost it, Doctor."

Chapter Sixteen

MY MISCARRIAGE WAS DEVASTATING. I DIDN'T KNOW how to think, feel or react after that Thursday. With so many weeks of not wanting the baby, of wanting to go through with an abortion, to finally understanding how important it was for me to have the baby and give it up for adoption, and then to suddenly lose it all? To not have to choose between abortion and adoptions. No more doctor appointments and baggy sweatshirts and eating a carton of ice cream a day. The next seven months that I had been planning were suddenly ripped away, leaving me hollow inside. My baby was gone.

Kiley called Nate after I had fainted, and he immediately got in his car and started the drive to Des Moines. I never even questioned him on how he convinced his parents to let him come on a weekday. Kiley and her mom drove me to Planned Parenthood and I regained consciousness sometime during the ride there. Dr. Romera gave me an exam and confirmed that I had suffered a spontaneous abortion, or miscarriage, something that is quite common during the first trimester of a pregnancy.

"But why?" I sat on the exam bed in room eight of Planned Parenthood, the same room and same bed that I sat on when we first heard my baby's heartbeat. "Why did this happen?" I cried, not understanding how or why another aspect of my life could go so horribly wrong.

"There are many reasons a miscarriage can occur," Dr. Romera said, peeling the latex gloves off her hands and depositing them in a wastebasket. She sat back down on her swivel chair and rolled closer to me. Placing a perfectly manicured hand on my arm, she continued, "In most cases, miscarriage occurs because there is a chromosomal abnormality, which simply means there is something wrong with the baby's chromosomes." I met her with a blank look. "If the pregnancy had continued, there is a strong chance the baby would have been born with some sort of a defect, or possibly several. A miscarriage is the body's way of recognizing the problem and stopping the pregnancy."

"So a miscarriage is actually a good thing?" I was confused. One of my elementary school friends had a mom who suffered through several miscarriages and she never seemed happy about it.

"It's tough to think of it as a good thing because it means a life was taken away. But you wouldn't want your baby to suffer in this world, either. Of course, there are other reasons for a miscarriage to happen—such as infections, age or lifestyle—but I don't think any of those apply in your case. I didn't see any infections during your exam, you're nineteen and quite healthy. Unless you suddenly picked up smoking, drinking, or doing drugs after you found out you were pregnant, which I also don't believe is the case." The doctor's tone was light-hearted, so I was sure she wasn't accusing me of doing those things, which I certainly wasn't. But what about my phone call with Nate?

"Doctor? Could it have happened because I was upset?" I asked, remembering how I was feeling when I talked to Nate about Stuart, about how I wasn't normal, screaming about how I hated my life. "I was really stressed and upset just before it happened. I mean, seconds before it happened." I looked into my doctor's pretty face, wanting to know the truth. "Could I have caused this?"

Dr. Romera's hand squeezed my arm gently. "Jasmine, I'll be honest with you. There are some people that believe stress can cause a miscarriage. Fact-wise, we don't know that. Some studies show that there can be a relationship between high stress levels and miscarriage, but again, this has not been proven. I will tell you that it is highly unlikely stress caused your miscarriage."

Highly unlikely, but not a definite no. I could have caused it. I let myself get carried away with anger, with self-pity, and that killed my baby. I should have controlled myself. I never should have gotten so upset in the first place. I did this to myself.

ෂාඥෂාඥ

"Jasmine?" My bedroom door creaked open and Nate's voice wafted through the quiet room. I was back at Irving and my apartment after Dr. Romera cleared me to leave, giving me a prescription for some pain medicine and a business card for a therapist. I didn't need a therapist, I already understood I caused the miscarriage, and I didn't want to take the pain medicine. I deserved to suffer for my actions.

"Jasmine, baby, you awake?" I didn't want to be. I wanted to be dead, like my baby. I killed an innocent child, a life that could have been brought into the world and loved. I squeezed my eyes shut, wanting Nate to just go away. He was a good guy. He deserved to be with someone who wouldn't deliberately kill his offspring.

Nate shut the bedroom door softly, and I could hear him setting down his overnight bag and slipping his shoes off. Lying on top of the covers, trying not to disturb me, he put one arm over my body. His head was suddenly right next to mine, and I could feel his rough curls on the back of my neck. I yearned to cuddle my body against his, to feel his love and warmth, but knew I couldn't. I shouldn't. I shouldn't need to be held and babied and loved. Not after what I did. All this time I was waiting for Nate to slip up, waiting for him to be the bad guy. What a joke. It was actually me that was the bad seed in the relationship. I was simply waiting for myself to fail.

I kept my face away from Nate's and tried to control my breathing. I let a hiccup escape and silently cursed myself for it. I didn't want Nate to realize that I was awake and crying.

"JJ, I know you're awake." *Damn.* "If you don't want to talk, I completely understand. Kiley and her mom filled me in and I called Dr. Romera from the car. Just know I'm here for you. Right here. And I'm not going anywhere."

After a length of silence, Nate sighed and started talking again. "Okay. I'll just talk. I can't believe this happened. You made me understand how selfish an abortion would have been. I was getting excited to be having this baby with you, even though we would put it up for adoption. We were going to do a good thing, give a family a baby. And that's huge. That would have been the greatest thing I have ever done in my life. And you showed that to me. You showed me how to be a better person, how to think about others instead of just ourselves. I wish you could understand how amazing you are, and realize the potential you have to help others."

How could I possibly help others? Look what I did to myself, to my baby, to that future family that would have been anxiously awaiting the birth of their adopted child.

I rolled over so I was facing Nate. His face was lined with worry and his eyes filled with hope and sadness at the same time. I had never seen him look so vulnerable, not even when we first found out we were pregnant. "It's all my fault," I whispered. I didn't want to say those words out loud, to admit my failure. The shame that filled my body felt tangible and it was sapping all my energy from me. I couldn't even lift my hand to touch Nate's face.

"It's not your fault, baby. It's nobody's fault," Nate whispered back to me, stroking my hair. "These things just happen."

I shook my head, wishing I could cry. But I just couldn't. All my tears had been leaked out, all my energy to cry and scream and kick and curse at the world was dried up. I could only whisper my apologies to my boyfriend. "It is, though. I was stressed when we were talking. I was mad at myself, at my life, at all the circumstances I've had to live through. I didn't even want to live myself," I admitted, the first time I really let my mind wrap around the idea of suicide.

Something flashed in Nate's eyes—fear maybe? Shock probably. "Jasmine, no. No, no, no," he said, not whispering anymore. He looked at me with such ferocity that goosebumps appeared on my arms. "Do not even say that. Do not think that."

"But it's true, Nate. And I'm sorry. But I was just thinking about how something always goes wrong. What could be next? And why do I keep putting myself through this? It was only for a second, I swear, that I thought those thoughts. The next thing I know I'm bleeding out my baby. You can't tell me I didn't cause the miscarriage."

"But Dr. Romera said the chromosomes were bad or wrong or there might be a defect…"

"She has to say all that. She's a doctor and has to speak medically. But I know, Nate. I can feel it. I did this to myself. To us. To our baby. And I'm so, so sorry. I'm just so sorry." The tears were finally able to come again. I shut my eyes and tried to block out the pain. The physical pain in my stomach and the searing emotional pain in my heart.

Nate wrapped both arms around my body, forcing me to tuck my head into his chest. His lips touched my forehead and kissed me softly. Once, twice, three times, over and over and over he kept kissing my forehead and cheeks and hair. "I'm going to take care of you, baby," he said in between kisses. "We'll get through this, I promise you. We'll get through this."

Even though it was only approaching seven o'clock at night, I fell asleep in Nate's arms, hoping and praying I would wake up the next morning and realize it was all only a dream. A nightmare. I would wake up tomorrow and still be pregnant and getting ready to tell my family and start the adoption process.

𝔰ℭ𝔯𝔰ℭ𝔯

When I opened my eyes again, the room was dark. The only sound was Nate's breathing, deep and even with just a hint of snore. But wait—there was another noise. The noise that had woke me up. What was that?

"Wah! Wah!" A baby? Was that a baby crying? In my apartment?

I lifted my head off the pillow and squinted at the alarm clock. The glowing green numbers informed me it was 1:48. I shook my head, trying to get the fog removed from my brain. I couldn't have heard a baby crying.

"Wah! Wah!" There it was again. Who would have brought a baby into a college apartment? Confused, I threw the comforter back and swung my feet out of the bed. Nate stirred, raising a hand and scratching at his face. I froze, not wanting to wake him up. After a few silent seconds, I stood, looking around. Now, where was that sound coming from? I placed a hand over my belly, wondering if dreaming of babies was part of being pregnant.

"Wah! Wah!" I seriously had to find the baby. It sounded terrified. Or hungry? I didn't know what the heck the difference could be between the two.

I walked past my dresser, glancing down at Cari's empty bed. I hoped she would come back to Irving soon. I was beginning to miss her foul language around the apartment.

The bedroom door creaked as I pushed it open and I tiptoed out to the living room. Fumbling in the darkness for a light, my fingers finally found the switch and flicked it on. Light flooded the room and I squinted, looking around. Everything appeared normal—my Skye Mitchell novel sitting on the couch, Kiley's blanket on the loveseat. Shoes and boots were stacked on the rug to the left of the front door. The kitchen table—whoa. What had happened there?

I walked over to the table, looking at the mess in front of me. The contents of my purse appeared to be spilled out and flung around. There was my wallet, my cherry chapstick, a few pens, even my missing gold bracelet. Why the hell was my purse overturned? Was someone trying to steal from me?

I heard a noise come from behind me, like a baby whimpering, and spun around. Nothing was in the room. But I had heard a noise. I was sure I had.

Then it hit me. My baby. Gone. The miscarriage. Blood in the bathroom and Kiley's mom and Dr. Romera. My baby was gone. I was being haunted. I was hearing noises from a phantom baby, the baby that I had I lost. The baby I had killed.

I sank to the floor, holding my stomach. My empty stomach. I was no longer housing a baby in there, I had lost it. Lost the baby. My face was wet with silent tears as I laid on the floor, curling up in the fetal position. An animal-like howl escaped my mouth, scaring me. But I kept crying. I cried and howled and kicked the carpet and clutched my stomach. The overwhelming feeling of failure, loss, pain, sorrow, was too much for me to handle. I couldn't take it.

I didn't know how long I laid on that little patch of carpet, crying my eyes out and making guttural noises from my throat. I remember Nate and Kiley both appearing in front of me and Nate lifting my shaking body into his arms. I remember Kiley holding my hand and placing a hot washcloth over my eyes and forehead, and the feeling of Nate's arm secure around me as I fell into a fitful sleep. But mostly, I remember the intense feeling of loss that refused to leave my body.

Chapter Seventeen

A MONTH PASSED. AFTER THAT AWFUL NIGHT OF hearing a baby crying and having a breakdown in the living room, Nate and Kiley convinced me that I needed therapy. I think deep down I knew I needed to go. I couldn't let myself continue to be haunted. My dreams had turned to nightmares, filled with babies and blood and other horrific images. I was losing weight so fast I was looking gaunt, and I couldn't find the energy to be focused on my classes. I found a great female therapist just a few blocks from campus who was recommended by Ann, my old (and Abby's new) therapist in Julien.

Nate attended some therapy sessions with me on the weekends. I could hardly believe my luck that I had found such a good guy. There were so many times where I thought for sure Nate would go running, but he stayed firmly by my side. It scared me to think how in love I was with him. And I knew just how special that was. I had finally given up waiting for him to make a mistake or be the bad guy. I wanted to slap myself for thinking that the past few months. I worried so much about what could happen instead of realizing what I was being blessed with.

Our therapist, Lisa, was very patient and understanding with me. It took some time but I finally began to realize that the miscarriage wasn't possibly all my fault. Lisa worked with me through all my feelings: the grief, the pain, the feeling of failure. We spoke about not only the miscarriage but my life in general. How not having a father had affected me in ways I didn't think it had. How my mother's addiction to gambling tied a financial noose around my neck. The sexual abuse from Bart and the physical abuse I endured from Kameron. Lisa touched on every subject in my life that had made an impact on me and helped me realize they were situations that I just couldn't control.

Going to therapy and working on my many difficult situations made me more focused and determined to turn my life around for good. I was no longer ashamed that I let myself get so down and depressed. After such an event—the miscarriage—it would have been impossible to live life like normal. And who knows? Maybe the miscarriage also happened for a reason. It forced me to get the help that I needed for a long time instead of letting myself get so upset over life's circumstances. I understood now how suffocated I felt each day, always waiting for the other shoe to drop. Always waiting for the next bad break. A weight had been lifted off my shoulders, from my whole body, and I felt lighter and full of freedom with each passing day. I knew I had tried to fake it when I came to Irving, to hide my problems from my new friends and even from myself, but it was better with everything in the open. I wasn't pulled down by the weight of my secrets. I was happy.

Maybe Nate was right, that everything happens for a reason. The abuse from Bart and Kameron helped me help Abby, Kiley and Cari in their situations. The gambling addiction my mom suffered helped me realize I could stand on my own two feet financially. If none of the events that happened in my life had taken place I would definitely not be the same Jasmine Jones. I didn't know that I would feel the same compassion and drive to make a difference for other girls like me.

"So you know what you want to do? When did you think of it?" Nate asked me over the phone.

It was a snowy December evening, the kind of night where everything was grey outside except for the mounds of white snow piled up along the streets and parking lots. The temperature was in the negatives with the wind chill, and residents of Des Moines were warned not to go outside if at all possible. I had been spending the evening having a nice roommate night with the girls, but ended up getting a brainstorm during our chicken spaghetti dinner.

"Just a few minutes ago when I was eating. I ran in my room to start writing stuff down in the middle of our meal." I looked at the note page, filled with my writing and bold exclamation points, underlined sentences and even some highlighted points. It was a jumbled mess but a warm rush of excitement was beginning to pulse through me. It was starting. My plan was really happening.

"Well, that's great! What do you have?"

"Okay. I'm afraid it might be a bit too much at first, you know? So if it seems like I'm getting carried away just stop me. I don't want to overwhelm anyone who is willing to listen to me."

"Just tell me your ideas, babe. I'm sure they're all great."

"Okay then." I took a deep breath, trying to start from the beginning. "I want to open a center here in Des Moines. That was one of my original ideas that I told you about. A place where girls can call or go to if they're having any sort of troubles. But I wanted something more, an extra boost to really give these girls confidence when they reach out for help. I want the center to offer classes, not like school, really, but classes on regaining confidence, maybe like a martial arts class to promote protection, have therapists on hand for sessions that can be done right at the center, that sort of thing. I think it's really important to offer girls whatever we can give them, not just some hotline number or a shelter where they can go and spend the night and then just go back home. I want to offer more services, classes, whatever, to motivate them to get the help. And then to really help them after they reach out, not just let them fall through the cracks. To make sure they recover from whatever ordeal they've gone through."

I chewed on my lower lip while waiting for Nate to answer. I hoped he didn't think my ideas were stupid or too outrageous to be done. I really felt like I was onto something, that people would like my idea and help me open a center.

"Yeah, I get what you're saying," Nate finally said. I breathed a sigh of relief. "I think you could be onto something here. There's nothing like that in Julien, just the crisis hotline for calls. And guidance counselors at schools, I guess, but that don't count."

"Schools!" Another flash hit me, and I quickly scribbled more notes on the paper. "I could go around to schools and give talks." When the Bart incident happened, I was only eleven. I hadn't learned in school yet that what he was doing was wrong. The only reason why I really knew he was doing something bad was because he said he would kill me if I told anyone. "I think elementary school kids need better education on these sorts of topics. If Bart would have made it seem like nothing was wrong I very well could have just continued with it. And that's not right. So I could talk to kids about what's right and wrong and at the same time promote the center and what it offers."

"You're on fire. Are you writing all this down?"

"Duh! I wonder if Lisa would help with therapy sessions or if she would know any other therapists that would contribute their time. This is obviously going to be a non-profit center. We could seek donations from the city and from sponsors, but that would be to build the center and open it. I don't think we could really afford to pay people, at least not right away." I hesitated. "Do you think people would still help even if they're not getting paid?"

"I do. I really do. People volunteer all the time and rich people love to donate their money. It's a tax write-off and it makes them look good. And I'm sure it makes them feel good too," he tacked on. "But what's your next step? How do you piece all this together?"

"Well, first I'm going to contact Lisa and ask if she would have therapists that would help. I think therapy is going to be a big part of this. Then I think I'm going to call Detectives Tilson and Brown and see if they could help at all too. Maybe they know someone who could offer martial arts classes or something? I'm going to try to put all these thoughts into an organized plan, then go to President Greer at Irving. She sits on a few different boards in the community, maybe she could help me get in front of people and present? I don't know, but I have a feeling that she'll know what I should do next. And she's told me before that her door is always open to students."

"Go for it. You can do this, JJ. I know you can. I'll be thinking about it, too, and if I have any flashes of brilliance, I'll pass them along to you. But I think you have that covered."

I blushed, hoping that Nate's confidence in my plan would be the same with President Greer and whoever else I presented it to. But deep down, I had a feeling that I really was onto something. And I wasn't going to let anything stop me from putting my plan into motion. I finally felt I was doing something good and I wasn't going to give up hope for anything.

As soon as I hung up with Nate, the bedroom door swung open. Cari and Kiley stood on the other side. "Girl, come on. Your dinner's getting cold," Cari said.

I stood and stretched my arms over my head. "Sorry about that. I just had a sudden stroke of genius and had to write some stuff down."

"About what?" Kiley asked.

"My plan for the girl's center. I thought of some ideas on how I want to make it unique."

"Well, grab your notebook and come back to the table. Maybe we can help you with some more ideas. But this bitch is hungry," Cari proclaimed, making me smile. It was nice to have her home again. Her case was still continuing, and it sounded like it would go to court. Turns out Uncle Brian didn't stop at just Cari. Unfortunately, his two daughters also came forward and said he abused them as well. Not unfortunate that they came forward, but unfortunate that their own father was abusing them. They were twelve and fifteen. I knew Cari found the good in finally telling her story because now she was saving her cousins. Who knows? If Cari had stayed silent, her cousins may have never come forward. Uncle Brian could have just gotten away with his disgusting behavior. The thought was horrifying.

Between the support of her parents, myself and Kiley and her twice weekly therapy sessions, I knew that Cari would be okay. She also spoke more openly to her parents about wanting to meet her biological parents. It sounded like her parents were still struggling with that, even more so after the abuse. Adoptive parents really had it tough in abuse situations. They were chosen to love and protect a child. Though it wasn't their fault for Uncle Brian's actions, I'm sure they still felt guilty over it. But with the therapy they were also getting, I could see Cari getting that chance to meet her biological parents in the near future.

I only felt it was right to tell Cari about my ordeal that occurred when she was gone. It wouldn't be fair to keep something just between me and Kiley. Cari was sympathetic and understanding, and supportive of my girl center project.

"Okay. Here are some of my ideas," I said, once the three of us were settled around the table again. "Tell me the truth what you think about them, even if you hate them. I want to present this to President Greer so I need to make sure they're good, okay?"

After Kiley and Cari promised they would be one hundred percent truthful, I went through my list of ideas. My roommates nodded their heads and murmured in agreement between mouthfuls of spaghetti chicken and pieces of Texas Toast.

"Oh, I have an idea!" Kiley said when I was talking about volunteers and non-profit work. "Maybe students from Irving could volunteer. We have to do so many hours of community service, anyways, so that could be an option for students to do."

"That's a great idea!" I said, noting that on my paper. "I bet President Greer would love that. It would just be another way for Irving to be helping in the community."

"Great idea. And maybe I have some more," Cari broke in. You said you wanted to offer some classes—like the martial arts class—which I think is a great idea, but what about more classes? What about something fun, like cooking classes? Or classes on how to write a resume or go on a job interview? Some of the girls using the center might be older and could benefit from those types of subjects."

I sat back in my chair, stunned as more ideas came from my friends. It was unbelievable. My little seed of an idea—start a center—was now becoming a full-blown project. If I could get President Greer to back me up, put me in front of the right people, big things could happen.

"I like what you're thinking," I said to the girls. "I feel like this could be more than just a center to help girls once they've been hurt. It could almost be a prevention center as well, and a community to give girls the tools and confidence to succeed. To not get pulled down by outside factors in their lives. Keep others off the streets and from falling into the dreaded bad crowds. Anyone could come and participate and who knows how many girls we could help. Giving them certain skills—like the job interview preparation and talking about sex and drugs and violence— could help them from making mistakes and getting put on the wrong path."

I was trying not to get too excited but the tingling sensation that was working through my body was impossible to ignore. "I don't want to get ahead of myself, but I think this is a great idea. Ideas. I'm going to type something up and see if I can talk to Greer tomorrow. She'll have to be on board, right?"

"Are you kidding me? These aren't great ideas, they are fan-fucking-tastic!" Cari gave her vote. "Greer would be stupid not to get behind you on this."

"I'm with Cari. She will have to love it. It could be something amazing for Des Moines, and to have an Irving student at the helm? That's a double punch for the president and the board she sits on. You are going to make her look good, too, and that's important in politics," Kiley said.

I pushed my plate away even though plenty of chicken spaghetti was still uneaten. "I want to go type up this stuff now. I don't think I can wait any longer." I pushed my chair back and picked my plate up. "I want to get all this done while everything is still fresh in my mind."

Kiley stood as well. "Why don't you just go, J? We'll finish cleaning up. We're happy to do it," she added when Cari made a grumbling noise.

"Yeah, yeah. We're ecstatic to do it," Cari said, shoving a forkful of noodles in her mouth. "But you're doing dishes tomorrow night then."

"You guys are the best! And I promise to do the dishes tomorrow. Maybe I'll even cook dinner!"

"You are not cooking for us! Stay away from the stove!" Cari yelled as I raced out the front door. "You need to take those cooking lessons!" was the last thing I heard as I took off down the hallway in the direction for the computer lab. I laughed to myself, but had to agree a cooking class or ten wouldn't be a bad idea for me.

The computer lab was almost full since most students weren't risking going outside in the nasty winter weather. I found an empty computer in the back and quickly booted it up and typed in my log-in information. It took me over an hour but I eventually saved my work and printed out four copies. One for me, one for President Greer, and a few extras just in case.

I bounded back up the stairs two at a time, exhausted, ready for bed, but excited. My vision was coming alive, I felt confident with my plan and I had my roommates and boyfriend backing me every step of the way. I took a moment to remind myself how lucky I was. The fresh scars of the hell I had been through the last few weeks were still memorable but I was learning to move past those feelings. I was accepting my past, all the details, good or bad, about me that stacked up.

I burst into the apartment ready to celebrate with Cari and Kiley, but the room was enshrouded with darkness. Only the minuscule gold lamp next to the loveseat was lit, leaving me just enough light to guide my way to the bedroom door. Cari and Kiley must have gone to bed.

I pushed open the bedroom door and was surprised to find the light still on. Cari was sitting up in bed, flipping the pages of my latest Skye Mitchell novel. It didn't appear she was getting any actual reading done judging by the speed of the page flips.

"Hey, girl. I didn't think you would still be awake," I said, setting my notebook and papers on the dresser. I pulled open a dresser drawer, grabbing out a pair of gray sweatpants to change into.

"I am. And actually, I wanted to talk to you about something," Cari said, closing the book and placing it on the floor. "Important," she added as an afterthought.

I turned to face her and noticed then that her usually pale face looked like milky chalk. Definitely too pale for Cari. "Okay. Is this about your case? Did the police do something? Did more girls come forward?" I fired off the questions, nervous at what the actual announcement would be.

Cari was shaking her head at my oral attack. "No, no. Nothing like that. But still—just sit down by me, please. It's hard for me to say."

I immediately crossed the room to sit beside her in the tiny twin bed. I grabbed her hand for good measure, pressing our palms together. "Okay. I'm here. You can tell me."

Cari paused before she spoke. I hoped she wouldn't back out. When the pause became a bit too long, I opened my mouth to try to get the ball rolling but Cari beat me to it. "You know I'm adopted." I nodded my head. "And you know what my Uncle Brian did to me." Another nod, though I didn't see the connection between the two. "I know that being adopted and being abused doesn't quite stack up to what you've been through in your life—"

"Cari! That has nothing—"

"Just listen to me," Cari cut me cutting her off. "I know you've been through bad things but so have I. They really affected me, especially when I was in high school and couldn't seem to figure my life out. I had all this pain and confusion inside me and I just didn't know how to make it go away. But then, I figured it out."

I waited, still not able to put the final piece in place.

"I would hurt myself. Physically. It would help take the pain away, the pain that was in here," she touched her head, "and here," she put a hand over her chest. "It became like an addiction almost. It was the only way I could keep myself sane. Calm myself down when I got upset. I couldn't stop."

"You hurt yourself physically? Like how? I don't understand."

"I would cut myself."

The image of Cari's ankle with a neat slice across it rushed into my mind. The night I was throwing up and Cari was locked in the bathroom. I opened the cabinet door and her razor fell out. Cari was cutting herself. She was taking a blade and putting it to her skin to harm herself.

"Oh, my God, Cari," I whispered, gripping her hand tighter. "No. I mean—why?" Tears pricked behind my eyelids, imaging the pain she inflicted on herself. How could someone feel that bad, that depressed, to be able to mutilate themselves?

Cari shrugged, looking at a spot behind my shoulder. "It was the only way I could calm down. To feel real. To remember I was alive. I realized my senior year that it was getting out of control. The scars were multiplying on my body and my boyfriends, or guys I was intimate with, would question them. I was embarrassed, ashamed. So I forced myself to quit. And it was okay," she went on, looking me in the eyes again. "I was getting ready to leave and come to college and start over. Be a new person. No one would have to know. But with everything that's happened, all these secrets I've told, the urge came back."

Something Cari had said stuck with me. She wanted to be a new person. Those were my exact thoughts when I started college. I didn't want anyone to know about my past. I wanted to keep Kameron, Stuart, Bart, the financial troubles, everything, swept cleanly under the rug. Cari wanted to hide all her flaws as well. We didn't last long that was for sure. But we told our secrets because the bond of friendship was so tight. We supported one another. And that was special.

"I think I need to admit to my therapist about the cutting this time," Cari was saying. "I got through it the first time by myself, but I'm not ashamed anymore. I'm ready to talk about it, to understand why I do it. What drives me to do it."

I agreed that Cari needed to tell the therapist. I couldn't offer any advice, any wisdom on that topic. I didn't know of anyone who cut themselves. I didn't know why someone was compelled to feel physical pain. To add physical pain on top of emotional pain? It sounded like hell to me. Unfathomable.

Cari promised to talk to her therapist at their next session. I would hold her to that promise. I couldn't stand the thought of Cari slicing anymore skin on her body. I wouldn't stand for it.

Chapter Eighteen

PRESIDENT GREER DIDN'T LOVE MY IDEAS. SHE WAS ecstatic for them. Before I even had all my thoughts spoken she was nodding her head and writing her own notes. That tingling feeling was coursing through my body as I watched her reaction.

"These are fantastic ideas, Jasmine," President Greer said. The two of us were alone in a conference room in the administration building of Irving. There was one long table that almost stretched from door to window and was the only piece of furniture in the room besides the chairs that lined it. President Greer sat on the east end at the head of the table; I was directly to her left. I felt powerful—and slightly intimidated when I imagined what other meetings and interviews took place in the room.

"Thank you," I said. "Thank you for taking the time and meeting with me and listening to me. This is—" I exhaled deeply, "This is really important to me."

President Greer pushed back the sleeves of her sleek black business suit. Leaning back in her chair and tenting her fingers, she asked me, "If you don't mind me wondering—why is this so important to you? You're nineteen and just starting college.

Most students are focusing on parties and finding dates. What is your motivation for doing this?"

I smiled, looking down at the notes spread out in front of me. I thought of all my friends that I had helped. I thought of the situations life had dealt me and all the times I didn't know where to turn. All the times I felt like an outsider or a freak or felt like I was simply destined to fail in life. And I thought of all the good the center could bring to girls like me, to give them hope to get past difficult experiences and have the best life they can. And that's exactly what I told President Greer. Even when I felt the tears come to my eyes I kept pushing through my speech. It was important that she saw how much everything meant to me. So other committee members and backers and the community could see just how important the center would be to me. I needed her to feel my passion, to feel my energy and excitement that I was putting into the plan.

When I walked out of the conference room thirty minutes later, I was floating on the carpet. Natalie Greer was behind me one hundred percent. Another meeting had been scheduled for early next week and that meeting would include members of the Greater Des Moines Committee. They were going to listen to my ideas and help me move forward. It was happening.

"So you have to present in front of all those people?" Nate asked me when I called to tell him the good news. "Are you nervous?"

"A little bit. I have a lot to get ready. I was thinking maybe a PowerPoint presentation? I feel like all big business meetings include PowerPoint presentations. Should I make booklets for everyone to look at?" I rushed out all my thoughts, staring down at my blank notebook. I had five days to get prepared for what would be the biggest moment in my life up to that point. I may have been freaking out a bit.

"JJ, you've got to calm down for me. We can get through this. How many days do we have?"

"Five."

Nate was silent. "Five. Okay, five days isn't much time. But we can do it."

I loved how Nate kept saying "we." We could do it. Together. And that's just what we did for the next two hours over the phone. Nate offered his advice on how I should start the presentation, end the presentation and everything in between. My blank notebook quickly filled with notes, Roman numerals, bullet points and arrows. In addition to what I wanted the center to stand for, what I wanted to offer, I also jotted down ideas for the layout and design, the staffing, how to secure volunteers, advertising and marketing, hours of operation and more. I tried to make the business plan as complete as I could. It definitely wasn't anywhere near finished, but it was a start.

We finally hung up the phone because our stomachs were growling too loud for us to continue on. But I felt satisfied. President Greer loved my plan. I was going to have the opportunity to present it to board members who could back me financially on opening the center. My boyfriend took two hours out of his day to help me plan my presentation and in that, injected more confidence in me and my ideas than I thought possible. I felt good. I felt complete. For the first time in my life I thought perhaps everything truly did happen for a reason. And that reason was to do good for others.

ಬಂಆಬಂಆ

"I think fitness classes are something important that should be incorporated. My personal trainer would be on board. She loves these sorts of opportunities," Maria Tolez said. She finished writing a note, then looked up. "I like this idea. It's fresh. It's new. It's just what Des Moines needs."

Maria was on the board of the Greater Des Moines Committee. She was the secretary of the board, but her full-time day job was as an OB-GYN physician at the downtown Mercy Hospital.

The time had come for my presentation. I went with my idea of a PowerPoint, which I wanted to think impressed the eight members that sat around the imposing table. There were five women and three men, all wearing serious business suits and matching serious expressions. They had a variety of full-time careers around Des Moines, including realty owners, philanthropists and lawyers. President Greer and the Director of Students at Irving were also at the meeting, and if it wasn't for the president giving me a subtle thumbs up before I started speaking, I may have run out of the room overwhelmed with fear before I even opened my mouth. But once I introduced myself and launched into my speech I was immediately at ease.

My speech flowed effortlessly because I believed in the words I was saying. And it showed to the members.

"Along with fitness classes, how about education on proper nutrition? That could possibly tie in with the cooking classes? Learning how to make balanced, proportioned, nutritionally acceptable meals is a large aspect the younger generation doesn't seem to grasp." This statement, which, hey, I had to agree with, came from a slightly overweight balding gentleman who had introduced himself as Gerald P. Wittington. That was really how he introduced himself. He was a retired banker and now focused all his energy on the committee when he wasn't traveling the world with his wife. I heard him say earlier how they had just returned from the Greek Islands.

"I have a suggestion," President Greer piped up. "None of you may know this, but I once participated in many, eh, beauty pageants around the Des Moines area." Her cheeks flushed, but I didn't know why. I wouldn't be ashamed of that. One of my dreams since I was a little girl was to be Miss America. "I still keep in touch with some of the women who work for the Des Moines Association of the pageants and I could bet they would help."

"Help how? Get the girls entered in the pageants?" A slender redhead with an abundance of gold jewelry asked. I think she had said her name was Gina, and she may have been one of the Realtors.

"Not necessarily. But in pageants, all the contestants go through workshops. They learn how to speak in front of an audience, walk with confidence, even how to choose professional clothes. Maybe we could have the reigning queen come in and talk with girls and then offer workshops that pageant contestants go through."

I didn't speak for a long time. The board members were off and running with ideas of their own—what classes to offer, possible sites for the location, how to staff the center. I took notes until my fingers cramped up, and wished I had brought a tape recorder with me. I couldn't believe how well my little idea was received.

"I think something to focus on is what you mentioned earlier, Jasmine. That this not just be a shelter, or a place to go if girls wanted to run away from home. This needs to be a learning facility, somewhere to inspire these girls," Katherine, a young lawyer on the board, spoke up. "We don't want them to think of it as a school, but rather somewhere they can go and have fun but still learn while there."

"Maybe we could focus on scheduling events and having girls sign up for them. Almost like school where you sign up for classes, but this will be better," I said, getting into her idea. "We could have them pick if they want to take a cooking class, or martial arts, or listen to the beauty queens talk. That way we could be organized, plan ahead to know how many people are attending."

"Great idea. Organization is going to be very important. We don't want just a hodgepodge of girls and activities happening randomly. And we'll want to keep track of the numbers, count how many are attending what classes, how many girls we have in therapy and so on," Maria said.

We continued talking about our ideas for well past an hour, until the board members needed to get on with their day. As the meeting wrapped, I stood up quickly to address the group again. "I just want to thank you for coming to this meeting and all the great ideas you thought of. This center means so much to me, and for that to be realized..." I trailed off, horrified that tears were coming to my eyes. I made it through a short synopsis of my experiences without crying and I didn't want to start then. "It just means a lot to me," I concluded before sitting down again. I stared hard at my notes in front of me, willing the tears away.

"Thank you, Jasmine," Maria spoke. I lifted my head and looked at her. Her pale brown eyes were looking directly at me. "We can understand how difficult this must have been for you, to put your idea and goal on the line like this and pitch it. It is remarkable how well you spoke to us. With the sheer drive behind your words, combined with a truly well thought-out business plan, it would be absurd for the board to turn you down. We will proudly back you and the center in full."

President Greer was the one who started clapping, but soon the entire board was clapping along with her. The noise resounded in my ears, enveloped me in a warm hug. I let the tears flow with no shame as the members came up to congratulate me and offer hugs of their own. I couldn't wait to get back to the apartment and let the roommates, Nate and my mom know that the center was a go.

ഇരുന്ന

"Cheers to you, Jasmine. Congratulations. I think I speak for both Cari and myself when I say that we are so lucky to have you as a friend. Without you, who knows where we would have ended up? I'm so happy I met you," Kiley lifted her champagne flute and clinked it lightly against mine. Tears shined brightly in her blue eyes, and I could feel the moisture in mine as well.

"Let me just say that none of this would have been possible without you two. What you've both been through, the courage you showed to face it head on is inspiring to me. You helped fuel my ideas. Without you girls—" I shook my head, forcing myself to speak through the lump in my throat, "without you girls, I couldn't have done it. None of this is just me."

And it wasn't. As I celebrated the news of the passing of the center plans with my roommates in our apartment, I couldn't put into the words the gratitude I wanted to express to them. To Abby. My mom. Nate. My sister. Everyone who had touched my life in some way helped me connect the puzzle pieces. I finally figured out how to answer the question of what I wanted to do with my life. What I wanted to be when I grew up. I was going to help people. I was going to make a difference.

"Well, this is getting emotional. Can we please eat now, bitches? We've been staring at our plates and making toasts for far too long," Cari said, tapping her nails against the table. "I'm starving!"

Kiley and I laughed, and I held up my flute. I was even drinking champagne that night. Well, I also had a can of Sprite next to me. The bubbles tasted weird, but it seemed necessary for toasting. "Just one more cheers," I said, and Kiley and Cari promptly lifted their glasses. Cari also picked up her fork with her left hand. "To friendship. I love you girls."

"To friendship!" We clinked glasses and started laughing. Cari cut into the chicken enchilada casserole, prepared by Kiley. I had bought the corn chips and Cari made a delicious taco dip. We ate dinner with a renewed enthusiasm. I knew my friends were just as excited about the center opening as I was. Both would be volunteering some of their free time there and planned on participating in some classes themselves. I knew we would continue learning thanks to the fantastic lineup of volunteers we had signed on. From therapists and detectives to chefs, martial arts experts, beauty queens and so much more. The fun was only just beginning.

∞⟡∞⟡

I was working in the computer lab a couple weeks later, pounding out more ideas and a tentative volunteer schedule for opening week. I checked my handwritten calendar, carefully transferring the dates, times and corresponding names into the computer. My name was written in for at least three hours each day, though I planned on being there much more. I had to make sure I didn't let any of my schoolwork get behind, so I wanted to make sure I didn't stretch myself too thin. But I knew I could also bring my assignments to the center to work on during downtime, so I wasn't worried.

I was just getting ready to hit print for the volunteer schedules when I heard a voice call my name. "Jas?"

I looked up to find Abby staring down at me, pregnant belly tucked into a pair of jeans and button-up shirt. "Abby? Oh, my gosh. What are you doing here?" I jumped out my chair, running over to my friend and throwing my arms around here. No matter what had happened in the past, the feeling of euphoria from seeing my friend standing before me made me realize how much I cared for and had missed her the past few months.

Abby was laughing as I continued to squeeze her. "I wanted to surprise you. I'm surprised Cari or Kiley didn't spill the beans."

"They were in on this? The sneaky devils didn't breathe a word to me! But what are you doing here? How did you even get down here?" I wondered briefly if she was coming back to school.

"I just came down for a long weekend," she said, reading my thoughts. "Tally has a job interview down here so I thought

I would come visit and keep her company as well." Tally was Abby's older sister.

"Well, that's excellent! I'm so excited you're here. Really, I am." I gave her another hug, not caring if the handful of other students in the lab were watching our reunion.

"I am, too. I wanted to come down and apologize to you in person. It just isn't the same over the phone."

"Here, let me grab my stuff quick and then we can go up to my room. It'll be quieter there." I saved my volunteer calendars to my personal drive, grabbed my notebooks and loose paperwork and swung my purse over my shoulder.

When we finally settled back in my bedroom, sitting side by side on my twin bed, I decided to speak first. "Abby, I really am sorry about how I took your news and how I acted when you said you didn't want to be at Irving and travel to Amsterdam. I was acting so selfish at the time, but I realize now that we are different people with different goals. I'm sorry I didn't see that before and wanted you to be like my clone."

"It's all right. Really. I should have mentioned it sooner that I didn't think Irving was right for me and that a travel major really didn't interest me. But I got swept up in your excitement that I just kind of let it happen. But I'm sorry I yelled at you that day, and that I was such a bitch leading up to it. I didn't know how to tell you about the baby and I knew you would be mad, and I just worked myself into being even angrier when you hadn't done anything wrong. I hope you can forgive me."

"Only if you can forgive me." The tears were threatening yet again.

"Of course." We embraced again, and I felt blessed to have my best friend back.

"Now," I wiped a tear from my cheek, "how are you and this baby doing? When are you due?"

"A little over two months still," Abby sighed, placing a hand on her baby bump. "I'm going to live with Mom for a while but me and Tally were thinking about getting a place together. It just depends on how her job interview goes."

"And things wish Jason?" I questioned, not wanting to get too deep into the subject.

"I haven't talked to him since the night I turned him in for assault. I don't want him around me. My doctor says it's not good for my stress levels, either."

I nodded, relieved, and really believing that she wasn't in contact with him anymore. Finally.

"Well, I think you make a cute pregnant lady. You haven't even gained any weight! You look like a stick with a beer belly or something."

"The first couple months were hell. I couldn't keep anything down and was so sick all the time. Morning sickness is not just in the morning, I don't care what anyone says. But I can tell I'm starting to gain weight, especially in my face. I'm going to have fat cheeks here real soon!"

"I'm sure you'll still look great. Do you want to get some dinner? Maybe we could invite Kiley and Cari to come out with us?" I was hesitant to ask because Abby hadn't been the nicest when she met them earlier in the year. But I didn't have to worry. Abby was very agreeable and Cari and Kiley jumped at the invite. I went out to dinner that night with my three best friends, and felt that all my puzzle pieces were finally clicked into place.

Epilogue

JUST A MONTH LATER, EVERYTHING HAD CHANGED.
My center had a home and was being worked on each day by
volunteers to get it in shape for the grand opening. One of the
realty managers on the board had secured three empty lot
spaces that were part of a strip mall in downtown Des Moines.
The lots were being transformed into smaller rooms that would
be used for classes and therapy sessions. The grand opening
was being set for the end of March, right after my twentieth
birthday. I couldn't have asked for a better gift.

We had hit one snag along the way, some financial backer
that thought my idea was crap and didn't want to support the
plans. He tried to shut down the entire project, trying to get
other backers and committee members to go against the green
light. I didn't know why he was so intent on shutting down a
business with the purpose to help others. I really thought we
had lost the support and tried not to let my spirits fall below
ground. I tried telling myself that I just needed to try harder,
maybe get a petition circulated, bring in more classes or
services. But with President Greer supporting me and our
plans, the man soon gave up his fight and my center was a go
once again. After the fear of almost losing it, I felt a deeper
connection and drive to make sure it saw the light.

I learned a lot about opening a business while preparing to launch my idea. I attended meetings on zoning, permits, financials, computer training and marketing. I signed letters, filmed TV commercials and was hands-on with all the scheduling. I realized that my organizational skills were up there, and had a newfound obsession with Post-it notes.

The opening of the center was initially going to interfere with my much-anticipated trip to Amsterdam. I couldn't miss the grand opening and the beginning weeks. I had worked too hard and was too excited not to see it all come together. After explaining to Reba why I would have to back out she immediately took action, working on pushing the trip back a month. Apparently, I had informed her right in time, where the travel dates could still be changed. I couldn't believe that nobody had any angry reactions to the news. All eighteen students took the postponement in stride, and our trip was now planned for mid-April. After working my tail off at T&T and also Activities, it looked like I was going to be in the clear financially to finally become an international traveler.

My roommates were still working through their problems, both still in therapy, and Cari was prepping for when her case went to court. We never heard what happened to John Raymond after he was removed from campus but maybe it was better that way. Detective Tilson did say that he moved out of Des Moines, so luckily Kiley wouldn't have to deal with any random run-ins with him.

Abby made a handful of trips to Des Moines to help with the center. I wouldn't let her do much—as she was nearing her eighth month of pregnancy—but just having her there meant everything to me. She hadn't seemed to gain any weight except for the volleyball poking out from her shirt and I was excited for the birth of her baby girl. Jason had been officially charged with domestic abuse and battery, and had spent time in the Julien jail. Abby also had a restraining order issued and I could tell she was working hard to get her life on the right track. She even enrolled in online classes through the community college in Julien, and wanted to learn to be an x-ray technician. I would have never guessed that would be a field Abby was interested in. Nate was right—we did have different interests and goals now. We grew up, found what we liked to do. And there was nothing wrong with that.

And then there was Nate. My own Prince Charming, knight in shining armor. He was coming down to Des Moines every other weekend and helping with the construction side of the center. He had gotten accepted to Iowa State University, only a thirty-minute car ride from Des Moines, and would be starting classes in the fall. We would no longer have the long distance between us.

My mom flew from Kentucky to Des Moines in March, and would stay for the grand opening. Telling my mom about the pregnancy and miscarriage was one of the hardest conversations I've had. I was so worried that she would be disappointed or disgusted with me, but those emotions never showed. She only hugged me hard and said she wished she could have been there with me. And cried, which was very disconcerting for me. I hated seeing my mom cry. I apologized again and again for not telling her sooner but she brushed those apologies away. What mattered were the present and the future, not the past, she had told me. And I believed that no one was prouder than my mom for the work I put into opening that center.

Her Way was officially opened on March 25. Many people wanted me to name the center after myself. I thought that was silly and egotistical. So many people contributed to the planning, designing and putting all those plans and designs together. It was never just me. Her Way was a place for girls to find their own way, to find inspiration, set goals and meet people who could help them. I loved the name.

The once empty lots of the vacant strip mall were now filled with cozy furniture, had paint on the walls and beautiful hardwood floors. There were separate classrooms that could hold a multitude of subjects—cooking, fitness, dance—anything we wanted we could do. All that was necessary was a volunteer. And the girls, of course.

I spent my mornings in class and every afternoon and most evenings at the center. I worked the phone lines, scheduled meetings with volunteers and even participated in a few cooking classes myself. I started giving speeches at elementary, junior high and even high schools on topics such as abuse. It was a great way to connect with students and free publicity for the center.

Her Way was open Monday, Wednesday, Friday, and Saturday for classes. Tuesday and Thursday were reserved for one-on-one and group therapy sessions, and were also times where girls could come simply to hang out or work on homework. Sundays were closed but the phone lines remained open. We had found excellent volunteers throughout the community that helped staff the phones twenty-four/seven.

Dr. Romera had heard about Her Way through the buzz in the community and called me to ask if she could help as well. Nate had told her the day I miscarried about our revised plans to keep the baby, and Dr. Romera told me how proud of me she was. She was going to give speeches about safe sex and the dangers of having sex young, and also offer free doctor visits for those who couldn't afford medical care. I thought she would make a great addition to our growing list of supporters.

As I cut through the ceremonial red ribbon on that first day and posed for pictures with the board members, I couldn't keep the smile off my face. We had an immediate response once the center talk had started floating around town. I saw many young faces in the crowd on opening day and felt relieved that girls were really stepping forward, some asking for help, others just wanting to learn a new skill or feel a connection with other girls. I loved that my idea was bigger and better than I initially imagined. Instead of a dark and depressing place that focused solely on abuse and the hardships of life, Her Way was filled with hope and optimism. I knew we would be a success. My list of volunteers was growing with speed, the donations were pouring in, the start of a foundation was in the works and with the support of my family, friends, Irving and the city of Des Moines, we together would change lives.

I looked around me that day and saw everyone that mattered in my life was there supporting me. My mom talking to Grace and Jeremy. I saw Kiley and Cari and their parents. Nate and his parents. Abby and her mom and sister came down, and Abby's belly had grown so big I worried she might give birth right there on the steps. I saw President Greer giving a media interview and members of the board shaking hands with just about everyone in the crowd.

But out of all the faces I saw, most importantly, I saw myself. I knew how far I had come, how much I had achieved and how determined I had been to make the center a reality. I saw my future, and it had never looked brighter.

I never expected my freshman year to go without a hitch. From all the curve balls thrown at me in my life, I knew something would have to shake up the year. But I can honestly say I had no idea it was going to include two pregnancies, more abuse than any girl should take from loved ones, falling in love, helping new friends and finally finding a way to turn all the negatives into a positive. I wasn't destined to fail. I was determined to succeed.

Acknowledgements

THERE are so many people that I have to thank- the biggest being my mom. Thank you for always supporting me no matter my goal is. To my family- Gina and Jon – for always having my back. To my Grandma- thank you for making me a reader and never doubting my talents. I miss you. To Mitch, my best friend of the last four years. Thank you for keeping me sane during this process, and putting a smile on my face every day. To Kira, my first college friend and wonderful proofreader. Thank you for such a strong friendship, inspiration, and for the courage you gave me to keep moving forward. To my crazy slew of friends– thank you for making me laugh, keeping me entertained, and giving me more ideas for future books.

To all the authors who helped me along the way- Cathleen Holst, Heather Wardell, Misa Rush, Kathleen Kole, Jackie Pilossoph, Shannon Hart, Casey Crow, Tess Hardwick and Lucie Simone. Without you ladies, I would have been stumbling into the publishing world without a clue as to where to turn. Thank you for your unselfish guidance and unending patience with my questions.

To the many ChickLitPlus followers- I can say with complete confidence Destined to Fail would not have seen the light of day if it weren't for you. The unwavering support, the encouragement and enthusiasm you gave me propelled me to keep churning forward. I am in awe of what a little book blog has helped me achieve. To name a few in particular- Kaley Stewart, Michelle Bell, Jenn Ladd, Jencey Gortney, Melissa Amster, Kate Supino, Laura Pepper Wu, Ashley Williams, Lacy Camey, JF Kristin, Kimberly Lin, Amy Lou Ellen, Heather Hummel, Nicky Wells, Jesi Lea Ryan, Georgina Scott, Jeanine Denzer, Amy Bromberg, Laura Chapman, and the many, many more that sent words of encouragement. Thank you for the bottom of my heart. And to Ashley Redbird, thank you for my magnificent cover that I have an obsession with!

A writer's journey is never a solo one. Thank you again for all the support, guidance, encouragement, and love that I have been lucky to receive. Enjoy Destined to Fail.

Samantha March

About the Author

SAMANTHA MARCH currently lives in Des Moines, Iowa with her boyfriend and crazy cast of friends. She also runs the popular book/women's lifestyle blog ChickLitPlus, which keeps her bookshelf stocked with the latest reads and up to date on all things health, fitness, fashion, and celebrity related. *Destined to Fail* is her first novel.

Please visit her website at http://samanthamarch.com